MEGALODON BLOODBATH

A NOVEL BY MICHAEL COLE

SEVERED PRESS
HOBART TASMANIA

MEGALODON: BLOODBATH

Copyright © 2021 by Michael Cole
Copyright © 2021 by Severed Press

WWW.SEVEREDPRESS.COM

All rights reserved. No part of this book may be reproduced or transmitted in any form or by any electronic or mechanical means, including photocopying, recording or by any information and retrieval system, without the written permission of the publisher and author, except where permitted by law. This novel is a work of fiction. Names, characters, places and incidents are the product of the author's imagination, or are used fictitiously. Any resemblance to actual events, locales or persons, living or dead, is purely coincidental.

ISBN: 978-1-922551-06-1

All rights reserved.

CHAPTER 1

"If you're fishing shallow and you're using a fifty, that's okay, but eighty is perfect. Regarding the drag, you see these numbers here near the spool? What that means is when I push this lever to a certain line, I know how much drag is there. When you look at this reel, I'll be pushing it up and letting him run. However, if I don't pull my drag, meaning literally pulling the line out, I could have too much drag—or not enough—and you'll end up losing the fish."

Captain Roger Washburn had given this speech maybe a thousand times in his twenty years of chartering. His client, Cliff Doel, nodded along, watching the rod as Roger explained the workings of swordfishing. Roger recognized the same lip scrunches and eyebrow raises of a man who barely understood anything being explained to him.

In his twenty years of fishing in the Keys, Roger Washburn could easily spot the difference between clients with knowledge on the art of fishing and those who had no idea what they were doing. Not that he minded showing them the ropes—it was what he was paid to do, after all. Those who were upfront about their ignorance weren't the problem. It was those who had no clue what they were doing, but wanted to present themselves as knowledgeable.

Judging by the smoking hot blonde Cliff had brought with him, he was clearly looking to make an impression. She was at least fifteen years younger than him. When they first met the previous day, she was in a bikini and taking snapshots of herself with her phone. *Instagram*, another tendril of the beast that was social media, consuming the attention of everyone in its grasp.

She was in jean shorts and a cutoff t-shirt. Once or twice, Roger allowed himself a glance of her figure. Nothing more than a visual appreciation, nothing more. Roger would never think of being with someone more than ten years his junior, and this chick was at least twenty.

Lately, his eyes had been wandering. Maybe he had been divorced too long. After his wife split, he kept to himself and refrained from mingling with women. Of the thirteen years of marriage, only the first two were pleasant. The rest was a hodgepodge of days where they didn't talk mixed with days they argued. Roger couldn't do anything right without her overreacting. If he went out for a drink, she'd claim he was getting wasted. If he smoked a cigar, he was a nicotine addict. It didn't matter that it was the first cigar in two weeks, he may as well have been a filthy drug user in her eyes.

Then came the divorce. She cheated on him, but of course it was his fault somehow. Then came the proceedings, allegations of abuse, demands for alimony, and the general desire to drain him of whatever assets she could. Lucky for Roger, she made one critical error. For one of the allegations of abuse, in which she claimed he struck her across the face during an argument, she used a specific date. She had been naming off dates of each incident, thinking it'd present some kind of credibility to her claims. The problem was that two of the dates apparently occurred when Roger was out of town, and had proof of his whereabouts.

That memory always made him smile. She hated that he saved his receipts, and claimed it just added to the clutter. During their divorce proceedings, those receipts *really* got on her nerves by blowing her whole narrative apart. The judge wasn't having any of it. She threw the book at the new ex-wife and dismissed her claims. Roger didn't owe her a penny. God bless that judge, as he figured he was doomed to pay alimony till he was six feet under.

Despite the win, the scars of the proceeding lasted quite a while. Roger avoided women like the plague. He wouldn't pick them up, take them to dinner, nothing. Eleven years of misery followed by the threat of his livelihood was enough.

Roger had watched the way this chick—Michelle was her name—hung around her man. She was well-spoken and didn't play dumb. Perhaps it was a genuine relationship. Still, Roger had a natural suspicion regarding men who liked younger women and women who liked older men. The guys were usually the womanizing types who skipped town as soon as they had enough, and the girls were usually trying to earn some coin from the stupid prick.

"So, what you're looking at is a relatively short rod. Fast action, bends at the tip, but has a lot of backbone. You've got a roller at the tip, built within the frame at the guide so it doesn't come off."

Cliff nodded. "What about that one?" He pointed at the rod behind Roger.

Of course he'd be more interested in the bigger one.

"This one is for down rigger. This is a Hooker Electric rod." Roger pulled the rod from the holder built in the gunwale of the boat. "This uses a motor that comes off if you want to make it a manual crank. Sixty-five pound test. It's heavier duty. The line comes to a ball-bearing swivel with a clip which can handle a lot of pressure. We put on a fifteen pound weight which obviously takes the tackle down to the bottom."

Cliff wiped the sweat from his brow with his cap. A North Dakota resident, he wasn't used to the heat down in the Florida Keys. Michelle, on the other hand, didn't seem fazed at all. She leaned against the gunwale, beer in hand, ready to watch her man bag the big one.

'Big'. Seemed guys were obsessed with size. Whether it was boats, fishing rods, biceps, or other parts of their anatomy, Roger couldn't deny that men were obsessed with size. As though bigger was always better. Sometimes that was the case, other times not so much.

His boat was a forty-foot striker. Roger had owned it for ten years, and in the decade before that, he owned another forty-footer. Fishing buddies often bragged to him, stating he should upgrade for fifty or sixty, while brandishing their big boats. Needless to say, with the size of the boat also came the size of the debts, and Roger was happy to pay off his vessel in half the time while those braggers still had years to go. He had his motto. "Bigger isn't always better. Bigger is worse." In Cliff's case, it would be humiliation to give the impression that he was an avid fisherman.

No, just another hotshot who caught a few bluegills and now thinks he's an expert.

Roger forced himself not to judge too hard. This couple was the first business he had in over a month. It was late July now. What was usually one of the most prosperous months out of the year had been completely sidelined after the big tsunami. Like the hand of God, it swept toward the southern East Coast, causing billions in damage and resulting in fifty deaths. Just as fast as the meteor that caused it, reservations were cancelled. Who wanted to spend their summer fishing in an area where first responders were searching for sunken vessels and dead bodies?

It took a little over a month before things were starting to return to normal. Cliff Doel took advantage of the new openings on Islamorada resorts, even managing to get a discounted price. Clearly, he wanted to get away for a while. Looking at the blonde he brought with him, it was easy for Roger to speculate what he had in mind. Of course, he couldn't help but notice the pale mark on Cliff's left ring finger. Separated? Recently divorced? Or out of town on a 'business trip'?

"So, you use salmon for bait, right?"

"Squid, actually," Roger said.

"Oh, you use squid! I see," Cliff said, trying to save face. Roger resisted the urge of saying something like 'that's *only* what we use for swordfish' but figured humiliating the guy wouldn't get him anywhere. At the end of the day, all he cared about was the paycheck. And to be fair, Cliff Doel was paying handsomely.

"How big do swordfish get?" Michelle asked.

"Up to fifteen-hundred pounds," Roger said.

"I heard they can get up to two-thousand," Cliff said, holding the rod like a knight with a broadsword.

"You're thinking marlin," Roger said. *There you go, thinking about size.* The captain climbed to the flybridge and looked at his chart. They were nearing the destination. Ten miles east of Islamorada and twelve-miles north of Cielo Nublado was his lucky spot for swordfish. In his cabin below, he proudly framed photos of his own catch, one with a fourteen-hundred pound swordfish, among images of his other trophies acquired over the years. "Alright, you guys ready to deploy the bait?"

"Damn right I am," Cliff said.

"You'll do great, babe," Michelle said. He slapped her ass then dug a beer from the cooler.

Roger pretended not to notice as he descended the ladder to the main deck. Couples having fun was one thing, but extramarital flings were something else entirely. When he arrived, Cliff was holding the Hooker Electric rod triumphantly.

"Let's get this party started."

The confidence in his face waned after the first hour. By the end of the second hour, Cliff was starting to subtly ask questions of other fishing spots. "Where'd you get that fish in the photo inside? How many places you usually fish?"

Roger knew the score. They were almost three hours in now. The time was nearing six. Despite what Roger had explained when they made their reservation, Cliff clearly thought he was going to hook a fish within a half-hour, reel it in, impress his girlfriend, then celebrate in their room upon return.

"Patience is the key," Roger said. "Often, I'm out for four hours before someone hooks a swordfish. Every day is different. Sometimes, the fish won't stop biting, other days, nothing."

Cliff sat in the fishing chair and watched the line extending from the rod. Michelle leaned against the transom, arms folded on the coaming as she looked out to the east.

"Was this where it happened?"

"Beg your pardon?" Roger said.

"The asteroid that hit. Wasn't it around here?"

"Oh!" Roger laughed. "No, it wasn't an asteroid. If that were the case, none of us would be here talking about it. It was a relatively small meteor, and no it didn't crash here. It landed about eighty miles east. Hit hard enough to cause a hell of a tidal wave, though."

"Did you see it?"

"I saw the wave."

"I mean, did you see the meteor? I figured it'd look like a shooting star falling toward the ocean."

"I saw the vapor cloud it created after it drifted this way. The thing was scalding hot after coming in through the atmosphere. They say it instantly vaporized a hundred-thousand gallons of water. Killed a bunch of fish in the area too. I volunteered in the search and rescue effort after a few yachts were reported missing. Found a bunch of floating fish, charred from the heat."

"Probably why we haven't found any here today," Cliff said.

"No." Roger chuckled. It was the only way he could keep himself from scoffing in a condescending manner. "I was out here a week ago on my own. Caught an eight-hundred pounder somewhere along this area. Took me about two hours. Just be patient, you'll get something."

Roger returned to the helm and bumped the boat forward against the current. Hopefully Cliff would get something. As Roger predicted, he wasn't the most pleasant of wannabe fishermen.

Another hour passed, and Cliff's line was still slack. He downed his fourth beer, then tossed the crust of a turkey sandwich into the water.

"Nothing's here," he said.

"Just be a little patient," Roger said.

"I've been patient. There's nothing here. I know it. Maybe the tsunami swept them away."

"It doesn't quite work like that," Roger said. "Fish move. That's why it's all about patience, regardless of what you're fishing for. It's all about finding the right area."

Cliff stood up out of the chair. "I thought you said this was where all the fish were."

"I never said that. I said this was where clients and I have experienced our best luck." Roger groaned. He knew where this conversation was leading. 'I didn't catch anything, so you owe me my money back.' Not only was this guy likely a cheating, unfaithful prick, but he was entitled. Hell, if his wife caught him with another woman, it'd probably somehow be *her* fault he was sleeping around. 'If you had done your job in the bedroom, I wouldn't be doing this.' Roger had seen those arguments made by asshats he once considered friends. Such types weren't easily negotiated with when they wanted their way. And Cliff Doel was definitely one of those types.

Cliff cracked open another beer and looked at the sky. "It'll be getting dark soon."

"You booked this charter for eight hours, starting at three o'clock," Roger said. "As for the results, there are no guarantees. Besides, you still might catch something." As far as Roger was concerned, there were two kinds of rich people. Those who simply enjoyed it, but didn't want to flaunt it. Then there were the power-hungry types, usually those who inherited it or otherwise obtained the wealth young. They tended to have a god complex, thinking they were entitled to everything they wanted. Apparently, Cliff was so entitled, he thought he *deserved* to have a swordfish embedded on his hook.

"You know what I think? I think you're a scammer," Cliff said.

"Oh, babe, stop it," Michelle said.

Roger nodded. *Yeah, listen to her, asshole. You're not impressing anybody, especially not your date.* It was clear that Cliff had no intention of being on the boat for the whole eight hours. He was certain he'd bag a trophy within two, then take her back to town, thinking she'd be all hot and heavy from witnessing his marvelous achievement. Roger cracked a smile. The guy didn't realize he probably would've been fighting with the swordfish for a couple of hours at best.

Cliff strutted around the deck, hands on his hips. He realized he wasn't doing himself any favors with Michelle by acting all tough with Roger. Apparently, she wasn't as impressed with attitude as she was money. Now, he was lost in the cycle of figuring out how to bounce back from this awkward moment.

Roger pointed at his line. "You might want to look…"

Cliff turned around. The line was taut. The drag growled as the line stretched out to sea. Something was bound on the hook.

Maybe this evening wasn't a bust after all. Cliff took the rod and began reeling in.

"Let it run for a few minutes first," Roger said. "Pull back, then lean forward quickly while reeling in the slack, then repeat. It'll take a while, so I hope you've got good stamina."

Cliff unbuttoned his shirt to reveal his sculpted pecs and abs. "Nothing to worry about there." He winked at Michelle, whose eyes were glued to the sight. A rich guy who wasn't fat. Not the most common of finds.

"If only she found one that wasn't married," Roger muttered under his breath.

"What?" Cliff said.

Roger cleared his throat. "Lean forward and reel it in." Cliff followed the instructions, cranking the reel as he leaned inward. "Alright, good. Now pull it back. It'll fight you, so just take it easy."

Cliff started to pull. His face turned red, his veins bulging from his forehead. "I…can't."

"Oh, come on, stud. Just lean back and put your shoulders to the chair."

Cliff groaned and tugged will all his might. The rod refused to move with him. "It won't move. It must be a *really* big fish!"

Once again, bigger is better.

"I'm sure it's big, but nothing your muscles can't handle."

"No, I'm serious. I can't even budge it."

Roger climbed down to the main deck. He felt the line to check if the weight had snagged something on the bottom. There was resistance. Whatever it was, it was gradually moving to the right, taking their line with it. A swordfish would be actively fighting them at the moment. Whatever had taken their bait was moving like a submarine, slow and silent, hardly taking notice of the attempt to haul it to the surface.

Suddenly, Cliff fell backward, the line coiling around the rod.

"Holy smokes! It snapped!" Michelle said.

"Damn it!" Cliff thumped his fist on the armrest, then tossed the rod on the deck.

"Whoa, man. Have respect for other people's property," Roger said. This time, he did away with keeping a nonaggressive tone.

"Property. You said that was a heavy-duty rig. And it snapped like nothing. I've seen kids' rods with better durability."

"It's not…" Roger looked at the coiled line. He'd seen fishing wire snap, but not that easily. It would've taken something with immense physical strength to break it with a simple tug.

The beer bottles clanged against each other. Roger felt the echo of something tapping the hull. The striker rocked backward, throwing all three occupants off balance.

Cliff went from agitated to alert. "What the hell was that?"

"Something hit the boat," Michelle said. She clung to his arm as they waited. Roger returned to the helm and looked at the water.

There, a couple hundred feet off the portside, he saw movement. From this distance, it was like looking at an enormous storm cloud calmly drifting under the waves. His brain went to work deducing what it could've been. A school of mackerel? He'd seen large clusters, though not traveling this shallow near a vessel, and not in that tight of a group. Whatever had hit the boat was a solid mass.

"What is it?" Michelle cried.

Roger couldn't answer. The thing was turning. Now facing the boat, it resembled a massive arrowhead. As though fired from a crossbow, it picked up speed.

It shallowed, a rigid blade-like ridge cutting through the surface. Roger Washburn now questioned whether it was *he* who drank all them beers, because either his senses were askew, or he was looking at a seven-foot dorsal fin.

The creature resembled a great white—except far bigger. Bigger in mass, bigger tail, bigger bite. It was his motto come to life. "Bigger isn't always better. Bigger, sometimes, is worse."

Like the arrow it resembled, the shark pierced the hull with its cone-shaped head. The hull imploded with ease, the striker folding into a V-shape as the hull and stern folded toward each other. With a thunderous *crack* the boat snapped in half.

Roger was swept off his feet by a raging wave. He could hear Michelle screaming. Within seconds, she already sounded as though she was hundreds of feet away. He summersaulted under the water, which proceeded to toss him about like a rag doll. It took all his might to reach the surface. When he did, the two halves of his boat had drifted hundreds of feet apart from each other. The bow was barely visible. It was moments away from descending to the depths. The stern side was twisting about as though placed on a merry-go-round, held afloat by an air pocket which would burst at any moment.

He grabbed onto a piece of debris, then rested. His frantic mind zipped back and forth between trying to comprehend what just happened and fighting for survival.

His boat was gone—sunk by a giant sea monster.

Michelle screamed again.

Roger propped himself up on the wreckage and scanned the horizon. She was north of him, about two-hundred feet away. Cliff was nowhere to be seen. Roger would look for him afterwards. First, he needed to reach Michelle. Drifting apart in all directions would only make it harder for Air-sea Rescue to find them—once they eventually started looking.

He kicked his feet with all his might. "Hold on! I'm coming over to you. Just keep your head above the water!"

"Hurry!" she cried.

Roger looked to the east as the remaining wreckage began to make its descent. The sight of the splintering deck, split hull, and the protruding ladder which formerly led to the flybridge brought his mind back to the shape that wrecked it. He scanned the water for that dreaded dorsal fin of impossible size. Even now, spitting saltwater every few seconds, his muscles aching from stroking the water, he was still questioning what he had just seen.

Every wave that passed by him made his heart jump. Every shadow that darkened the water gave him pause. He was trapped in a watery nightmare. The only way out was to keep going forward.

"Help!" Michelle cried. Roger just had a little ways to go. The poor girl was struggling to stay afloat. She had no life vest on. Half of her energy had probably been drained by the panic she was experiencing.

"Grab on!"

Michelle latched herself to the slab of deck and rested her head. "Oh my god! What was that?!"

"I don't know."

"I thought you knew all the fish that were in these waters!"

"I—" *She seriously expects me to know about a ninety-foot shark?* Roger allowed himself to take a deep breath. The girl was frightened and probably wouldn't have a rational thought until they were on dry land. He lifted his head and looked past her.

He saw a white shirt fifty feet away, and a head with brown hair clinging to a piece of hull. "There! I see Cliff."

Michelle looked over her shoulder. "Cliff! We're over here!"

Cliff remained still, his head slumped over the wreckage. Unconscious, maybe?

"Stay here. I'll go get him and bring him over." Roger pushed off the deck piece and swam toward the half-drunk adulterer. With the water calming, he was able to close the distance faster. He grabbed the piece of hull to hold himself up. "Cliff, you alright?" The man didn't answer. "Hey! Wake up!" He smacked the client across the face. Still no answer.

Roger groaned. That damn booze combined with the trauma had made him pass out. He reached across the hull and grabbed a fistful of Cliff's hair. "Come on, wake up!" He lifted his head off the hull, then stared silently at the pale face of a slack-jawed man with half closed, glazed-over eyes. Roger lowered his head and stared at the white shirt. It was torn to ribbons, waving free as a flag and twisting over itself, as though there wasn't a body it was fitted over to give it definite form.

Something wasn't right with this image. Roger grabbed Cliff by the shoulder and lifted him. The first thing he noticed was how light Cliff felt. The second were the strings of flesh and jagged bone fragments protruding down from his torso. Everything below the shoulders had been bitten off.

There was no doubt in his mind now. There was indeed a giant shark in the water.

Roger screamed and raced back toward Michelle.

"What are you doing? Why are you leaving him?!" she shouted. Roger couldn't reply. He closed within ten feet, then stopped. Michelle saw the look on his face. "What's going on? What did you see?"

It wasn't what he had seen, but what he was *seeing*. The water under Michelle darkened. That shape that took his vessel had returned. Growing larger with each passing second, it 'split' revealing white, jagged triangular shapes attached to red lines.

The mouth broke the surface, the teeth clamping down on Michelle. Like a steak knife through a hot dog, she was cut in half in a split-second. The jaws snapped repeatedly, scooping up every bit of its prey before facing the third victim in the water.

Clouds of blood surrounded Roger. He was literally in the middle of an ocean of red. A bloodbath.

The red water parted, and the huge mouth emerged. The next world of red was from his own guts spilling from his body as he was diced in seven-inch teeth and swallowed.

CHAPTER 2

"Hey, Chief. I've got a call for ya."

Just by the tone of Suzy O'Rourke's voice on the radio, Nico Medrano knew his peaceful morning was about to be interrupted by nonsense.

"I suppose it's why they pay me the big bucks," he said, looking down at the badge on his sweat-stained shirt. "Let me guess: Dan Huckert is taking issue with vacationers?"

"You surprised?"

"Oh, OF COURSE I am!" He and his dispatcher shared a laugh.

"To be fair, this might be a legitimate complaint this time, Chief."

"Oh really?"

"You remember those jet skiers from the other day?"

Nico closed his eyes and threw his head back. "Oh great. Those idiots again? The ones that almost ran over the people swimming by their luxury yacht?"

"Seems like these guys get their kicks out of annoying boaters."

"It's looking that way. Go figure they'd pick Dan Huckert to annoy and harass. I'll give him credit for calling us, though. Usually, he brandishes the shotgun first." He sighed. "What's his position?"

"Half mile northwest of the weather buoy. They're not using jet skis this time. Jet BOATS instead."

"Fabulous. Alright, I'm on my way." Nico stood by the anchor, allowing himself a few extra moments to keep an eye on the kids swimming at the south beach. It was shallow, and the boating activity was sparse on this end of the island. Still, the parental side of him was overpowering. Since being appointed Chief of Police three years ago, there hadn't been a single drowning along the shores of Cielo Nublado. The only injuries and fatalities were further out, usually involving alcohol and misuse of boating equipment.

Better get moving, or the next fatality will be homicide.

He hauled the anchor up then pointed his boat northwest. "Time to work."

The journey to his destination took the Chief along the west side of the island. It was eight in the morning and already the heat was a killer. People were getting on their boats, laying their towels on the beaches, swimming, and partaking in the various other luxuries the island had to offer. Charters were departing, with clients paying thousands of dollars per day in hopes of a single snapshot of them with a two-thousand pound marlin. Some succeeded while others returned empty-handed. Then there were the adrenaline-rush types who preferred to parasail and jet ski. In this heat, Nico couldn't blame them. Life was too short not to have fun.

Then there were the types like the Klingberg brothers. The *Three Stooges*, as Nico preferred to think of them, they were always causing some sort of issue. Two days ago, his office received complaints from a fishing charter. The Klingbergs were zipping around the boat while the client had a thousand pound marlin on the hook. The incident presented two issues: the annoyance of the charter and its passengers, and the risk of injury to the jet skiers themselves. The bill of a marlin was no joke. It didn't happen often, but with the right angle and enough force, those things could run a man through. And these jokers from Texas were carelessly speeding around it like flies around shit.

At the end of the day, the Klingbergs were cowards. They enjoyed annoying people until the law showed up. Nico's reputation preceded him. He had heard through the grapevine that most of the resorts would give friendly warnings to all their guests about misconduct. Apparently during these 'briefings,' as Nico thought of them as, many resort staff would state that they had the Wolf of Waco as their police chief.

His ten years as lieutenant in the Homicide Division was his selling point when campaigning for the relatively cushy job as Cielo Nublado's Police Chief. Twice, he solved cases that achieved national attention. There was the Wilbur Shooter, who ambushed the CEO of an electronics company. Nico's investigation of the case not only led him to the whereabouts of the killer, but his investigation of the victims themselves provided insight to the motivation. As it turned out, the shooter was paid off by an up-and-coming business rival who wanted to stir chaos in the competition with the sudden death of its CEO.

Then there was the Phil Treece murder. A famous Rockstar on tour in Waco met a fateful end, supposedly due to his addiction to heroin. The local media at the time was quick to push the headlines of 'Phil Treece: Death by Heroin Overdose.' For Nico, attention to detail went a long way. The scars from Phil's previous injections were always on the inside of his elbow. The new needle wound, however, was in his forearm.

"Interesting that he'd change spots on the exact occurrence that killed him," he had said. Though the autopsy revealed his death was indeed by heroin, the state of the bedsheets and couch indicated a female was in the room with him. Again, not a surprise, as Phil Treece enjoyed his sexual encounters. Except DNA results showed that this latest woman wasn't just a fan eager to give herself to her hero for a night.

Three years prior, Phil Treece had made headlines when a woman accused him of sexual assault. Though it went through the usual news cycles, nothing came of it. The charges were dropped, the woman's lawyers backed out, leading many to believe Phil had paid them off.

Nico's investigation of his death revealed that the woman who slept with him on that fateful night was no other than the accuser's younger sister. Out for vengeance, she spent a vigorous night with him, then as the Rockstar was sleeping, she injected him with an overdose of his own drugs, then departed.

If Nico learned anything from his experience as a detective, it was that nothing was as simple as it seemed at first glance. Some believed that was his reason for transferring to the island paradise of Cielo Nublado. Nico let them think that, as there was no need for them to know why he wanted to get the hell out of Texas.

As much as he tried to put the last weeks of his former life out of his mind, it always returned to him as he watched the kids playing on the beach. That *one* attention to detail he missed had cost him everything.

The rush of ocean wind on his face just from operating the police boat was welcome. It helped to distract him from the gloomy memories that lingered in his mind. He had grown to love being on the water and couldn't imagine any other way of life from here on. The job was simpler, the scenery was nicer, the people were friendlier, and most visitors just wanted to have a nice time before returning to their normal lives.

The worst thing he had dealt with since taking the job was the tsunami. The island was fortunate to suffer minimal damage, largely due to his preparation efforts. He had heard the report of the meteor entering the planet's atmosphere. When it was revealed how large it was and where it would land, he realized disaster was near. He issued an emergency broadcast, sent his chopper unit to alert all boats in the vicinity, closed the beaches, and mandated everybody move inland.

Cielo Nublado did not suffer a single casualty. Many labeled Nico Medrano a hero for his efforts. It was hard for him to accept being called that. How can one be a hero for simply doing his job? Letting people get caught in the inevitable wave would make him a bad leader and a worse human. Regardless, he was grateful that, so far, that was the worst thing he had faced in his three years. Compared to that meteor, jokers like the Klingbergs were a walk in the park.

I suppose something's gotta keep me on my toes.

As Nico passed the southwest cove, his radio crackled. *"Hey, Chief. You need any assistance?"*

He chuckled. Renny Jackman displayed the eager qualities of a rookie but with the skill of a professional. He was always volunteering for overtime, was usually the first one to show up at calls, and to keep the already high morale boosted, would host barbeques for the officers and EMS staff.

"I don't think it's anything I can't handle."

"You sure? I can take the chopper and provide air support!"

"Ha! No need for that. This isn't Vietnam. Just keep an eye on the beaches, will ya?"

"You got it, boss."

Nico clipped his mic back to the collar of his shirt and kept course. After a few minutes, he spotted a yacht roughly a thousand feet to his ten o'clock. A fisherman was on the desk, seated in a chair, with a few peers cheering him on. The rod was bent, the fisherman leaning forward and spinning the reel quickly, then slowly pulling back.

As he took the boat northwest, he gradually neared the vessel. The green and white stripes on the side made it easily identifiable as Burt Nelson's striker. The distance closed to five hundred feet as he passed them by. Cheers erupted from the deck as the marlin on the end of the line breached the surface like a missile. The fish looked to be twelve feet in length and possibly eight hundred pounds.

Burt Nelson's voice came through the radio. *"Hey, Chief! I see ya over there! You ought to come check this out."*

"I see it from here," Nico said, waving to the boat captain. "Hell of a way to start the morning. Unfortunately, I can't stop by. I'm on my way toward adventures of my own. Maybe if you're still at it, I'll swing by on my way back."

"The odds are in your favor. This bad boy isn't going down without a fight. It'll be a couple hours before he's in the boat."

"Good to know. In the meantime, wish your customers good luck for me."

****

"Will do." Burt put his radio down on the console and proceeded to watch the spectacle from the flybridge. Tony, the fisherman in the chair, grunted as he heaved the rod back. His two kids were bouncing up and down on their toes, eager to see the fish leap once more.

His wife patted his shoulder. "Keep at it, hon!"

"Come on, Dad!" the older son said.

"Working on it," Tony said. He leaned forward and cranked the reel. The fish jumped again, its bill slicing the air like a sword.

"Allow yourself moments to rest. It's starting to run. Let it wear itself down," Burt said.

"Okay." The rod wavered in Tony's hands. It felt like it would be yanked from his grasp at any moment. Keep it in the holder, and for godsake, don't let go.

His younger son stood at the transom. "Hey...what's that?" He pointed to their one o'clock.

Burt raised his binoculars to his eyes and looked. "Uh-oh."

"What's wrong?" the wife asked.

"Looks like somebody's interested in your prize, Tony."

"Huh?" Tony was too busy fighting the marlin to look.

"Oh, I see it," his wife said. "Oh my! It's a shark!"

"It's a big shark!" the younger son said.

The older one rushed to the transom. "Wow!"

"How big is it?" Tony asked.

Burt chuckled. "Just a mako. Maybe twelve feet long. However, it is moving toward your marlin."

"Wait... it's gonna eat my fish?!"

"It might try and take a chunk out of it," Burt said.

"Can't we stop it?"

"I'm afraid there's not much we can do regarding that."

"Except get it on video." The older son pulled out his smartphone and started recording.

Tony shot him a glare. "Figures you'd record *that* and not your old man reeling in this fish."

The kid didn't take much notice of anything his father said. He watched the shark, keeping it centered on his screen. For a few moments, the dorsal fin moved along the surface directly toward the struggling marlin. Detecting the second threat, the marlin went to dive.

"Looks like the mako's following," Burt said.

"Aw man, we're gonna miss it!" the older son said.

The predator moved in for the kill. The target was weak and not making distance. The shark had no understanding of the nearly invisible wire that prevented the marlin from escaping. Its brain was fixated on the struggling motion and the small hint of blood that leaked from the wound caused by the hook. Blood and struggle were major indicators of easy prey, regardless of size.

Its target was still attempting to dive deep, its body wiggling like that of an eel. It was swimming in place, not gaining any additional distance. The mako, on the other hand, was not bound by external factors. It had free range, full strength, and an empty stomach to fill. Just a few more feet and its inch-long teeth would shred a five-pound chunk from the marlin.

It snapped its jaws. The teeth intertwined over nothing but useless water. The marlin had turned around and darted for the surface, right for the boat carrying the humans.

Before the shark could pursue, its lateral line detected a new distortion. Something large, moving fast. These were not struggling movements or even cruising speed. They were fast, growing steadily stronger. And nearer.

The predator was now the prey, and unlike the marlin, the mako had hesitated too long before fleeing. It turned and shot for the surface, making no more than a few yards before being engulfed in the titanic jaws. It felt the brief and agonizing sensation of huge teeth cutting through its body like slabs. Even as death took it, it still saw the water's surface growing ever closer and brighter, giving it a vain hope of escape.

"Whoa! The line went slack!" Toby said. He cranked the reel rapidly.

Burt descended to the main deck and stood by his side. "Did the line break?"

"No… I think—holy shit!"

The ocean splattered the deck as the marlin breached within a few feet of the stern. Its bill struck the transom, splashing the family a second time.

"Hurry! Hurry! Hurry! Reel in the slack! You've almost got it!" Burt said, twirling his hand near Tony's wrist. Tony cranked repeatedly, successfully bringing in the line before the marlin could make any real distance. It was just a few feet from the boat. Burt put on his gloves and went to the side. The marlin breached again, thrusting its bill like a fencer. Burt grabbed it and wrestled the fish down. "Nice work, Tony! You've got it!" He pressed the bill to the board. "This might be around six-hundred pounds. Not bad for your first catch."

He was surprised not to hear the family cheering. Instead, he heard one of the kids ask, "Dad, what's that?" When he looked over his shoulder, he saw they were looking straight out with flabbergasted expressions. He followed their gazes and spotted the bright red cloud of blood in the water.

"Did the shark bite my fish?" Tony asked.

"No. It's completely intact as far as I can see." Burt plunged a hook into the fish's gill slit and held it in place. "Keep that line tight. I'm gonna hold it here for a sec, then we'll get a line on its tail and haul it up. Then we'll—"

"What's that?" the youngest son said.

"I see something in the water," the wife said. "It looks like a—AHH!" She cupped her mouth as the decapitated head of the mako shark broke the surface like the projectile cork of a champagne bottle.

CHAPTER 3

At a quarter after eight, the north beach was crowded with over five hundred people taking advantage of the relatively cool morning. Parents played with their kids in the shallows, various groups set up volleyball nets, and people eager to relax in the water started pumping air into their inflatables.

For Renny Jackman, the best part of his job were the women who sunbathed with their bikini tops undone as they lay face-down to avoid that pale line screwing up their tan. Just one instance was all it would take. A volleyball kid stumbling out too far, an unplanned adjustment to get more comfortable, *anything.*

"It's not gonna happen."

Renny glanced over his shoulder at the officer with the short tomboy haircut, barbed wire wrist tattoo, and .357 magnum at her waist. Despite the sunglasses, he could detect the judgement in her eyes. Nothing new, she did it all the time. Likewise, Renny would do something to aggravate her. It was a natural part of their daily banter.

"I don't know what you're talking about."

"Uh-huh." She sipped her coffee and handed him his cup that she bought from the local café further down the beach. "You're not fooling anybody, Renny. You can stare all you want, but us ladies are well-trained against creeps like you. You're not getting a tit-peek, no matter how hard you try."

"What?!" Renny pretended to be offended. "I'm clearly looking out for the wellbeing of everyone on this beach. I swore an oath to this community, and—" He watched Carley text something on her phone then await the response with a grin on her face. "What did you do?"

"Just texted your wife to let her know her husband's being a perve again."

"Ah, THANKS!"

Her phone chimed. Carley smiled again as she read the response. She typed a quick reply, then lightly smacked Renny on the chin.

"HEY! What the hell was that for?" Carley held the screen so he could see his wife's text. *"Go ahead and slap him for me."* To which Carley replied, *"Will do."* "Oh, I see how it is!"

"That's what you get."

"For protecting and serving—oh…"

Carley followed his eyes at a pair of athletic blondes wearing bikinis a size too small for the good they covered. "I guess I should've smacked you harder."

"Oh, I'm sure you're offended. Like you don't check out the dudes on this beach."

"Whenever I see one without a beer gut."

"Ha! I see how it is. So it's okay for you to look around, but for *me* it's taboo."

"You're waiting for these chicks to lean up or roll over without putting their tops on. Not the same thing. If I notice a dude, and I'm not confirming or denying I do, I'm admiring his figure. Not watching for their trunks to fall off."

"But if they did…"

Carley rolled her eyes and shook her head. "How the hell did I go down this rabbit hole?"

"I don't know. Because you're jealous, maybe? I hear flat-chested women are envious of their well-endowed counterparts."

Carley pointed a finger. "Keep that shit up and I'll slap you for my own gratification." Renny suppressed a laugh long enough for him to drink his coffee. The two of them proceeded to watch the various activity on the beach. Swimmers moved out to the shark nets which were three hundred feet from shore. Beyond those barriers were a couple of sailboats cruising by, operated by college-age people.

When Carley glanced back at Renny, she noticed him watching a woman walking along the beach. "You're on a roll this morning, aren't you?"

"What?"

"What do you mean 'what'? What's the matter? You not getting any at home, so you having a little mental porno."

"I do that even when I *am* getting some," Renny said. "But I'm innocent in this specific instance. I'm just watching the kids."

Carley looked to the woman in question and realized she was walking along the shore with two toddlers. The little boys, three and two, giggled as they splashed the water with their tiny feet.

"Oh, I see. Living up to the Chief's expectations. Guy's very protective of kids."

"He has good reason to be."

"Why? Ever since he came here, he has always emphasized protection of children. Not like there aren't a hundred lifeguards on this island with that exact responsibility. Also, it's not like this island's known for drownings."

"It's not meant to insult your intelligence. Nico's just, uh… it's a little personal. That's all I can say."

"You've mentioned that before. Sounds like the Chief has a soft spot for kids."

"Yeah, that's fair to say."

Carley waited for Renny to follow that statement up with something, only nothing came of it. Usually, Renny had no issues telling secrets and spreading a moderate amount of gossip without letting it get out of hand. The fact that he kept his statements about Nico and his overprotectiveness of kids indicated that he was respectful of the Chief's privacy. Still, it felt a tad insulting that he wouldn't let her in on the secret. They'd been working together for ten years, with him getting hired just a couple of months after her. They attended each other's weddings, were always addressed as 'work husband' and 'work wife', and were such good friends that neither spouse had any issues with them going to concerts or to the bar together.

Whatever background he had on the Chief, it had to be strictly personal. It couldn't be criminal or immoral—Renny wouldn't have issues spilling the beans to her on that. With that in mind, she suspected he came into this knowledge by accident. Nico was a nice man and a good leader who made a strong bond with his officers. He had been fairly open about his personal life during casual chatting. They'd talk sports—he was a *Dodgers* fan—they'd talk about boats, movies, marriage advice. Nico was married once for ten years, though Carley didn't know about the details of the divorce. It didn't make sense that there was something he would only want Renny to know and not the others.

"What time is it?" Renny asked.

"Eight-twenty."

"Ugh."

"What? Got a date?"

"No, I'm hungry."

"Already? Didn't you have an egg biscuit sandwich already?"

"I did. It wore off."

"How the hell did it wear off after an hour? It's not like you're pumping iron or jogging."

"I don't know. Ask my stomach. Regardless, I can't take it anymore. Go over to that breakfast stand and get me a bacon and egg burrito."

Carley turned to face him, eyes wide. "Um, ex-CUSE me."

"You heard me, woman."

Her jaw dropped. "Oh…OH!" She smiled, suppressing a range of responses. It wasn't that she was afraid she'd offend Renny, but she was a uniformed officer in public, and a few vulgar statements wouldn't bode well. Instead, the smartphone came out.

"Getting me in trouble again?" he said with a chuckle.

"Damn right I am. I'm seeing to it you sleep on the couch tonight."

"Joke's on you. I'm gonna work my charm when I get there. All it'll take is a quick stop at the store. I'll grab a bouquet of flowers, a romantic card, some chocolates. Not only will I sleep in bed, she'll be *insisting* I do." He laughed as his partner continued to text. "You're telling her my master plan, aren't you?"

"Hey, look at that! You're actually a tad smarter than I gave you credit for."

Renny downed the rest of his coffee then proceeded to eyeball the crowd. "Well, if I'm sleeping on the couch already, I guess any transgression from here on is free." In his peripheral vision, he saw Carley smirk. Her thumb was still hitting the keyboard. "You're gonna tell her I said that too, aren't you?"

"Mm-hmm."

"Couch it is." He went to finish off his coffee, only to lower it. Both eyebrows raised as the sunbathing women pushed to their feet and turned, breasts fully exposed. "Whoa…"

As soon as they turned, they started running, along with the rest of the crowd. Screams echoed across the beach. Those in the water were racing for the shore. On the other side of that shark barrier, a massive swell approached. Beneath that wave was a dark mass, making a straight line for the beach. It struck one of the sailboats, flipping it over and launching its occupants head-over-heels into the water.

The shark barrier folded inward, the buoys holding in place skidding along with the swell.

Renny and Carley ran into the crowd. "Move! Move! Get out of the way!" They waved their hands, directing people out of the mass' path.

"What is it?" Carley said. Renny didn't answer. He took her by the arm and ran to the left.

A big black head rose over the water. It struck the shoreline, generating a massive cloud of sand.

Renny and Carley caught their breath and watched as a fifty foot sperm whale writhed along the beach.

"Whew!" Renny rubbed his forearm over his brow then slowly approached. "Everybody alright?" He saw a few kids with iPhones approaching the creature. "Don't get too close."

The forty ton creature settled and released a wet mist from its blowhole. It lay motionless on its side, the sand around it turning red.

Carley carefully moved to her left, getting a view of its underside. "My God... Renny, you see this?"

He nodded. All along the whale's body were massive craters where the flesh had been torn away. "That's not normal."

"What the hell could've done this to a whale this size?"

"I don't know. Orcas, maybe."

"I'll get ahold of Dispatch," Carley said.

"Tell them to get EMS up here and a boat patrol unit." He took a deep breath and waited for the adrenaline rush to settle down. As he did, he watched the crowd to make sure they were keeping their distance. A pair of women stepped out, frantically looking for their tops. Renny shrugged. "At least something good came out of this."

Carley groaned. "There's something wrong with you."

"It gets worse. I'm still hungry."

CHAPTER 4

When Nico located Dan Huckert's boat, the Klingbergs were nowhere to be found. All it took was the knowledge that police were on their way for them to depart.

Dan Huckert was sitting on the deck of his boat. He wore a constant sneer on his face, like a wild canine guarding a dead squirrel. A fifty-three year old man, recently retired from twenty-five years of service in the Florida Department of Corrections, he looked twenty years older. Two-and-a-half decades in one of the worst occupations in the country, with constant mandatory overtime would do that to a human being. Despite his unfriendliness, it was still painful for Nico to see Dan looking so worn. He knew the average life expectancy of corrections officers was around fifty-eight. Judging by how rugged Dan looked, he predicted he was going to fit that statistic perfectly. It made it all the more frustrating that his retirement was being hindered by hotshots in their early twenties. Yeah, Dan Huckert was known as the black sheep of Cielo Nublado, but the guy did serve his community honorably. And knowing a few correctional staff that went wayward, sneaking contraband, taking bribes from inmates or family members of inmates, Nico thought Dan turned out okay considering.

Nico pulled the boat up near Dan's. "Good morning, partner."

"Wish it were!" Dan said.

The Chief read the tone. No point in small talk. For once, Dan was pissed off for good reason. There was a large red marking on the starboard quarter of his fishing yacht that wasn't there before.

"I'm guessing they did that."

"Damn right. They're lucky I didn't shoot their sorry asses."

"They're lucky, I'm lucky, and *you're* lucky," Nico said. "It's been long enough since I've had a murder case. Don't ruin that streak for me, please."

Dan looked down at the marking on his boat, then shot Nico a glare. "Don't worry. You would've never known. I'd just let the bastards sink. Let the sharks have a little midnight snack."

"That's…that's great. I'm glad you felt the need to let me know. I—" Nico closed his eyes and remembered there was no use carrying on. "Which way did they go?"

Dan pointed to the north. "They bucked it a few moments after I called your dispatch."

"Gotcha. Was it all three of them?"

"Yep. Got 'em on video here." Dan pulled his smartphone from his pocket, put the recording on the screen, then tossed it to Nico.

Nico saw the date and time at the top of the screen. Gotta love modern technology. Makes cases such as these far easier. He pressed play and watched the three assholes speeding around Dan's fishing line.

"Get out of here!" The retiree was met with middle fingers and laughter from the Klingbergs, who sped around in two rented jetboats. Cruising in the red one was Ralf. He was the oldest of the Klingbergs, easily distinguishable by his height. He was at least six inches taller than his two brothers, both of whom were around five-eight. At the helm of the second boat was Fredrick. He was easily identifiable thanks to his shaggy hair which, if dyed any color, would officially give him the appearance of a clown. Considering his behavior, it would've fit. In the passenger seat was Nate, a skinny bastard whose arms looked as though they'd snap off if he attempted to lift a dumbbell.

As the video continued, Nico watched as the morons sped closer and closer to the stern of his boat. As the one named Nate passed by, he inadvertently put himself on a collision course with Ralf, who swerved and sideswiped Dan's boat. Instead of having an 'oh shit' moment and considering that they had gone too far, the three of them spent the next minute laughing and hollering, despite Dan's increasing profane threats.

Nico reflected on his previous encounter with them. Two days ago, they were reported speeding near one of the beaches, close to the shark nets. After numerous complaints and one interaction with one of his officers, the Klingbergs moved out to sea. Afterwards, they found a fishing charter to harass. Nico was already out on his patrol boat and responded to the complaint. When he arrived, he saw the jerks hauling ass to the south side of the island. He ordered Officer Renny Jackman to standby at the docks, where he intercepted the brothers after they came ashore.

Nico hoped it would be a simple matter of taking their names, giving them a stern warning with the threat of being kicked off the island should they not comply. That hope lasted a few hours when they decided to harass a waitress in a bar later that afternoon. That incident, unfortunately, wasn't reported until the following morning, after Nico had to deal with another incident regarding them. He was called to respond to an altercation at Roscoe's Diner between Ralf Klingberg and—of all people—Dan Huckert. Like immature high schoolers, they were making a ruckus, which angered the retiree who was simply trying to enjoy a quiet breakfast.

Like this occasion, they vanished, though Nico suspected it wasn't due to police response, but to avoid getting a beating from Dan. They talked tough, had high opinions of themselves, but at the end of the day, they were children in adult bodies.

"It's about damn time you did something about them," Dan said.

"Thanks to this, it will be done," Nico said. "Once I figure out where they are, they're going to get a boat ride to Miami. That, of course, will come after a few nights in a jail cell and a hefty fine. Bob Greek's gonna be pissed too, after he sees the damage done to his jetboat."

"Well, get to it then!" Dan said, throwing his arms in the air. "Just like yesterday, you were late to the party."

"Oh, come on, Dan. Sounds to me like you had it under control!" Nico's smile faded. He should've known his humor was lost on the miserable prick.

"If they come near me one more time, I won't be wasting my breath calling your sorry ass, Chief. I'll handle the situation myself." Dan held his shotgun high. Nico felt his throat dry up. Just the fact that Dan had the weapon so close meant he was seconds away from brandishing it—or worse, using it—against the Klingbergs.

"Come on, Dan. You know better. You've worked in a prison all your life. You don't want to go back—especially not as an inmate. Won't bode well for you once your new neighbors discover your occupation. And you know as well as I do, they will."

"Only if I'm caught."

"Oh, right! Not like you bragging about it here won't make you the first person I'd look at if anything happened—you know what? Never mind. I'm gonna track them down and take care of the issue. Anything else happens, just radio me directly. Alright?" He tossed Dan's phone back to him. "Do me a favor and email me that video when you get a chance."

Dan hauled his anchor up then returned to the helm of his boat. "Yeah, fine."

"Don't do anything foolish now. Please. I'm asking nice."

"Foolish? Give me a break. I'm the nicest guy you've ever met, Chief." Dan started the engine and took off.

Nico shook his head. "I'm gonna press X to doubt on that one." He cut the wheel to port and took the boat north. With nobody on the horizon, it was likely the Klingbergs had either moved back to the island, or, considering how far out they were, had probably rented a boat to haul the jet skis back and forth. Knowing how rich they were and enjoyed throwing money around, it was probably the latter.

As he reached for the radio to radio dispatch, a series of transmissions came through.

Carley Amburn was the first. *"Unit Four to Dispatch, we have a weird situation over on North Beach."*

"Go ahead."

"Bear with me on this one. We just had a whale beach itself."

"You found a whale?"

"No, it found US. It plowed through the shark barriers and threw itself onto the sandbank. Like the freaking devil was after it."

"Unit Five here. She's right, Dispatch. I think it's dead now. I'm not sure if it was trying to escape a pod of orcas or something, but it's practically been gutted," Renny Jackman said.

"Can you get EMS en route, please. We've got a couple minor injuries over here. We also need a patrol boat unit to help some people in the water."

"Getting on the horn now," Suzie replied.

Nico pointed his boat to the island and maxed the throttle.

"Unit one here. I'm on my way. Keep everyone back."

"Way ahead of you, Chief," Renny said.

"Good man." He clipped the speaker back and watched the island come into view. The Klingbergs would have to wait. Nico exhaled sharply, replaying the radio transmissions in his head. "A freaking sperm whale racing to shore? What the hell would cause it to do that?"

CHAPTER 5

It wasn't normal to see the northern beach so quiet on a summer morning. When Nico arrived, there were two boat units patrolling the water, five car units on the beach, and three ambulances.

Even from a few hundred feet out, he could see the huge bite wounds in the whale's hide. They were nearly seven feet wide and at least a yard deep, if not more. The only thing that made sense was a pod of orcas, though it was weird that there wouldn't be any smaller wounds from individual bites.

Then again, I'm no expert on the way killer whales hunt. Maybe they focus on a couple of key areas to bite.

He waved to the other boat units then passed by the shark net. At least, what was left of it. A large portion had been ripped down the middle as the whale made landfall. It would have to be replaced by the island maintenance division.

Carley Amburn and Renny Jackman were standing by the dead whale, along with the island mayor and a few of his staff. Behind them was a fairly large crowd watching the corpse with anticipation, as though they expected it to spring back to life at any point.

A hundred yards east was a small harbor. Nico moored the boat and walked down the beach. His eyes went to the nearest ambulance. A few young twenty-somethings were being treated for sprains. While walking, he overheard their statement to the officer with a notepad.

"We were just sailing, then boom! The thing emerged."

"It struck your sailboat?" the officer asked.

"Not directly. We got caught in the swell. I never thought something so big could move so fast."

"I always thought whales washed up on the beach, not deliberately swam there," the girlfriend said. "This one seemed pretty damn eager."

Some of Nico's officers were putting caution tape around the animal. A few local press snapped pictures of his arrival, then rushed into his path with pens pressed to their notepads.

"Chief?! What's your opinion on this bizarre event?"

"Will the beaches be closed?"

"How do you address the injured swimmers who are planning to sue the island?"

Nico put his hands up. "Whoa! Let's not get too far ahead of ourselves, gentlemen. No, the beaches will *not* be closed. Don't be ridiculous. We're talking about a dead whale on the beach, not a great white picking off swimmers. As for the lawsuits, that's not my department."

"People are saying the whale swam to the beach with intent."

"Well—*yeah*! It was probably attacked by a pod of orcas and was trying to flee."

"Should we be worried? If killer whales are this eager to attack an animal of this size, are our swimmers at risk?"

Nico chuckled. "Have you ever watched the *Discovery Channel*? This sort of thing happens all the time—minus the whale charging through a crowd of swimmers to escape. Plus, I don't think there's ever been a case of orcas attacking humans. Now, if you please."

He squeezed through the blockade of reporters and made his way to the caution tape. He ducked underneath it and gazed at the whale. "Damn!"

"Fun morning, isn't it, Chief?" Renny said.

Nico glanced over his shoulder to make sure the journalists weren't eavesdropping. "About as fun as a hernia. We're damn lucky this thing didn't kill anybody." He faced the two officers, remembering they were on the beach when it happened. "How 'bout you guys? You alright?"

"Oh, yeah. We're fine," Carley said. "Just happened so fast. One moment, the world was normal. People were swimming, tanning, Ren was being a prude, as usual."

Nico grinned. *Renny's gonna get us in trouble one of these days.*

"Then the ocean opened up like in some Greek mythological story. Next thing we know, this fella slams into the beach. Died about a minute later."

"With gaping wounds like this, it's a wonder how it survived up to this point," Renny said.

"Adrenaline, I suppose," Nico said. He stepped closer to the wounds. "Jesus, I can *fit* into one of these." He looked at one of the bites in the stomach region. It was so deep the internal organs were exposed. The smell was atrocious enough to keep Carley and Renny at bay. Nico, on the other hand, was no stranger to horrible odors. Being a homicide detective for ten years, he had seen too many bodies in various stages of decay. There were suicides that went undiscovered until the smell grew so horrible. Murdered victims stuffed into trash bags and cans, which were hidden behind alleys where nobody wandered. It was enough to make one question humanity. For Nico, a dead whale was the least disturbing 'homicide' he ever reported to. At least, from what he could see, this was simply nature taking its course.

He walked around the back, finding one more bite wound along the whale's head. Every wound had the same basic shape. Despite his attempts to convince himself it was a pod of orcas, Nico still found it bizarre how each wound looked like a single bite.

"Nah, can't be. Had to be killer whales. Nothing in the water that can make bites that big." He walked to the fluke. Interestingly, it was untouched. "Okay, now that's strange."

"What's strange?" Carley asked.

"Orcas would've attacked the fluke. Keep their prey from being able to swim efficiently."

"You seem to know a lot about killer whales," Carley said.

"I've got a little inside knowledge," Nico said.

"Yeah? Big fan of *National Geographic?*" Carley said.

Nico shrugged. "Sure." Carley noted the slight change in his tone. It was a 'sure' that sounded more like 'I'm done talking about this'. Subtle, not rude, but just enough for her to know to not pursue.

Okay. Apparently, his expertise on sea life is a touchy subject.

Nico's gaze moved to the small dorsal fin on the whale's back. "Ah, damn it."

"What's the matter?" Carley said.

"It's got a tag. Whoever was tracking this thing probably won't be too pleased."

Renny laughed. "What? You think they'll want us to arrest the orcas that killed it?"

"No, smartass. But we will have to give the institution a call. They'll probably want to send somebody to get a look at the thing before it gets hauled out to sea."

He heard the pull of caution tape as Mayor Robert Zahn ducked underneath. "Did I hear you right, Nico? You're gonna hold up the operation to get this thing off the beach?"

"Relax, Rob. There's other beaches where people can gather. It's just a hundred feet around this thing that's being blocked off."

"But the smell!"

"It's only bad when you're right next to it. The thing will be taken out of here before it gets worse. But it's got a tracking tag, meaning it was being studied for research by..." Nico glanced at the label on the end of the tag, "Ah, hell."

"What?"

Nico shook his head. "Nothing. It's being tracked by the University of Florida."

"Why's that so bad?" Robert asked.

"It's... nothing." Nico took a deep breath and forced a smile. "Mayor, I'll have this out of your hair... or lack thereof."

"Oh, funny!" Robert said.

"It kind of is. Just leave it to me. It's a courtesy that we inform the institution that's studying this. I'll let them know if they can't make it today, we'll have no choice but to haul it out before the gasses build up inside it."

Robert groaned. "Alright. I'm holding you to that, Chief." He returned to the other side of the barrier and resumed addressing the journalists crowding around him.

Nico's fake smile quickly vanished. He dug out his phone and called Dispatch. "Hey, Suzie, it's the Chief. Hey, can you look up the administration number to the University of Florida for me?... Yep, take your time." While on hold, he watched one of the paramedic crews treat a twelve-year old child who appeared to have suffered some scrapes during the chaos.

Renny stood beside him. "You know, you could just have Suzie call them herself."

"Better if I call them directly," Nico said.

"That where *she* works?" Renny asked. Nico didn't reply, which in a way served as an answer. "It's not likely they'll send her."

"Last I heard, she's doing some researching along the Islamorada Keys. They'll send her."

"Interesting... how do you know that? That's not something you'd see on the news." Again, Nico didn't answer. "You've been peeking at her on social media, haven't you?" Another non-answer, but a cold stare. Renny smiled. "If they send her, I can meet with her. You don't have to stay. You can go home early, or to the office, or..."

"No, I'll do it," Nico said.

"You sure? I can—"

"It's better if I do it."

"Better?! What's there to do better? All there is to do is say, 'Hey, Doc. This whale of yours decided it wanted to be a land whale. Unfortunately, it didn't realize it needed blue hair and a *Twitter* account."

That sparked a smile. "No, she knows I'm here. If I'm not the one greeting her, it'll be obvious I'm hiding."

"I've told you before, Chief. I'm sensing unresolved issues," Renny said.

"I didn't ask," Nico said. Finally, Suzie came through with the University administration number. "Thanks." He wrote it down then placed the call. "Hi, my name is Nico Medrano, Chief of Police on Cielo

Nublado. I'm calling to inform your marine biology department that we have one of their whales..."

****

"Uh-huh. Cielo Nublado? You sure there's nobody else that can head over there?"

"Doctor, there's nobody else in the area to inspect the specimen. Tracking that whale was your project. I'd like you to inspect the injuries and make sure it wasn't done by fishermen."

Denise Reta exhaled slowly and shut her eyes. "Alright. I should arrive there within the next two hours or so." She hung up the phone and leaned back in her chair. "You've got to be kidding me. Cielo Nublado, of all places."

Her assistant, Cameron Royle, stood up from the leather seat in the galley, squeezing his sagging midsection from the dining table. "That really such a big issue, Doc?"

She looked up at him. "Well, we've got these specimens here that we're studying. I don't want to leave this area, in case they move off..."

Cameron laughed. "Denise, you've got those creatures tagged already. You've got two carcasses frozen in the cargo hold. Nothing's gonna discredit you from your findings."

"*Our* findings," she said with a smile. "Don't discredit yourself."

"I do kick ass," Cameron said. "But don't change the subject by flattering me. I know the truth. It's not that you don't want to leave. You just don't want to go to Cielo Nublado."

"Ugh. I knew I never should've opened up to you."

"You know I sympathize with what happened in your past, but this might be a way for you to confront it," he said. "Look, I've known you for twelve years. You haven't been the same since... *it* happened. And frankly, I think you and Nico regret how you guys handled things."

"It's too late now," she said.

"Too late to undo what you did? Maybe. But, if nothing else comes of it, maybe it's time you guys get some actual closure. Go out for a cup of coffee with him."

She smirked. "Can't I have you do that for me instead?"

"You know? Nico would probably say yes to that, because I think he's feeling exactly how you are. Our whale has presented an amazing opportunity... Speaking of which, I'm eager to find out what killed it."

"According to the boss, Nico thinks it might have been orcas, though the bites described don't add up. I guess the only way to find out is to head on over." She stood up and went out on deck. It was time to untie the deck lines and set sail. The sooner she got there, the sooner she could leave.

CHAPTER 6

Miami, Florida.
9:08 a.m.
Late. Now, Ed Thatcher's adrenaline had practically doubled. He pumped his Remington pistol-grip twelve-gauge and pulled his ski mask over his face. On his right hip was a Glock 17 and three spare magazines. A bullet-proof vest covered his thick torso. Though muscular, he was down ten pounds from two weeks ago. His jittery hands weren't just from the anticipation of what he was about to do.

His habit started around Christmas time. It wasn't his first exposure to cocaine and meth, but it was the first time the claws of addiction had seized him. Some days, it felt like his insides were burning, and the only way to extinguish the flames was to fulfill the urge. Over the course of the year, it gradually got worse. Now, he was at the point where he needed at least one hit per day just to focus. Such a supply demanded sufficient funds, which even an experienced criminal like Ed Thatcher struggled to scrape together.

Thatcher watched the road around their black SUV. Traffic wasn't too horrible at the moment. It was a Thursday, and most of the world had already arrived at their place of employment. It was the very reason they chose this time, as the original plan was to arrive five minutes to opening, catch one of the tellers on the way in, then force the staff to open the vault.

They were thirteen minutes behind schedule. Embarrassing. Even rookies weren't this far off. Thatcher's blood was boiling. Now, they had to adjust to the change in their environment. They couldn't abandon the mission. Roberto Rosing would not stand for it. He had arranged to meet them tomorrow with ten kilos of purified cocaine. Such a package demanded seven-hundred grand—something Thatcher didn't have on hand. Not at the moment, that is.

In the driver's seat was Kris Hebron, a tan-skinned, dark haired runaway from Louisiana. He and Thatcher had been making runs for the past thirteen years, stealing cars, delivering drugs, and now they had upgraded to robbing banks. Only now, it wasn't for the thrill of the steal, but to supply Thatcher's pathetic habit.

Kris had his automatic H&K in his lap, courtesy of arms dealers out of Mexico. He looked over at his business partner.

"You good, Thatcher?" He always referred to him by his last name. For whatever reason, Thatcher hated the name Ed. Maybe he had received jokes about *Mr. Ed* too many times as a kid. Regardless, it didn't exist as far as Thatcher was concerned.

"Damn right I am. Let's do this."

"You sure?" Allen Lo said. He pointed at a couple walking to the front door. "That's the fourth time we saw someone go in. We weren't planning on this."

"Oh, quit being such a pussy," Carl Heard said. The bearded man pumped his shotgun and pulled his ski mask over his face. The area around the cheeks puffed out due to his thick beard.

Allen Lo yanked back the cocking mechanism on his submachine gun. He hated being called a pussy, and his constant efforts to prove that fact wrong were obvious. He was the first to step out. The rest of the men followed.

Kris gave the road a quick glance. No cops at the moment, but that could change anytime. They needed to work fast and efficiently. If the presence of customers helped in anyway, it would be the added sense of terror. Screaming clients would get the bank manager to hustle, especially if Carl smacked a few around. And knowing him, that was bound to happen.

Like a military fireteam, they rushed the entrance. Except, instead of taking strategic breaching positions, they simply opened the front door and marched right in. All eyes turned toward them. Seven clients, two tellers, a manager, and a notary. Eleven people to keep an eye on. Eleven people to strike fear into.

Thatcher raised his shotgun. "On your knees! Right at this moment!" Screams filled the room. Five of the seven customers dropped to the floor. The other two, stricken by fright, were caught in a deer-in-the-headlights moment. In a way, Thatcher was happy about that. He approached the nearest one, a woman in her late forties, and struck her in the forehead with the butt of his shotgun. She fell to the floor, crying and pressing her hands to her bleeding face. The other, a male of similar age, turned to aid her, only to be kicked in the groin and struck across the temple.

Allen Lo stood by the end of the teller counter, watching the entrance while remaining out of view from the lot. Kris hopped across to the other side and forced the tellers away from the counter.

"Don't even *think* about hitting that button."

Carl went into the manager's office and found a scrawny, long-haired man in his mid-thirties shaking at his desk. The man raised his hands.

"Don't hurt anybody."

"That depends on how well and how fast you cooperate." Carl grabbed him by the tie and dragged him into the lobby. "Get your keys, boss man. Into the vault we go. If you don't have those keys out in thirty seconds, I'll put a shell into one of your precious tellers." He pointed his shotgun at the counter. Both people on the other side raised their hands.

"Get a move on," Thatcher said. "I'm losing my temper fast. I'm not looking to kill anybody—at least, I wasn't. But now I'm starting to have a change of heart."

"Go fuck yourself," a client on the floor muttered.

Thatcher spun on his heel. "Who was that?" Three of the other clients did not hesitate to betray the male in his early twenties. Youngblood, feels like he needs to talk tough. Thatcher grabbed him by the collar, lifted him to his feet, only to knock his front teeth out with his shotgun. He proceeded to kick the young man after he fell, cracking a few ribs in the process.

He looked at the manager and pointed his shotgun like a pistol. It waivered in his grip, both from the weight, and the withdrawal that was clouding his reflexes.

"I don't see them keys."

"Want me to demonstrate our resolve?" Carl said.

"No! I got the key!" the manager freed them from his belt, dropped them onto the floor, and quickly lunged for them. "Here! Here!"

"Take us to the vault," Thatcher said. "The rest of you, stay on the floor and don't even consider doing anything stupid. We'll shoot all of you and, who knows, maybe we'll take a couple of you ladies along for the ride. Something to keep in mind if you're considering being a hero."

"Don't forget, heroes tend to die young," Carl said. He and Thatcher pushed the manager around the back, with Thatcher grabbing one of the tellers for insurance. He put the muzzle of the shotgun against the back of her head.

"Get that thing open," Thatcher said. His voice was like a cobra's. His tongue stuck between his lips with every other word. His associates often wondered how he never bit himself.

"I'm getting it. I'm getting it...there! I got it!"

The manager opened the cash vault. Before he could step aside, he was grabbed by the neck and thrust face-first into the wall by Carl. Thatcher pushed the teller forward and struck her in the back of the head with the shotgun butt, rendering her equally as unconscious as her boss. Both criminals hurried into the vault, placed their weapons down, and began loading their bags with cash.

"Go, go, go!" Thatcher said. "Hurry it up."

"Quit pestering me," Carl said, scooping blocks of money into the bag. He filled the first bag, zipped it up, then began filling the second.

"You counting how much you're putting in?"

Carl turned around. "Enough, that's all I can say. I don't have time to count every dollar. We're lucky the cops aren't on to us yet. Hell, it's only a matter of time before somebody walks—"

The manager stirred and lifted his head. He saw the robbers, yelped, then tried to turn around. In doing so, his hand inadvertently came down on Carl's shotgun.

"He's going for it!" Thatcher said. He scooped up his shotgun and blasted the manager in the ribs, killing him instantly. His fresh corpse, bleeding from the midsection, rolled toward the door, his white shirt now red.

The blasts echoed through the lobby, drawing Allen and Kris' attention to the door.

"What the hell?"

In that moment, two customers ran for the door.

"Shit! Shit! Shit!" Kris said, pointing! "Get 'em!" Allen tried to run after them, but tripped over one of the other customers. As he hit the floor, one of the men went for his weapon. Both he and Allen wrestled for it for a brief moment before Kris hopped over the counter and put a spray of bullets into the man's back. He then rushed out through the doors, pointed his H&K at the two fleeing customers, and hit them both in the back with a spray of bullets.

Cars slowed down on the road, their drivers alerted by the sound of gunfire. Some people screamed in the distance, while those on the sidewalk turned and ran. Right then, Kris realized his instinctive reaction was not the right choice. They would've been better off just letting the idiots go. Now the whole city was on to their activity.

He stepped back inside. Allen was watching the teller, making sure she wasn't going for the police alarm. Kris shook his head.

"Won't make a difference at this point." He leaned over the counter and looked to the back hallway. "Hey, Tha—" He came close to making a second error: using names. "Boss! We've got to go *now*!"

"What the hell happened out there? We heard shooting."

Kris scoffed. *What happened out here? What happened in THERE?! What was THAT shooting all about?*

"I'll explain later." He moved to the other side and entered the vault.

"Grab a bag," Thatcher said. "This should be enough."

Kris groaned as he lifted the heavy duffle bag. "Yeah, I think so. Come on, let's go!"

"You're not calling the shots!"

Kris glared at him. "Don't let that shit you're hooked on make you forget that I'm always looking out for you, dickhead." Thatcher wasn't in the mood for lectures.

"Go on!"

The three men moved into the lobby and went for the door, while Allen watched the whimpering crowd.

"Nobody better make even the slightest move until we're out of the lot," Thatcher said. "Or I'll have my boys unload on this building if it's the last thing we do."

They rushed out into the lot. Kris used the remote to start to get the engine running. They gathered near the back and threw their bags into the trunk.

Flashing lights and blaring sirens drew their attention to the west road. A police interceptor mounted the curb and bounced up onto the lot. It came to a screeching halt and both officers jumped outside. Using their vehicle for cover, they took aim with their Glocks.

"Throw your weapons on the ground and show me your—"

Carl was the first to open fire. Tight pellet groupings tore into the police vehicle, shattering the windows and driving the officers behind cover.

Thatcher pushed Kris into the driver's seat and took his submachine gun. He could hear the officers radioing for backup. He unloaded the magazine into the driver's side, flattening both tires. He reloaded and went for his seat.

"Get in, Carl."

Carl opened his door and began to step inside. The cops emerged from cover and returned fire. One round caught him in the small of his back, dropping him to the pavement. He squirmed on the ground in agony, his mouth wide open, unable to scream. Despite the pain in his spinal column, he refused to give up. He pulled his own Glock and fired back. His shots went wide while the cops continued hitting him with bullets. Blood spat from a half-dozen holes in his chest. Finally, the brute known as Carl Heard was dead.

Thatcher leaned out of the open door and fired back. His spray struck one of the cops in the neck, dropping him and forcing the other to tend to his aid. Another set of flashing lights appeared in on the road behind them.

"Close the damn door! He's dead! We can't help him!" Kris said. He floored the pedal as Thatcher latched his door.

"Shit! SHIT! Goddamn!!!" He hit the dashboard, then watched the side mirror. One of the patrollers was right behind them and closing in.

The officer in the passenger seat leaned out the window, Glock drawn. Bullets pierced the back of the SUV, causing Allen to duck down.

Thatcher rolled his window down, leaned out, and fired back. A line of bullet holes formed across the windshield. Suddenly, the interceptor veered off to the side and went into the opposing lane, where it struck another vehicle head-on. The cop in the passenger window was flung forward, his body waving like a flag through the open window. The jerking motion from the sudden stop, at the very least, had twisted his spine—if not snapped it completely.

"Keep going! Take a turn here…alright, now a left here…alright…"

"Thatcher, I know how to drive," Kris said. He took a few deep breaths and slowed the SUV down. For the moment, they were lost in the crowd of vehicles. With the bullet holes in the trunk, they couldn't blend in completely. "We need to ditch this vehicle."

"No shit." Allen cupped his hands over his face. "Any chance of making it to the airport?!"

"Oh, sure. We can definitely make it there," Kris said. "Getting past security, on the other hand."

"What about the highway?" Thatcher said. "Take South Miami Avenue, take it to twenty-fifth Road, and get on I-95 North. We can take that to West I-395 and take that to 836-West."

"We'll never make it to the bridge in this vehicle," Kris said.

Thatcher checked his watch. "If we just go now…"

"We've killed *at least* two cops and God-knows how many people at the bank," Kris said. "And now they've got Carl. Once they identify him—and it won't take long—our faces are gonna be all over every TV in the state. We go on that bridge, I guarantee we'll be spotted. Especially in this bullet ridden thing."

Thatcher pounded the dashboard. "What about your truck?"

Karl laughed. "My truck?! That rust-bucket? Yeah, I agree on switching over to it, since the cops are on the lookout for this SUV. But no way am I taking that thing on the highway. That thing's broken down on me twice. We break down on the bridge, we're far past fucked."

"We're already far past fucked if we don't get out of here."

"We go on that highway, we're dead meat," Kris said. "Same with that airport. Right now, we're Public Enemy Number One."

"Alright, fine!" Thatcher said. "I have an alternative plan. I know a buddy with a boat. We'll take that toward the Keys. We just need to find someplace to lay low where the cops won't think to search. Any ideas?"

Kris thought for a second. "I know a guy."

"Good. Where is he?"

CHAPTER 7

Cielo Nublado, North Beach.

It was eleven in the morning and, for the most part, life on the beach had gone back to normal. People were swimming, sunbathing, and boating as they normally did. The only difference was the two-hundred block of space that was isolated for the whale. Not that anyone wanted to hang around it anyway. The gasses were starting to billow from inside it, and a horrid stench was permeating the nearby area. There was enough of a breeze to keep it from getting too horrible, but Nico Medrano knew that within a couple more hours, the mayor would be throwing a fit.

At a quarter after eleven, the mayor's fits were the last thing on his mind. He saw the eighty-foot research vessel approach from the northwest. He had seen images of it on *Facebook*, but had never viewed the vessel with his own eyes. It had a main deck as well as a pilothouse twelve-feet above it, supported by a fly deck which gave foot space in a U-shaped area around the controls. He could see clothes drying off the guardrails.

He figured Denise slept in her private quarters, never taking advantage of the hotels on site wherever she was assigned. For the last three years, she strived to be on the water. It was the only way to distract herself from the misery they shared.

"You alright, Chief?"

Nico glanced at Renny, who stood by his side with the expression of a concerned friend. "Yeah, I'm good. Thanks." He noticed Carley standing a few yards back. "You guys been talking?"

Renny shook his head. "She's asked out of curiosity, but she's not being nosey. I told her it's a private ordeal and we left it at that. This subject matter—it's not something I take lightly."

"I appreciate it," Nico said. "I suppose it's alright if she wants to know. Just don't broadcast it across the department."

"No. I would only do that on occasions such as you accidentally getting on that gay dating website."

Nico closed his eyes as the embarrassing memory flashed in his mind. "I typed in the first letter, didn't pay attention to the option, since I thought it was suggesting the same gun site I always go to…"

"Yeah, yeah, yeah, keep telling that story. I might have to tell your ex I caught you on *bromodates.com*. 'Best site for single men to meet gay lovers.'"

Nico allowed his officer a moment to chuckle. Usually, when he would look at *Browning Arms Company's* website, he'd simply type in the first letter and the search-bar would provide the rest. He'd simply click on it and browse the site. Usually, if it suggested something else, he'd type a few other letters until he got what he wanted. As luck would have it that fateful day, he was only paying half-attention and clicked on the link...only to see images of men in romantic situations.

To top it off, Renny Jackman walked into his office at that very moment.

"You mention that, I'll stuff you in that whale's mouth," he said.

Carley perked up. "What? You guys talking about the gay site thing?"

"Yeah!" Renny said. "Chief here says he's having seconds thoughts. Might broaden his horizons and revisit it."

Carley raised her coffee cup in a toast. "Mazel tov, Chief."

He shook his head and feigned annoyance. "You two—I swear, I oughta—I'm gonna go to the docks."

"You should write on your profile that you enjoy walks on the beach!" Renny said. Much to his amusement, Nico raised a middle finger as he walked off.

The butterflies in Nico's stomach were flapping their wings. It was the first time in three years he had laid eyes on Denise Reta.

Reta...he still wasn't used to that. Not that he took issue with her family name, but the fact that she was using it again was just another reminder of the left turn his life had taken. Naturally, he wondered about her love life, while attempting to convince himself he didn't care. Who was he to judge? He'd been on a couple of dates these past few years, though none of them went anywhere past dinner.

The vessel was docking. He saw somebody on the main deck tossing the stern line to an officer on the pier. Nico recognized the balding head and goatee. Cameron Royle! Still wearing the same kind of camo shorts and green t-shirt. A far-cry from his Marine days, the guy had put on an additional twenty pounds since Nico last saw him.

Who am I to judge? Nico looked down at himself. He wasn't fat by any means, but that six-pack he used to have had finally disappeared under a couple layers of insulation. An hour every other day at the gym wasn't cutting it anymore.

He set foot on the pier as the research assistant finished securing the bow line. "Hey, just so you know, that twenty bucks you owe me builds interest after three years."

Cameron turned and smiled. "Nico! Hey man!" They hugged each other.

"What's new? Spending your days sailing the high seas?"

"Got to do something to keep me going," Cameron said. "Frankly, I was bored on the mainland anyway. Was falling behind on the house payments. Now, since I'm practically living on the *Water Stallion*," he tapped the hull of the boat affectionately, "there was no point in even keeping it."

"Too bad you live like a slob."

Both men looked up to the fly deck. Dr. Denise Reta leaned on the guardrail. A fit woman who embraced her feminine features, most men pegged her in her early thirties. Most would be shocked to learn she was actually forty-four. Her blonde hair still fell to her shoulders, never an inch longer. The only imperfection on her face was a small scar on the left cheek where she had a mole removed. Her brown eyes were fixed on Nico Medrano.

"Denny. How you doing?"

First time in three years he used that nickname. It simply slipped, a habit that refused to die. During the divorce proceedings, whenever they had a private session, she made a point for him to refer to her as Denise, not Denny. It was as though any fragment of their affection was condemned to die and be forgotten. To his surprise, it garnered a smile.

Perhaps with time came hindsight, and whatever grudges she held against him had dissipated.

"I'm okay, actually," she said.

Actually. Were you not expecting to be? Common sense struck. He remembered how *he* felt when he realized he'd be seeing her again. How could he blame her for feeling the same way?

"Good. You...you look good." *Cliché.* What was one supposed to say in these situations?

"Thanks. You're looking alright too, Chief. You've put on a tan, I see."

"Living the island life," he said.

Denise climbed down to the pier. Seeing Nico face-to-face, she froze. All the memories flooded back at once. The good and the bad. With those memories came three years' worth of accumulated self-doubt all at once. Naturally, she looked at his ring finger. Nothing there, except a pale line. It had taken him a while to stop wearing it.

Renny and Carley watched from the edge of the barricade. The distance and number of people moving about in-between could not conceal the body language between the Chief and the marine biologist.

"I'm sensing a history between them," Carley said.

Renny nodded. "You can say that."

She glanced his way. "Must be pretty serious if even you are willing to keep it under wraps."

"Well, it is." By the look on his face, Carley knew he wasn't being sarcastic. Usually, Renny had a shit-eating grin on his face when interacting with her. The guy was nonstop with his child-like antics, so when he was serious about something, Carley knew it was genuine.

Renny took a sip from his water bottle. "Her name's Denise Reta. Up until September of 2018, it was Denise *Medrano*."

"Oh…they were married?"

"No, they're cousins!" he quipped.

"Well, how am I supposed to know?! She could be his sister."

"I figured you'd catch the hint."

"Well, all you said was in 2018 her last name changed. She could've gone from Medrano to her married name of Reta. Makes sense if it's his sister. Hell, could be Nico's *mother*, for all I know."

"Why the hell would I imply she's his mother?! Just LOOK at her!"

"Hey, you're the one who chose to speak in riddles…"

"Alright, alright! Damn!" Renny groaned. "Gosh, and you call me the obnoxious one. Yes, they used to be *married*."

Carley smiled in delight of the mental anguish she inflicted. "So, what happened? I'm assuming you know."

Renny's tone shifted back to seriousness. "They used to live in Texas. He was a detective, she was a researcher, mainly doing lab work. Both worked shitty, nonstop hours. With Nico being a homicide detective, you can imagine what that life was like."

"So, they just drifted apart?"

"He hinted they were suffering a little bit from that. Not that they were on bad terms or anything, but couples do need time together to—be a couple. But that's not what did them in. He, uh…*they* used to have a son. He was four. Well, those long hours took their toll.

"You see, they lived on a lakefront property. Long story short, Nico got a rare day off after working a case nonstop for like a month, with only a couple hours of sleep a night. It was a Wednesday, the wife was at work, Nico was at home with the kid. They were playing outside. Nico nodded off. When he woke up, the kid wasn't there."

Carley covered her mouth. "Did he…"

"Yes." He sighed. "So, as you can imagine, it screwed both their minds, especially Nico's."

So many things made sense to Carley now. "His obsession with watching kids on the beach."

"He absolutely hates himself for it. He never said that outright, but I can tell," Renny said. "One moment, he was playing with his boy in the sand. A moment later, he sat back in the chair. Didn't even feel himself dozing off. So, that wrecked their marriage. My suspicion is that Denise couldn't even stand to look at him after that. She didn't demand alimony or anything of the sort. She just wanted to be away. So, they sold everything, split it fifty-fifty, and went on with separate lives. Neither could stand to live in Waco anymore after that. So, she went into research and Nico came out here."

"Damn, now I feel kinda guilty for being happy he moved here," Carley said. "How did you find out about all this if he's so private about it?"

Renny scratched his head and grinned nervously. "My bad habit of barging into his office without knocking. I caught him in the middle of looking over old photos of the kid with some tissues in hand. Wasn't sure what was going on, so I asked if he was alright. Turns out it was the kid's birthday... or would've been. Since I was there, he gave me a quick rundown of what happened. Probably knew it was better to let me in on the truth, thinking I'd let it slip that 'I found the Chief crying like a little girl in his office.'"

"And you would've?!"

"Depending on the reason." Renny smiled again.

"You're an ass," Carley said. She watched the Chief interacting with his ex. Whatever they were talking about, it was pleasant. There was laughter and their body language did not seem hostile. "I'm sensing they still have feelings for each other."

Renny snorted. "You *sense*? You have magic powers or something?"

"I do. It's called woman's intuition. You're married. You should know this by now."

"I don't know. The only power I've seen from my wife is the power of spending my money." The phone came out again, and Carley's thumb went to work messaging the missus. "Do you take joy in cockblocking me?"

"Abso-fucking-lutely," Carley said. A moment passed, then Carley smacked him on the back of the head.

"Hey! You spilled my coffee!"

"You had it coming."

"Let me guess; my gorgeous wife told you to do that."

"No, she hasn't responded yet. That one was for me."

"I should start texting your hubby and say something like 'hey, she thinks you don't make enough money.'"

"You do that I'll kill ya."

"Oh! So, you can do it to me, but I can't do it to you? Is that how this works?"

"Damn right." Her phone chimed. She read the text then looked at her partner. Renny cringed, thinking he was gonna take another tap to the head. Nothing came.

"What? No specific instructions? She tell you to knee me in the balls?"

"Wow, you've got better insight than I thought."

Renny thought about that for a moment. "Wait… she actually told you to do that?" She showed him the text. *'Knee him in the nuts for me. He won't be using them for a while.'* "Great! Thanks. Can't wait to get home tonight. Fortunately for me, you won't get to go through with that request of hers. Here comes the Chief. Better look professional now."

"You've lucked out," Carley said.

"You wouldn't *actually* do that…right?" Carley didn't reply. In a way, that was worse than an answer in the affirmative.

****

"Well, let's get down to business," Denise said. "The University informed me that this thing arrived on the beach as though fleeing something. Is that right?"

"That's correct," Nico said. "Had a few patrol boats out here after it happened. Nobody saw anything. I can't think of anything that could cause those wounds other than killer whales."

"That's a fair guess," she said. "You seem to know a lot about whales."

"Well, I had a good teacher."

Denise laughed. *I suppose you did pay some attention to my ramblings back in the day. Before…* That laugh faded away as horrible memories took hold. Her defense mechanism erected like a steel wall. Work. She buried herself in work. It was all she had left at this point.

"Let's take a look at him, then."

They ducked under the caution tape and approached the carcass.

"Whoa," Cameron said. "They really did a number on this thing. I've never seen them make such injuries like this before."

"Nor have I," Denise said. "These wounds look oddly identical. Almost…" she chuckled, knowing what she was about to say was going to sound crazy. "If I didn't know any better, I'd say they looked like shark bites."

"Ha!"

All eyes went to Renny, who quickly turned away and pretended he wasn't the one who laughed…while pointing a finger at Carley.

Cameron took a look at the fluke. "No bite marks here. I don't see anything smaller than these large wounds."

"I thought that was strange," Nico said.

"Orcas are like ants," Denise said. "When hunting a large whale, many will strike at different points of the body. Some will go for the head while others attack the fluke. I would say they're capable of making injuries like this if the whale was already dead. Not while in active pursuit." She pulled out a tape measure and extended the tip to Nico. "You mind?"

He took the end and pulled it across one of the bite wounds.

"Seven feet, three inches," Denise said. They went to the wound along the stomach area. "Same. Seven feet, three inches. That's very interesting."

Nico understood the tone. "You think these *are* bites."

"I'm not *saying* anything, though it is a very odd coincidence that these are the same radius."

Nico scratched his forehead and gazed out at the blue horizon. "What the hell could actually make bites this big?"

CHAPTER 8

"Tom? It's those guys again."

Tom Wilder was not a violent man, but these assholes in the jetboats were pushing his mind to places he never thought he'd delve to. There were three of these idiots, one in a red boat, and two in a silver one.

The red boat zipped by the stern of their yacht, spraying the deck, and his girlfriend Tris. She exclaimed a series of curse words while pulling her now-wet towel off the deck.

"You guys get your kicks out of pissing everyone off?"

The silver jetboat slowed down and passed by the starboard side. The passenger idiot stood up and leaned over the side to gaze at her. "Hey good-look'n! Show us your titties!"

"Get out of here!" Tom Wilder yelled. The imbeciles launched like teenagers and continued to speed around the yacht.

Tris wiped the water from her face and looked up at him. "Tom? I can't take this anymore. Can we go somewhere else?"

"They'll just follow us," he said. He contemplated his options while the pricks continued to circle the yacht like sharks. All he wanted to do was hang out with his girlfriend, let her get tanned and tipsy, which would hopefully lead to better things later on. Not only were these guys screwing with his own relaxation, but judging by how agitated Tris was, his hopes were going down the crapper. "We'll head in."

"Huh?"

"We'll head toward the island," he said. "We'll let the police know that these guys are screwing around out here."

"Can't you… I don't know, throw something at them or something? I don't want to head in."

"All we're successfully doing out here is getting pissed-off. If we retaliate, we'll just egg them on further. I know the type. They *enjoy* getting into trouble and getting a reaction out of people."

The red boat neared them. "Hey, darling! This guy not taking care of you? You look miserable as hell."

"Fuck off, man!" Tom shouted, despite what he just said to Tris five seconds ago.

The guy in the boat laughed. "The boys and I, we're sorry we splashed you. Just can't help but give you attention because you're the finest woman we've seen on this side of the island. If I was that guy up there, I'd be fixing you margaritas all day long."

"Yeah, uh-huh, sure," Tom said. "Guys, you mind going away. When we go on vacation, the last thing we want is—" A wall of water struck his face as the silver jetboat zipped by and cut sharply to the right, pointing its propeller right at him. He stood, hands out to the side, water dripping from his Hawaiian shirt. He turned to the other boat and waved his fist. "I'm gonna kill you! I'm gonna..." He went to turn, only to step on his dropped beer bottle, which rolled and took his foot along with it. As though a rug had been pulled out from under his feet, Tom hit the deck.

Laughter erupted from the trio of troublemakers. Already, the silver boat was circling back to spray them again.

Tom grabbed the guardrail and started pulling himself up to his feet. "I'm gonna kill you—" Another jet of water struck his face and flooded the flybridge, making him slip and fall back down.

After circling the boat a few more times, the red boat slowed by again. Its operator eyed Tris and made kissing noises. "Seems your so-called man is struggling to stay on his feet." He laughed maniacally. The other boat slowed near the starboard quarter.

"So, what about showing them titties?" one of them said.

"Christ," Tris muttered.

"Do it! Do it! Do it! Do it!" Like a tribe from a long lost civilization chanting to their ancient god, they vocalized their desire for the bikini top to come off. "Do it! Do it! DO IT! DO IT! DO IT!"

At this point, Tris didn't care. Arguing wouldn't help. Tom was too much of a wuss to do anything about these guys. And it would take forever for any cops to get out here.

She undid her string and flashed her breasts.

"WHOA!" The troublemakers cheered, raised their beer bottles, and slapped hands, nearly falling in the water as they reached over to the other boats.

The guy in the red boat smiled. "You're a class act, darl'n." He looked up at Tom as he started speeding away. "She's a keeper, dude! Don't let her go!" The three boaters sped to the north, whooping nonstop.

Tom looked down at his girlfriend, who was retying her bikini string. "What did you do?"

"Played along. Getting pissed off was only spurring them on. Not like you were gonna do anything about it."

"You actually showed them your—"

"Yeah, and they're gone now. At least one of us thought outside the box." She went below for a new blanket.

****

Ralf Klingberg couldn't wipe the smile from his face. He couldn't believe that the chick on the yacht actually did it. No way was she irritated enough to do that. She had probably worked in modeling, in a strip joint, or otherwise was extremely comfortable with herself. Either way, he wasn't complaining.

Nor were Nate and Fredrick, who sped alongside his boat. After moving a third-of-a-mile out, they slowed down.

"Where to next?" Fredrick shouted.

"Next? Hell, I'm wondering why we don't head back?!" Nate said, pointing his thumb back at the yacht.

"Ha! Maybe later. I'm thinking she likes me," Ralf said.

"Hey—" Fredrick paused to burp, then pointed up ahead. "Is it just me, or is that the same old prick from the restaurant? Dan-What's-his-name?"

Ralf dug for some binoculars and gazed up ahead. "Well, would you look at that! Old timer's still out on his boat reeling in an empty hook! Well, I'm up for some more fun! What about you assholes?"

"Beats going around in circles," Fredrick said.

"I don't see any cops around," Nate said.

"Alright." Ralf fixed his shades then fastened himself into the seat. "Let's go!"

Being natural shit-stirrers, the Klingbergs were not sufficed with the rush of wind in their hair and the adrenaline of moving fast. Their kicks came from the cause-and-effect of agitating others. Every Friday, they would go into a crowded movie theater. Unlike the rest of the crowd, their entertainment didn't come from the movie, but from flinging popcorn at people in lower rows. On one occasion, they were at a bar, seated near a husband and wife. When Ralf happened to catch the name and address on the husband's license, a sinister plan came to play. The three brothers scraped together some funds, hired a prostitute, and sent her to the address, stating she had arrived for her meeting with Howard Putnam. They sat in a car, cackling as they watched the aftermath play out. The wife, infuriated to discover that her husband had apparently been hiring prostitutes, kicked him out of the house then and there, while he pleaded innocence. It escalated to her throwing his belongings onto the lawn, smashing a prized guitar, and keying his car. Eventually the cops arrived and broke them up.

Such successful endeavors only emboldened the Klingbergs to continue wreaking havoc on the happiness of others. Once in a while, they would have a recurring victim. Here in the waters along Cielo Nublado, Dan Huckert was that recurring victim.

Like street racers, the two boats zipped ahead side-by-side. Within a few seconds, they closed in on the fishing striker. Ralf sprayed the bow and Fredrick zipped by the stern. Dan stood up from his chair. Before he could curse at them, a fountain of water struck his face.

"Ha! I'm getting good at this!" Fredrick said.

"When do I get a turn?" Nate said.

"Next year!"

After speeding a couple of hundred feet away, he hooked to the left, then crossed paths with Ralf who was also swinging around. He was laughing while looking over his shoulder at the infuriated retiree.

"Again!" he shouted.

Fredrick nodded then pointed the jetboat back at Huckert. Once again, the brothers sped side-by-side, this time with the intention of both crafts splashing by the aft deck. Two consecutive jets of water to soak the guy, ruin his day, before they would return to the island for refueling.

Ralf took the lead. He angled the bow right, carefully watching the position of the striker. His eyes went to Dan Huckert. Only now was he appearing on deck after a brief trip to the cabin. There was something in his hand. A stick or a rod of some sort.

He recognized the rounded muzzle, pump action, and stock of a shotgun. "Oh, SHIT!" All desire to piss-off Dan Huckert had vanished. He veered to port and sped to the east, Fredrick following. There was a crack of a gunshot and the clunking of buckshot against the hull of the silver jetboat.

"Whoa!" Nate cried out. "That guy's got a gun!"

"Oh really? You think?!" Fredrick said. He followed Ralf to the east. It was obvious he was planning to return to the island. All it took was a little serious pushback to ruin the thrill of causing mayhem. First, they would have to figure out how to explain the damage to the guy they rented these boats from. A scrape on the red one—that could be easily written off as an accident. 'We simply got too close to another boat.' The shotgun blast was a different story. Maybe they could state that Huckert tracked them down and started shooting.

The sound of impact filled his ears. In the first split-second, he thought he heard another gunshot. Then he saw the wall of water in front of Ralf's boat. The tidal wave parted, and a triangular shape emerged. Black eyes rolled back and a massive jaw extended, lined with serrated teeth.

A shark! A shark that would terrify even the devil!

Fredrick heard Ralf scream before the jaws seized his boat and took him under, propeller still shooting water.

"Oh my God!" Nate shouted. Fredrick veered to the right, the boat bouncing along the huge swells.

"That—that was—"

The giant head burst through the surface, jaws agape. Dangling from its teeth were pieces of hull, and ribbons of Ralf's white t-shirt...along with some skin.

"—Shark?!"

Fredrick pushed the throttle to the max, shooting the jetboat westward. He looked over his shoulder and screamed as the jaws snapped. They slammed shut within a yard of the propellors. That mouth was large enough to swallow a damn forklift. It wasn't machinery this thing was after. It was flesh. *Their* flesh.

The fish dipped under the water, the tail fin generating additional waves as it pushed its enormous mass.

Fredrick kept watching. He could barely see its shape under the waves. Was it keeping pace? Where did it come from? How long would it chase them?

"Fred!" Nate shouted. He ignored his brother, still trying to watch for the beast. The waves settled, the shape disappearing from view. "Where'd it go?"

"FRED!"

"WHAT?!"

"MOVE!!!"

When Fredrick realized they were speeding right for Dan Huckert's boat, it was too late. The retiree was at the transom, shotgun shouldered. The buckshot struck him right in the chest. Nate screamed in horror, grabbing for the helm. It was too late.

The jetboat struck the fishing yacht, the impact generating sparks which ignited both fuel tanks.

****

"I just—I can't believe it!" Tom said.

Tris laid her fresh towel out. "Will you lay off?!"

"Lay off? You seriously expecting me to lay off when you're taking your top off for a bunch of biker wannabees who are—" His voice trailed off as he stared to the northwest.

"What's the matter? Tongue-tied?" Tris said. Tom said nothing. He removed his sunglasses and squinted. Tris heard the rumble. It was like thunder, except there was hardly a cloud in the sky. She sat up and saw the huge fireball rising in the distance. "What the—?"

Tom dug his phone out. "Come on, come on!" To his amazement, he managed to get a signal. He dialed 9-1-1. "Yes, get the fire department out here. There's been an explosion."

CHAPTER 9

"Alright. We're almost there. You guys really owe me for this."

Kris Hebron was glad to hear this, not only because it meant they were out of Miami jurisdiction, but because it was likely the last time he would have to listen to the boat owner, Enrique, bellyache about the risk.

He tried to count his blessings. If listening to Enrique's bitching about money was the worst thing he would have to deal with from here on, he'd take it. The day had been a miserable experience so far. It was hell driving through Miami with a bullet-ridden vehicle that the whole planet was looking for. They had ditched it in favor of Kris' pickup truck, which itself stuck out like a sore thumb. The thing had a tendency to break down, and was awaiting a trip to the junkyard. No way were they going to risk a trip on the Seven Mile Bridge on that thing. And Allen didn't drive, and even if he did, he'd probably get them into an accident. It took him until they were out on the boat to quit his jittering.

Enrique, a former associate two years out of prison, was reluctant to take them in. Being pinned down and sodomized on a semi-regular basis in prison made him wary of partaking in the habits that got him there. He had made drug runs with Kris and Thatcher in the past, including an incident that resulted in a shootout with a rival gang. It was when he was attempting a solo operation—a 'pocket money job' as he called it—that he was caught and arrested. Five miserable years in prison followed. It would have been more had the police and prosecutors been able to link him to his other crimes.

His answer was initially "No" when the gang came to him. That sentiment increased with the news of Carl's death. Carl's distinguishing features made it easy for police to identify him as a member of a four-man crew who robbed a bank in Atlanta three years ago. It was a heist that led to a brief shootout and the death of a bank guard. Thanks to fingerprints and poor masking, their identities were uncovered by investigators. Now, that mistake was really coming back to bite them.

Kris was correct when he predicted their faces would be all over the news. It only took twenty minutes before the local radio reported the names of the 'likely' suspects. Ed Thatcher, Kris Hebron, and Allen Lo, the last known associates of Carl Heard.

An interview with a detective who reviewed the security footage stated that the physical description of the three men was identical to what is known about them. The radio host announced that mugshots of the men would be on all local news screens, and that a ten-thousand dollar reward would be granted for information leading to the arrest of the three men. State police were on the lookout and alerts were placed in all neighboring police departments.

Two cops dead and three civilians, Ed Thatcher and his gang were being regarded on a similar threat level as terrorists. It seemed like the whole state was about to come crashing down on them.

The promise of money was their only leverage. And thanks to that damn reward, they had to fork up more than ten-grand to outbid the city to keep Enrique from ratting them out to the cops. It was Enrique's financial troubles that were their saving grace.

Though supposedly done with his criminal life, he struggled to adapt to the day-to-day routine of normal folk. He had just gotten fired from his third job in a row, and unfortunately for him, this most recent termination came before he had enough time there to qualify for unemployment.

His boat wasn't anything special. It was a twenty-two-foot cruiser inherited from his dead uncle. With the cousins living further north, nowhere near a body of water, Enrique was given dibs on it. Free boat? Why not? If nothing else, he could sell it.

Instead, he was taking the FBI's most wanted into the Florida Keys.

He watched the island grow larger in view. This was his first visit to Cielo Nublado. From what he heard, it was a resort community with a population consisting of more tourists than residents. He did a quick *google* search of the place, and based on what he read, there was little in the way of crime. With a little luck, the cops would be lax around here. And with so many boats and people visiting from all over the country, it wouldn't be too difficult to blend in.

Enrique was back into his criminal life. He was committed now. If he returned to the mainland, they would be spotted, arrested, and he would be tried as an accessory to their crimes. At least, that was what he told himself up to this point.

They watched a police chopper take to the sky. In the distance were flashing lights. Police boats were in the water, heading east. Whatever was going on, it was serious. *Maybe as serious as a shooting that left five people dead.*

Regret was making him nauseous. "I'm telling you, man. If this doesn't work out, I'll shoot you myself before I get caught."

"Relax. They're not heading towards us. Whatever they want, it seems unrelated," Kris said. Both men turned around to the sound of groaning. A shaky Ed Thatcher was stumbling on the aft deck, undoing a tinfoil wrap.

"You're doing drugs on my boat?" Enrique said.

"Just a bump. Need something to get me focused."

Kris clenched his teeth to keep from shouting at him. "Dude, there's cops around. If they see you—"

Thatcher pressed his nose into the powder and inhaled. He leaned his head back and moaned while the drugs coursed through his system. "Oh. Oooohhhh. That's better."

Enrique sneered. "That looked like more than a bump. And you're spilling some on the deck, you moron."

"You want to make money or not, Enrique?" Thatcher said.

"Hey, I can still turn you in to the police. All I have to say is that you've forced me to take you out on my boat."

The sarcasm was lost on Thatcher. He pulled his pistol from his waistline and pointed it at the boat operator. "Go ahead. Just know, it won't get you very far."

Kris smacked Enrique upside the head. "How dumb are you? You seriously think telling him that will go over well."

"Hey! We're on *my* boat!"

"Doesn't mean jack shit to me," Thatcher said. "I'll shoot you and take your damn boat."

Allen Lo marched onto the aft deck. His face was pale, his eyes dark. He had vomited twice since getting on the boat, due to a combination of seasickness and shot nerves.

"Will everyone relax?!" As if the strain of barking those words put him over the edge, Allen leaned over the side and heaved. Thatcher winced and backed away.

Enrique turned to operate the boat. Sooner he got done with these idiots, the sooner he'd be on his way back home. Hopefully without them.

"Kris, call that buddy of yours. Figure out where the hell I'm supposed to take you."

Kris got on Enrique's phone. The first few tries, he failed to get a signal. After they got closer to the island, his call finally went through.

"Yeah, Pedro, it's Kris. We're almost there. Tell me where to go… No, nobody knows we're on the boat… Yes, I'm sure… I'm pretty sure the authorities still think we're on the mainland… Ugh! We've been over this. We just need to lay low for a few days until we come up with a plan… Uh-huh… East side of the island, tan house near the hill. Got it." He hung up and turned to Enrique. "He'll be out to meet us. The private oceanfront residences are on the southeast side of the island."

****

Pedro Contreras used to go by the nickname of the Iron Bolt. He was a farmer when growing up in Texas, branding cows and other livestock. In his daily activities, he'd fire a metal rod into their brains, killing them to be sliced into steaks.

That was the life he had before getting into drug trafficking. What started one day as a simple run-in ended up leading to a payoff. He found a small band of dealers sneaking across the border. The men had cash. *Lots* of cash. They offered a whole block of hundred dollar bills for a quick ride to their meeting place.

Money defeated conscience that day. He took the money and did the job. It was more than he had ever made working on a slaughter farm, and it was done in the span of a half-hour. Thus, his life took a turn. He snuck back and forth across the border, shipping drugs, weapons, and people in his truck. He maintained the farm during the day, as it kept him from drawing attention to himself. Pedro had perfected living off three or four hours of sleep, so rest wasn't an issue.

What was an issue was the rival gang that intercepted his route. Someone had slipped them the details of his operations. They knew right where to strike. What they didn't know was that he carried a mini-pistol in his lap. He may have killed the thugs, but it only worsened his overall problem. One of the killers was related to a drug lord in Nuevo Laredo.

Pedro knew to act fast. He gathered his belongings, and all his cash savings, and got the hell out of dodge. He traveled through Georgia and Florida, eventually changing his name, and moved into the Keys, ultimately settling in Cielo Nublado. The life of crime was over. His life literally depended on it.

All the events leading to his current residence flashed before his eyes as he watched the cruiser dock along his pier. Kris and Thatcher approached while the other two moored the boat. He could hear the one named Thatcher mumbling under his breath.

"This guy better be solid."

"Shh!"

It was hard to tell who was the actual brains of the operation. However, it wasn't for Pedro to judge. He owed Kris a favor—after all, he was the one who tipped him off about the drug lord.

"Iron Bolt! Good to see you."

"I wish I could say the same," Pedro said. He pointed his thumb to the living room window. "Just wait till you *gilipollas* see the news broadcast in there."

Kris exhaled sharply. "Yeah, we're kinda feeling the weight."

Pedro pointed at the cruiser. "You are absolutely, positively sure that nobody's looking for that thing? Or that guy operating it?"

"You have my word," Kris said.

"I hope we're sure of that," Thatcher said. He watched the sky then looked at Pedro. "I saw a police chopper flying around. I didn't think the police here were too busy. You know anything about that, Pedro?"

"There was a boating accident further east. Couple idiots on jetboats ran into a guy's striker. Caused a big explosion from what I've heard. But rest assured, I'm sure they've received descriptions of you guys."

The other two men approached. Pedro knew Allen Lo thanks to his mugshot on the news. The other one was the boat owner Enrique, whom Kris named in their initial phone call.

Allen was the most nervous. He continuously glanced to-and-fro at the neighboring properties. They were fairly well spaced out, but still within view. "Mind if we get inside before we're seen?"

"That depends on Kris," Pedro said. "I might owe you a favor, but the risk I have far outweighs what you underwent." Kris pulled out a wad of hundred dollar bills and handed it to him. "Alright, *now* you can come in. There's sausage on the stove and beer in the fridge. Figured you guys would be hungry."

"Dude, you're a lifesaver," Kris said. As soon as he stepped inside, he went right to the kitchen.

"For whatever that's worth," Pedro said. "But don't get too comfortable. This is a temporary thing, guys. You can't stay here more than a couple days."

"A couple days is all we need," Thatcher said. "That, and a phone. Mind if I borrow yours?"

"To do what?"

"I need to call and make an arrangement."

Pedro's expression hardened. "What kind of arrangement?"

Thatcher grabbed a piece of sausage from the stove and helped himself to one of the beers in the fridge. "Roberto Rosing. He's got product for me. We were originally supposed to catch a flight out to the Bahamas—"

"Yeah, you can kiss that hope goodbye," Enrique said. "And don't look at me. I'm not taking you that far. You can forget it."

Thatcher looked at Pedro. "What about *you*? Where's your boat? I'd be willing to pay handsomely for a trip out to our destination."

"Did you *see* a boat in my dock?" Pedro said.

"Wait... you don't have a boat?" Thatcher said, his face turning red. Pedro shook his head. "How can you live on an island and *not* have a boat? Isn't that like sacrilege?"

"Newsflash—not all island residents own boats. Personally, I'm trying to keep my expenses down. If I need to get somewhere, I take a ferry. As far as I'm concerned right now, this island is my world. And no way am I going to let you wreck that—you're not using my private phone to call a drug dealer. No freaking way," Pedro slashed his hand across the air. "You want my contact information linked to him in the event he ever gets arrested? You out of your mind?"

He looked to the television. The reporter on screen was speaking about Ken Teegle, the manager who was murdered in the bank vault.

Who am I kidding? Of course he is.

Thatcher downed half the bottle then slammed it down on the counter. "I *have* to make that call."

"Exactly what kind of *product* are we talking about?" Pedro said.

"Just look at that speck on his upper lip," Enrique said.

Pedro leaned forward for a better look, then nodded. "Yeah, that's what I thought." He tilted his head northwest. "There's a payphone at the corner up there. You can use that."

Thatcher spat his next mouthful of beer. "Payphone?! You crazy?"

"I might be just for letting you guys bunk here," Pedro said.

Thatcher went to the rear window and looked at Pedro's garage and shed. His van had a sticker on the side. *Pedro's Landscaping and Maintenance.* The shed doors were open. The wall was lined with tools, weedwhackers, gas cannisters, and various other supplies for his business.

He sniggered. "Why's that? You living the straight life? Paying taxes? Being a 'good' citizen?" Thatcher said.

"Beats looking over my shoulder every twelve minutes. Also beats going to prison," Pedro said. He glanced at Kris, who read the expression in his eyes. *If I didn't owe you a favor...*

Thatcher returned to the window and tried to see if he could see the road. "How far is that payphone?"

"About a hundred yards."

"Not too far. You said the cops are occupied?"

"Yeah, doesn't mean you won't get recognized by anyone walking by," Pedro said.

At this point, that didn't matter to Thatcher. The need to make that call was as strong as the addiction itself. "I'm going."

Pedro pointed a finger at Kris and Allen Lo. "If he gets caught, my official story is that you guys broke in here. I'm not falling on my sword for you." He dug into his closet and tossed Thatcher a ball cap, some sunglasses, and a white shirt. "Put these on. At least look like you're here on vacation."

"Fine." Thatcher changed his shirt and put on the hat and sunglasses. He checked his pockets. "You got some quarters?"

Pedro laughed. "You stole maybe a million dollars from the bank and you don't have spare change?"

"Do you have quarters or not?"

Pedro grabbed a few out of a jar and tossed them over. "Don't take too long." Thatcher was immediately out the door. Pedro rushed out after him. "Hey! Psst!"

Thatcher turned, his expression combative. "What?"

Pedro pointed at the gun tucked in his waist. "Might want to leave that here. Or at least make some kind of effort to conceal it better."

Thatcher looked at the weapon. "Oh." He moved it to the back of his pants then turned. "This better?"

"Yeah."

Thatcher followed the sidewalk to a small road which led to the main street. He took a right, then kept his head down while he walked. If he was in the city, he'd throw a hoodie on to keep his face hidden. But here, with everyone wearing thin clothing, he wouldn't have a more effective way of drawing attention to himself.

Most people walking about didn't pay him any mind. They were too occupied with their own activities to worry about some random guy walking down the road. He quickened his pace when he spotted the payphone. Nobody was in it, but that could change in the twenty seconds it would take for him to reach it.

Almost there. Almost there...FUCK!!!

Someone stepped to the phone. For what felt like enough time to pass into the age of space exploration, the guy was digging through a little pocketbook for the number he wanted to call. Then there was the digging in his wallet for change.

Thatcher repeatedly tapped his finger against his leg. It was the only way he could get rid of his nervous energy. He couldn't pace or do anything else to indicate distress. He was lucky nobody had their eyes on him already.

The worst urge was that to grab the moron at the phone and throw him in front of a passing car.

By the time the guy finished his call, Thatcher felt a decade older. He sprang for the phone as soon as the guy stepped away, as though fearful that someone else would cut in front of him. He pulled a paper from his pocket with Roberto's contact information and dialed the number.

Waiting for his dealer to answer was worse than waiting for his turn on the phone.

"Who's calling?"

"Roberto, this is Ed Thatcher. I'm calling from a payphone in Cielo Nublado. I have your money."

"I know you do, you clumsy fool."

"Huh?"

"What do you mean 'huh'? Your face is on every television screen in the state. How can you be so sloppy?"

"The situation got out of control is all," Thatcher said, keeping his voice low. "Listen, I can't talk long. I have your money."

"What makes you think I'm willing to do business with a top priority suspect?"

"Money, that's what," Thatcher said.

"Money won't do me good if I'm seen doing business with you. What are you doing hiding out in Cielo Nublado anyway?"

"I have a contact here willing to let me hide out. Listen, we can meet and make the transaction."

"We'll see about that," Roberto said.

"What does that mean?"

"It means we can do business if you can afford the extra risk. You see, the price went up. One-point-three million."

"One-point—" Thatcher clamped his jaw shut and inhaled deeply. "That's atrocious."

"You've filled four duffle bags worth of cash. I'm sure you can afford it."

Thatcher groaned. The longer he stayed out in the open, the greater the risk of being recognized. Everything was in Roberto's favor. Thatcher needed Roberto more than Roberto needed him. Even time was on Roberto's side, and he knew it.

"Alright, fine. When do we meet?"

"Tomorrow. I know that area. There's an area roughly two miles southeast of there called Jacquez Grave. It's a wreck site, good place of reference. We'll meet there. I'm gonna show up in my seaplane, assuming the Coast Guard isn't there. After we land, pull up next to us with your boat. We'll make the exchange, and you can go back to evading the police."

"Wait, you want to do this on the water?"

"That's as close to isolated as we're gonna get," Roberto said. "I feel stupid for even making this deal to begin with. Ten o'clock tomorrow. If I don't see you there at that exact moment, my crew and I will turn around and head back. We won't even bother landing."

"But..." Thatcher's heart raced. Enrique had the only boat and he was planning to return to Miami shortly. Pedro had expressed his desire not to be any more involved beyond housing them for a couple of days.

"But what?"

"I don't have a boat..."

"*Better find one. Ten o'clock tomorrow. Jacquez Grave. I don't see you there, you're out of luck.*" The line went dead.

Thatcher placed the phone back and began the stroll back to Pedro's house. He kept a hand to his forehead, not to obscure his face from view, but to nurse a headache. He didn't have a boat, nor would he know the exact location that Roberto described. His only hope were two people who didn't want anything more to do with him than what they were already paid to do.

Unless he was able to bribe them to assist.

Time to go over some accounting.

CHAPTER 10

Nico wasn't sure if all the planets had aligned or what the hell was causing all the chaos in the world, but today was throwing more at him than he cared for. He was angry at himself for not tracking down the Klingbergs. They were troublemakers for sure, but he never expected things to escalate to this level.

Never take things at face value.

He thought that lesson was engrained in his mind. Apparently, he had gotten too lax in paradise. Now, he was staring at the aftermath of a boat explosion. The paramedics had just finished peeling Dan Huckert's charred corpse from what was left of the aft deck. He was burnt down to the bone, which was black as dirt. Not too far from him was his shotgun, almost equally black.

The young couple that reported the explosion had reported three men harassing their boats. The descriptions were identical to what Nico saw in Huckert's video. Fragments of one of the jetboats were embedded in Huckert's vessel. One of the Klingbergs were flung forward onto the striker, while the other was fastened in the driver's seat.

"Hey, Chief."

Nico looked east, where the chopper, piloted by Renny, hovered over the water. "Go ahead."

"Looks like they found the other jetboat."

Below the chopper was an EMS vessel and a tugboat. The winch strained as it hauled something up. Divers broke the surface and climbed up on deck of the EMS rescue boat.

"Hey guys, give me an update."

"Not sure exactly what happened, but something did a number on that boat," one of the divers replied through the radio.

"Signs of impact?"

"I guess so. You can see for yourself when it comes up. From what I can tell, it looks... well, crushed rather than smashed, if that makes sense."

No, it didn't make sense. But Nico wasn't going to make the diver clarify if he could just observe the vessel himself. It beat watching the other paramedics peel the boat driver from his seat.

"Hey, Chief?" one of them said.

"Yeah?"

"Bring your boat a little closer, will ya? You might be interested in this."

Nico turned the helm to port and slowly hooked his boat around the jetboat until he was nearly parallel with the EMS rescue boat. The paramedics had the corpse in a body bag and loaded it onto their deck. The Lieutenant was still on the jetboat, which was literally lodged into the striker like an arrowhead. He pointed to the back of the leather seat.

"Buckshot in the seat. There's some tissue damage in the driver's chest cavity as well that doesn't appear to be caused by the burns."

"We'll have to see what the coroner has to say," Nico said. "Still, it doesn't add up. The Klingbergs liked to stir up shit, but they weren't suicidal murderers. Why the hell were they flying at top speed straight for the boat?" He thought for a moment, remembering the maneuvers he saw in Huckert's video of his earlier encounter. "I suppose, maybe he was playing a prank, and was going to make a sharp turn at the last second. Then Huckert shot him before he could cut the wheel."

The Lieutenant nodded. "That makes enough sense. Good thing that's not my department."

"Still, it doesn't explain what happened with the other boat," Nico said. He redirected his patrol boat toward the other crash site. The red jetboat had been lifted to the surface by the cable. The crew aboard the tugboat secured lines around cleats in the stern for towing. Its bow was crumpled as though caught in a giant vice. The outboard motor was intact, and the entire back half of the boat appeared relatively untouched.

"No sign of the operator?"

"We'll keep looking, but so far, there's no sign of the guy."

"Great," Nico said to himself. "With my luck, the guy will float up near the beach. That'll help tourism, I'm sure." He could only imagine the public reaction to a bloated corpse appearing in a crowded beach.

"Want us to keep sweeping the area, Chief?" Renny asked.

"No. Nothing more you can do. I'll be heading to Dock Four in a few moments."

He looked at the surrounding ocean. The only other boats in sight were way off in the distance. It seemed unlikely that *both* people would crash into separate vessels at the same time. Even so, the damage the red jetboat sustained wasn't reminiscent of a head-on crash. The bow would be smashed in. It was crumpled, but not by impact, but more reminiscent of damage caused by compression.

Another oddity caught his eye.

In the hull were small breaches. Each one was roughly six inches long and a little over an inch thick. He could see a line of these odd cuts on the underside, as well as a few up top—right in the compressed areas of the boat.

"Any ideas what these are?" he said to the Lieutenant.

He shook his head. "Beats me. We'll inspect the wreckage a little more once we tow it to our garage."

"Keep me updated." He checked his watch. "If you need anything, let me know. I need to head in. There's a whale that needs to be towed. Mayor's gonna be on my case as it is."

CHAPTER 11

"Listen, Cameron. It's nothing. He was just being polite was all."

"Yeah, yeah. I know he's being polite. He's the Chief of Police. He can't express his feelings for you in a public setting."

"Oh, jeez." Denise secured the line around the whale's fluke. They would need police supervision to keep swimmers at bay before they could line up the boat to hook it up. Then they would be off to sea to haul it out. Whatever killed the thing could finish it off.

"I can tell you're feeling disappointed," Cameron said.

"Disappointed? That we don't know what did this?" She pointed at the dead whale.

"No. That he had to run off so quickly."

She laughed. "No. It's no big deal."

"Yeah, you say that. But I've known you long enough to know when you're lying."

"I don't lie."

"HA!" Cameron double checked the loop, then approached her. "I saw the twinkle in your eye when you stepped off that boat. You weren't just playing nice. You were *delighted* to see Mr. Detective again."

"Looks can be deceiving, Cameron."

"Yeah, sure." He watched as she continued to inspect one of the bite marks with her forceps. "You can pretend to be interested in that all you want. I'm not laying off this topic."

"I *am* interested in this, thank you very much," Denise said. "In case you didn't realize, this whale we've been tracking for two years has a bunch of holes in it." She scraped her tools around the inner layers of flesh and blubber. "There's puncture marks and scraping. This might give me a clue as to what did this."

"And yet, your mind is on Nico."

"Oh, for crying out loud," she said. She lowered her tools to her side and looked at him. "Cameron, this isn't funny. You know exactly why I can't...why *he and I* can't be a thing anymore. It hurts too much. For both of us."

"What's funny? Who said I was joking?" Cameron said. "Everything I said was pure fact based on observation. Science, if you will. A PhD like you should appreciate that. When he was called off to take care of the boating incident, you pretended to be unfazed. But I know all the subtle signs that state otherwise. The parting of your lips when you wanted to say something, but couldn't get the words out. The looking away, conveniently in the direction of the whale, when Nico said he had to go. I noticed the disappointment there."

"The disappointment is having to listen to you," she said. "Cameron, you need a date."

He patted his stomach. "Yeah, I think that ship has sailed. Listen, just because we have to haul this thing out to sea, doesn't mean we can't stay on this island a little longer."

"We *can't* stay longer," she said. "You forget what discoveries we've made? Creatures that we thought died out eons ago? You want someone else to take credit for these finds."

"Of course not. But I still think you talking with Nico is more important, even compared to that. If nothing else, you'll get full closure. That's something a courthouse can't provide, Denise. Million year old crustaceans and fish don't hold a candle to the connections we have as humans."

Denise scraped the tissue some more in an attempt to pretend she wasn't listening. Then she remembered it was Cameron Royle she was talking to. She wasn't going to win with silence, especially when he was right.

She smiled. "You ought to write romance fiction."

Cameron shrugged. "Hey! If it helps earn us more grant money."

"Hopefully, we'll get more once we turn in our reports…" She noticed the tilting of his head and squinting of his eyes. *You're deflecting again.* She sighed. "Yeeeees. I'll make a point to talk with him."

"That's good!" He crossed his arms and smiled. "Hey, you never know! If nothing else, it could lead to a nice little romp in the sack for old times' sake."

"Ugh!" Denise pushed the cackling assistant. His laughter increased in volume, partially out of surprise for the level of force behind that shove. He stumbled back toward the wound and held his hand out to break the fall. There was a squishing of wet flesh followed by a disgusted groan.

"You had that one coming," Denise said.

"Maybe, but I still stand by my statement," Cameron said. He pulled his hand away from the coagulated blood of the injury. "Bleh! That's just lovely. Got some on my shirt too!"

"Well, if we're staying here overnight, I'm sure there's a public laundry you can use," Denise said. She started putting her tools away in her kit. When she looked back at him, Cameron was willfully toughing the flesh. "What are you doing?"

"There's something here," he said. "Something hard."

"You being crude again?"

"No... Not that I'm above that. But seriously, there's something in the meat. It can't be a bone, it's too shallow."

Denise put on a fresh pair of gloves and inspected the spot. Cameron was right. Something rigid was embedded in the flesh. Whatever it was, it was deep enough to keep her from getting a decent view of it. Cameron was right—it was not bone.

She retrieved her forceps and inserted them into the laceration. The thing was small enough for the tools to clamp down on it. When giving it a small tug, she felt the item shift. It was wedged tight, requiring her to squeeze the handles with both hands and pull back with all her strength. There was a wet sound of flesh being sliced, along with the spilling of blood.

The object came loose.

Denise and Cameron gazed at the item with unblinking eyes. After a minute, their eyes met the other's.

"Is that what it looks like?" Cameron said, pointing at the triangular bony object in the forceps.

"It..." Denise could hardly speak. It was as though all the air had been driven out of her lungs.

"Denise... I think it's fair to say we'll *definitely* be staying a little longer."

"Yeah. I think so. The dean is not gonna believe this one until he sees it," Denise said as she gazed at the seven-inch tooth in her grasp.

All of a sudden, those enormous bites made perfect sense. With that realization came a kind of intense excitement that only a researcher could feel... and a little bit of dread.

"We need to find this thing," she said. She looked at the dead whale and smiled. "And we have the perfect bait to lure it."

"Just so we're on the same page, the 'it' we're referring to is in fact..." Cameron pointed at the tooth.

Denise's smile widened. "Megalodon."

CHAPTER 12

"I'm telling you right now, Matthew, it's either me or the boat."

For six years, Matthew Lodes had heard one version or another with that threat. Two years into their marriage, it was the dog. He bought a German Shephard puppy, she didn't like the shedding—or the dog itself for that matter—and made him choose between it and her.

So he chose her.

Then he bought himself a lizard. An animal that lived in a twenty-gallon glass aquarium couldn't bother the missus, right? No shedding fur. No upkeep, except for a cleaning once in a while, which he'd take care of himself. But no, she thought the little thing was hideous to look at. After two weeks of debate, she made him choose between it and her.

So he chose her.

Three years into the marriage, he was gifted a pack of Cuban cigars. Matthew loved cigars, as they were relaxing and brought back fond memories of his father. On his eighteenth birthday, he lit up his first cigar with his dad, and every Saturday each summer, they'd smoke until Matthew got married and moved to Upper Matecumbe Key.

This latest gift from his work friend at the office contained forty Cubans. Considering himself a moderate smoker, he was set for the whole year. Until he lit one up in his backyard.

Julie Lenner-Lodes hated the smell. The fact that the cigars were a once-in-a-while thing made no difference to her. It sparked another argument which concluded with her using her pocket ace argument.

"It's either the cigars or me."

So, he chose her.

It was that way for the motorcycle. It was that way for the jet ski. Too dangerous, she had argued. Counseling made no difference. Paying extra attention to her made no difference. Julie was a schoolteacher and many of her hours at home were spent grading papers. Whatever time she had left, she wanted his undivided attention.

The one that almost broke Matthew were the *Miami Dolphins* season tickets. Constantly heading to the mainland to watch a bunch of dudes slam into each other? No way. Julie wasn't having it. It was either her or the tickets.

He reluctantly chose her.

Feeling like a prisoner in his own life, getting more miserable by the day, Matthew found himself resorting to retail therapy. He made good money from his sales job, but a man needed more than a good job to be happy. His friends often invited him on trips, which he'd turn down in fear Julie would get mad. That led to humiliating remarks from them about him being a cuck.

"Guess we know who wears the pants in your household."

It hurt because it was true. He bent to her will on everything. He never discussed his marriage issues with his father, but only because he didn't have the heart. His dad was never giddy about his son's marriage to Julie. He had mentioned casually that they were different people with different interests and personalities, and often such opposite types didn't mesh well in a marriage. The guy was right.

Finally, with a bunch of money saved up, both from work and the gifts he was pressured into selling, he bought himself a small cabin cruiser. He even assumed Julie would want to spend time out on the water with him. How could she not? They were in the Keys, after all.

Nope. Her idea of enjoying the ocean was being on the beach working on her tan. It was a Bayliner 285 SB, only twenty-eight feet in length, and better yet, less than a hundred-grand in payments.

Julie didn't waste time using her pocket ace argument with this one. Standing there in the living room, she was as irritated as though the boat were another woman.

"You don't need that boat, Matt. Return it, sell it, I don't care. But you're not keeping it. I can't believe you bought that thing without consulting with me first."

Matthew thought of everything he had been denied under her rule. Yeah, she had a point there. Any married person should keep their spouse in the loop when making such big purchases. Then again, this was Julie he was dealing with.

"Would it have made any difference?"

"Yes, actually. I would've kept you from signing the papers, and we wouldn't have this headache right now."

Matt shook his head. "I think I'm gonna hang on to the boat for now." For the first time, watching her face turn beet red made him want to smile.

"I've about had enough of this, Matt. I said it once, I'll say it again—"

"More like you've said it a hundred times since we got married," Matt said.

Julie paused, her face swelling with anger. "—It's either me or that stupid boat. Make your pick."

Matt looked away for a moment to let his courage build up. When it arrived, a smile came over his face.

He looked back at her. "Baby, if I have to choose between you and the boat, I choose the boat. See ya!"

In his peripheral vision, he watched her facial expression change from that of someone in command to someone in total shock. He shut the door behind him, not a hard slam, but with enough force to signify confidence. By the time he was out on the dock, she stepped outside. He debated for a moment whether to look back at her or not. He decided to do so in case she wanted to negotiate further.

Nope. Balled in her arms was a huge pile of his laundry.

Damn. That didn't take long. Did she already have those set aside for this dramatic moment?

"Enjoy your stupid boat. Hope it has a bed!" she shouted.

Matt laughed. "It does, actually. Better yet, I don't have to listen to anyone snore while I'm sleeping on it!" Her gasp triggered another laugh. She literally could not stand the idea of someone standing up to her. She would occasionally brag how she set an unruly student up for suspension or detention if they didn't cooperate in class. Not that Matt believed students shouldn't be disciplined, but she seemed a little too giddy each time she did it. Power hungry madness was all it amounted to.

Never had Matthew Lodes felt more triumphant than the moment he stepped aboard his cruiser. He worried that he'd experience instant regret with this action, but so far he was feeling on top of the world. If only he could go back in time and keep his dog, lizard, and cigars. That would change once he found himself a place to live. In the meantime, he would celebrate his triumph with a cold one out on the water.

First, he got on the phone with one of his buddies. "Hey, Harry! You and Lana want to come out on the *Cruis'n Cigar*?"

"She's letting you keep it?"

"She's tossing all my belongings out on the front porch as I speak to you."

"Holy shit! You serious?"

"Serious as a heart attack."

"Well, in that case, it's time we celebrate. We'll be out in front in five."

"On my way now!"

****

With a beer in hand and a cigar in his mouth, courtesy of his friend Harry Daniels and his wife Lana, Matthew pushed his boat to its top speed of thirty-eight knots.

"Whoa!" Lana screamed with joy as they hit a wave. It wasn't exactly an Olympic speed, but it was enough to get the wind rushing through your hair. And right now, the three of them were content with that.

For two hours, they cruised the water, going further and further southeast. The sandbars had disappeared. They were in the open ocean now. Living in the shallow waters of the Keys, it was somewhat ominous to watch the bottom disappear from view.

It was enough to make Harry slip into his life vest. He handed one to Lana. "Might want to wear this."

"Nah, I'm good. I hate wearing those things," she said.

"Babe, it's safer this way."

"Have another beer," she said.

"I agree with her!" Matthew said. He slowed down to puff on his cigar and downed the rest of his beer, then pushed the boat to its max speed. He was flying—flying away from his misery, from his marriage, to the freedom of the open ocean. He eyed the openness of the world ahead. Usually he didn't overthink simple details, but he couldn't help but wonder if the vast openness ahead was symbolic of his future. There were so many directions he could take that it stirred his adrenaline just to comprehend them.

"You need a place to stay?" Harry asked.

Matthew didn't hear him over the roar of the motor. He was lost in the thrill of the new direction in life. He imagined the divorce proceedings would be swift. He was more than happy to let Julie have the house. At the moment, he didn't need that much space anyway.

Harry tossed his beer tab at the back of his head. "Hey!"

Matthew slowed the boat down. "What? Too fast for you?"

"Hell no, but I'd like to be able to puff this thing without all the smoke being forced back into my throat," Harry said, holding up in his cigar. "Not to mention, I don't know how much fuel this thing holds. I'd like to *not* get stranded in the open ocean." He looked behind them. They had gone at least ten miles southeast. Over the course of time, he watched the Overseas Highway become a thin line in the distance. Now, there was only bluish-green horizon behind them.

A better marker of where they were at was the speck of land up ahead. They were maybe a mile-and-a-half northeast of Cielo Nublado.

"Hmm, you know, I've never been there," Matthew said.

"It's a nice place," Lana said. "Why the sudden interest? You wanna move out to paradise?"

Matthew shrugged. *Maybe.* It wasn't a bad idea, as far as he was concerned. If he couldn't find a decent place to stay in Upper Matecumbe, maybe he could find something on Cielo Nublado.

"You didn't answer my question," Harry said. "You need a place to stay tonight?"

Matthew turned to look at him. Harry was sitting next to his wife enjoying his cigar and beverage. Unlike Julie, Lana didn't mind the cigar smoke. In fact, she thought it smelled manly. If Matthew would need any help from Harry, it would be advice on how to find a woman like her.

"What was the question?"

"Since you're getting kicked out of the house, do you need a place to stay tonight?"

Matthew shrugged. "I haven't thought ahead that far. My mind's caught up in the upcoming divorce procedures."

"Yeah..." Lana took a drink of her beer. "If you didn't hate Julie before, you'll definitely hate her during that."

"No shit."

"With a little luck, we'll agree on what to split and get it over with relatively quick," Matthew said.

"Ha!" Lana wiped her lips and tried to conceal her smile, but it was too late. "Sorry. I don't mean to laugh at you, but you obviously have no idea how divorce works."

"You've been married to Julie for six years," Harry said. "You're honestly telling us you don't think she's the type that'll delay every chance she'll get just to squeeze every inch of income from you she possibly can?"

Matthew's uplifted spirit started to sink. "I, uh, I guess I haven't really thought it through."

"That's obvious, bud. Not trying to ruin your day, but since you've got this boat, the court's gonna look at that as evidence you have disposable income to be split."

"But... I saved up for this..."

"That's the court system for you, buddy. Rest assured, her lawyers will look into this purchase with the intent of presenting to the judge that you're withholding income."

"Are you serious?" Matthew's beer was wobbling in his hand, threatening to fall free.

Harry nodded. "Sorry, bud."

"You're saying me owning this boat ultimately benefits Julie in the eyes of the court?" His two friends nodded. Matthew's face turned beet red. "That's completely illogical!"

"Sorry, *Spock,*" Harry said. "That's the court system for ya."

Matthew sank into his seat. Suddenly, the ocean didn't seem so blue anymore, the boat no longer a flight to freedom, but another shackle in the prison that was his marriage.

He couldn't believe it. In a way, Julie had won the battle before it even started. It didn't matter whether it was morally right—morals were often lost on the court system.

It wasn't often he was tempted to cry. Usually he'd simply lose his temper if things didn't go his way. Never did Matthew resort to weeping like a child. Today, though, he could feel himself welling up. It was a sense of injustice and hopelessness.

"No freaking way," he said. "I'll sink this boat before she can use it against me."

"Won't make a difference," Lana said.

"Not unless I claim she sabotaged it," Matthew said.

"I don't think it works that way," Harry said.

"Oh, just you wait. I'll get photos of the damage 'she' caused, and present that in court."

"You'll need a police report," Lana said. "The investigation will likely reveal the truth. You're good at selling your company's clothing brand, Matt, but you're not good at selling lies."

"Plus, didn't you get insurance for this?" Harry asked.

"Yeah..."

"That'll probably cover the damage anyway. At least, that's how the court will look at that unless there's concrete evidence Julie damaged it." He puffed on his cigar, while wishing he waited a day to bring this ugly truth up. "Sorry, buddy. I don't mean to be a killjoy. I just want you to know the truth."

"Yeah. Should've held on to that money you were saving," Lana said. "Could've bought this boat afterwards, once everything was finalized."

Matthew tossed his beer into the water then smacked the console with his palm. "I hate that bitch." Suddenly, he didn't want to be out on the water anymore. Whether the information Lana and Harry were telling him was accurate meant nothing at this point. He regretted buying this boat. Now, he was trapped. Even if he returned it, it would show in his financial records, which Julie would exploit.

This boat was the freaking death of him.

In five minutes, Matthew went from loving the *Cruis'n Cigar* to despising it. He throttled to twelve knots, then began circling back.

"Heading home?" Harry asked.

"Yep."

"Aw, come on. Don't let Julie ruin the thrill of this purchase," Lana said. "You've been wanting a boat for a while."

"I'd sooner see this thing hit by a freaking torpedo and broken into a thousand pieces. Preferably with—" His throat tightened as he completed the turn. All three people aboard stood up in shock as they witnessed the huge swell barreling toward their boat. It wasn't a tidal wave. Just an isolated swell pushed by a large mass.

The oncoming object took form. Fins protruded out of its side, its front a cone-shaped mass, coming right for their boat like...

A torpedo. Only this torpedo had a mouth lined with huge teeth.

A shark! An EIGHTY FOOT shark!

There was no explosion, though there might as well have been. The bow of the cruiser imploded in a split second, the vessel itself flipping backward.

All Matthew felt was the water. It had engulfed him, for he had been flung several yards back. It sucked him down like a vacuum. At twenty feet, he regained enough of his bearings to determine which way was up.

Halfway there, the sight of the enormous mass caught his attention. He froze, watching the fragments of his cruiser rain down in front of him. It was like an asteroid field of wreckage, and weaving in-between it all was the enormous shark. Black eyes reflected the sunlight, its mouth partially agape to allow water through its gill slits.

All of a sudden, those jaws extended to the max, revealing the dark tunnel that was its throat. Matthew's heart fluttered as his eyes registered its target. Ten feet in front of it was Lana. Her blond hair floated over her scalp like seaweed reaching for sunlight. Like him, she was disoriented and was just starting to swim for the surface. Air bubbles exploded from her mouth as she screamed.

The jaws clamped down around her, crushing her skull and her heels together. The scream came to an instant stop. Matthew could imagine the crunching of bones as her skeletal structure was fragmented. The seeping of blood through the shark's gills...along with a severed hand...completed that horrific mental image.

The panic drained his already dwindling oxygen supply. Matthew shot for the surface, then filled his lungs with air. Looking to the east, he saw his capsized boat. It only had a few moments to go before it was completely submerged. Floating right toward him was the very life vest he neglected to put on. He grabbed it, slipped it under his arms, then allowed the current to take him where it willed.

More screams echoed in the distance. Squinting, Matthew leaned forward. A few hundred feet away, he saw Harry. He was looking around, unaware that Lana was already in the shark's gullet. Most of her, at least. He splashed the water, growing increasingly flustered with each passing moment.

It all culminated in a titanic explosion of water. The shark emerged from underneath him. For a split-second, the fish resembled an eighty-foot bird hovering over the ocean, surrounded by mist. Protruding from its closed jaws was Harry's writhing torso. A moment later, it fell free, squiggly intestines whipping about. The shark hit the water with a tremendous splash.

As the water settled, the dorsal fin reemerged. More thrashing of water followed as the shark tracked down the remains and engulfed them. Afterwards, the fish coursed the surface in search of any leftovers.

Matthew could feel his own rapid beating heart. No doubt, the fish would detect it and come for him next.

Damn that boat. It really was the death of him.

I wanna be back with Julie. I don't care anymore. The devil I knew before was better than this. At least she was a wildcat in the sack, and was fun whenever she was in a good mood.

"I got rid of the boat," he said out loud. "Julie, I'm sorry. I just wanna go back. The insurance money will cover the boat!"

He watched the fin draw within fifty feet. As he feared, the shark detected his heartbeat and was closing in.

Then it stopped. The fish slowly submerged, its mass only supported by movement in addition to levity from its giant liver. The fish hooked to the south and darted away, its giant caudal fin generating swells that carried Matthew away. He watched the dorsal fin, then its trajectory.

A pod of dolphins were leaping in the distance. It was like a happy family gathering, unaware that their motions were attracting a giant predator. If they detected something was coming, they probably mistook it for a humpback whale.

By the time he heard the squealing of panicking dolphins, Matthew Lodes passed out.

He dreamed of being back home with Julie, having made amends. Even that was preferable to being in the gullet of a huge shark.

CHAPTER 13

It was rare that Nico Medrano endured a scathing verbal reprimand from the mayor. Robert was generally very happy with the Chief's performance in his job, especially after the meteor strike and the resulting tsunami. Of course, the guy took a little credit for himself, utilizing Nico's success as indication that he had good judgement in selecting his staff.

Nico couldn't blame him today. In fact, he blamed himself. He should've let Renny take the chopper out and search for the Klingbergs. It seemed an easy matter to just await for them to arrive back at port.

Nothing is as simple as it seems.

He leaned back in the chair across from Robert Zahn's desk. The crowning hairs around the guy's bald scalp were almost on end as he ripped into the Chief, his finger pointed as though making a passionate case to a jury.

"...And now, Dan Huckert's dead. You realize how this will impact business on our island?"

Nico held back before responding. His initial tone would've sounded insensitive to the tragedy that occurred. Yes, the Klingbergs were jackasses, and Dan Huckert wasn't necessarily the star resident of Cielo Nublado, but none of them deserved to die in a boat crash. With that in mind, Nico doubted it would affect tourism. It was a boating accident. These things happen.

The only difference this time was that he could've stopped it. If not for that damned whale...

"I accept full responsibility, Rob," he said. "I allowed myself to get distracted with what happened at the north beach. I'll make a press statement as soon as I'm out of this office."

That didn't seem to ease the mayor's nerves at all. "Great. That's just what we need."

"Pardon?"

"Already, we're at risk of deterring people from coming here thanks to the news of this thing. People want to barbeque, not *be* barbequed. In addition to that, the last thing we need is them to think our public safety is incompetent."

This time, Nico chuckled a little. "Uh, Robert... first of all, it's only local news, and they have a right to have the truth as we know it so far. A boat crash isn't going to make headlines across the country, so you can relax. Secondly, it wasn't a mass shooting or a terrorist bombing. It was a boat accident, caused by—with respect to the deceased—a bunch of unruly morons."

The mayor leaned back in his seat. "I recall there's more to it than that?"

"Such as…?"

"Your report mentioned something about a shotgun blast. That Dan Huckert might've killed one of those people?"

"He had a weapon on his boat. It's not illegal to carry firearms on vessels, and I've checked him in the past. He had all the permits. My guess is that the Klingbergs harassed him again and things got out of hand." He noticed the look in the mayor's face. "Look, our forensics guys are looking into it, but that doesn't change the obvious fact that it all resulted in a boat crash. Even if Dan Huckert killed one or more of those guys, what do you expect me to do about it? He's dead, and he wasn't exactly a threat to the public."

"What about the missing person?"

"Our divers still can't find him," Nico said. "He might've been swept north by the straits. Hard to say. But his boat suffered some sort of damage, and from what I've seen, there's nothing Dan Huckert could've done to cause that."

"Then what could? A three-way boat crash?"

Nico shook his head. "The damage isn't consistent with any kind of collision."

"And what about that whale on the beach?"

"Officer Jackman reported that the researchers hauled it out to sea on our behalf."

Robert Zahn leaned forward. "What? You let the researchers handle it?"

"Yeah." Nico shrugged. "What's the problem? It's *their* whale?"

"The union contracts state that the island maintenance division has custody of that assignment. They could file a grievance that non-union personnel was performing their tasks."

"Oh, cut it out with that bullshit," Nico said. "Tell you what; next time a whale beaches itself here, I'll let them have first dibs. Now, if you excuse me…" He stood up and went for the door.

"Chief? One more question."

It took a moment for Nico to get rid of his annoyed look before turning around. "Yeah?"

"I've been seeing an odd increase of police activity on the island today. More than usual."

"There's been more activity today than usual," Nico said.

"Not more than what the staff on shift can handle. Certainly not enough to warrant hundreds of dollars' worth of overtime."

Hundreds? This guy's worked up on HUNDREDS of dollars?! It's pocket change compared to the taxpayer money he throws around.

"Rob, you've heard of the shooting in Miami, right?"

"Yeah." The mayor chuckled. "You don't honestly think those crooks are *here*, do ya?"

"It's just a precaution. They haven't been found yet. Which means they're hiding out wherever they can. We're easily within traveling distance."

"Yeah? Well, so is North Key, Key Largo, Windley, the Lower and Upper Matecumbe, Fiesta Key…"

"Yes, yes, I get it."

"They'd have to come in by boat or seaplane. We're nowhere near the Overseas Highway."

"Like I said, it's a precaution. It's our responsibility to be on the lookout as best we can."

"Alright, fine. It's just that, with everything else going on, we don't need residents around here on edge."

"Nobody's on edge except me, Mayor. And, judging by the way that vein is sticking out of your head, you. Have a Scotch and relax. Leave the worrying to me."

Nico stepped out of the office and went to the lot. He sat in his truck. With nobody around, he didn't have to keep up the façade of confidence.

Four people dead. Something he could have prevented had he had taken swift action. Back in his mind, he knew it wasn't entirely his fault. At the end of the day, responsibility went to the Klingbergs who thought they could act foolishly without consequence. But he was the Chief, and the safety of everyone on this island and its surrounding waters was his concern. Nico had allowed himself to get distracted today. Just as he did July 2018.

July. Is there something about this month that's haunted?

Once upon a time, Nico loved this month. Now, he wished he could skip it every year. Reduce the calendar to eleven months instead of twelve. But he couldn't. He had to live with it.

The time on his watch read four-forty-six. Nothing from Denise. Maybe after hauling the whale out she simply returned to wherever she was researching. At least he was off the hook. Hiding made him feel like a coward, facing her made him feel like the failure he saw himself as.

He started the engine. "Please, God. Let the bullshit be over with."

CHAPTER 14

"No. NO! Absolutely not taking part in this insanity, dude." Enrique stood up from the basement sofa and went straight for the stairs.

Ed Thatcher realized his proposal to the group was quickly going downhill. Kris and Allen were on his side, though reluctantly. Whether they liked it or not, they were stuck with Thatcher. They couldn't risk letting him go his own way, for if he got caught, he would easily spill the beans on their whereabouts. And with his mind clouded by his addiction, they couldn't trust him to operate alone.

"Enrique, wait," Thatcher said.

"No way, man. I'm going home. I did what you paid me to do. No way am I going to be caught doing a drug deal."

"We're *not* going to be caught," Thatcher said. "Pedro knows the local waters. The police don't go around inspecting every boat. The meeting will be relatively brief. Roberto doesn't want to stick around longer than he has to. It'll be a brief exchange."

"You assume I'm willing to help you," Pedro said.

Thatcher turned around to face him. Being at another man's mercy was excruciating. It wasn't something he was used to. His ego was burning so hot, he felt he could fire solar flares from his eyes. On any other occasion, Thatcher would have Pedro beaten to a pulp and left on the side of the road. Such action wouldn't help him in this case, as Pedro was the only one who could locate that wreck.

"I'll pay you."

"I'm not keen on having drugs in my house," Pedro said. "*Especially* knowing you'll be snorting it up all night. God only knows how crazy you get when you're high."

"Likewise, I'm not riding around with drugs on my boat," Enrique said.

"Oh, but murderers are okay," Thatcher said. He had no qualms with calling himself what he was. The bank wasn't the first time he squeezed the trigger. Maybe the most newsworthy time, but not the first. And he would do it again to keep himself from going to prison.

Enrique looked at Kris. "My favor to you guys is fulfilled. I'm outta here." He ascended the stairs.

Thatcher ran up after him. "Enrique, I need you!"

"I don't want to be part of this anymore."

"Yeah? What are you gonna do when you get home? You think you can land another job? Sounds like you've tried the straight life and it spat in your face. Face it, you'd be near broke if not for this little job. Now I have another for you. All I need you to do is drive the boat."

Enrique stopped at the front door. "Let's pretend I agree. Why do I have a feeling you're gonna come up with some other task for me after this?"

Thatcher smiled, revealing stained teeth. "Because I will. You see, after tomorrow's deal, we'll have to figure out where we're going next. Might head into Mexico. Not sure yet, but regardless, we'll need a boat."

"Dude, you're insane." Enrique grabbed the doorknob and began to twist it.

"Call me as many names as you want," Thatcher said. "But I'm offering you one-hundred grand—for a few days' work."

It was as though Enrique was suddenly frozen in time. He stood motionless, his hand still clutching the door handle. The latch had just come undone, yet the door remained shut. Slowly, he let the knob spin back. It was the phrasing that made the light bulb go off.

The last few years, he had been working all kinds of crappy jobs for scraps. Fifty bucks a day to lift hundred-pound bags of grain? Spraying decks. Hammering pallets. Then Uncle Sam took his fair share. It was all an ex-con could get, at least so they say.

At the end of the week, he'd have a few hundred bucks.

A few days, a hundred grand. Damn, I wish Thatcher didn't phrase it like that.

If only Pedro's boat was in commission.

Enrique considered the details of the task. The deal tomorrow would be quick. Roberto would give a sample, Thatcher would test it, then he'd pay the money and Roberto would hand over the rest of the supply. Even if somebody could see them, would they really know what was going on unless they were up close?

Now, the traveling was a different story. It's not like his boat was a yacht that could travel the world. It was just a small cruiser.

BUT...if Thatcher pays up front, I can get out of here in the middle of the night and head back to Florida. Pedro won't give a shit, and it's not like the gang will retaliate, as they don't want to be anywhere near Miami.

He faced the gang leader. "I want payment as soon as the deal is complete."

"Half," Thatcher said.

"Full. And another five grand to cover fuel."

Thatcher gnawed on his lip. "I'll think about it."

Enrique's hand was back on the door handle. "While you're thinking, I'll be heading home."

"Alright, fine!" Thatcher shouted. He squeezed his eyes shut. He was begging. He HATED begging. "Money up front. You have a deal."

Enrique was a bag of mixed emotions. On the one hand, he loved the prospect of making some serious cash for a fairly simple job. Of course, that came with risks. But whoever got ahead without making risks? Besides, this was a one-time thing.

The two men returned to Pedro's basement, where the gang would be staying. If Pedro were to get a surprise visitor, he didn't want to risk these guys being seen or heard. It was his neck on the line too.

Unlike Enrique, Thatcher didn't have the leverage of poor financials to persuade Pedro to assist in his operation. Plus, he was running out of funds to begin with.

He stood with his back to a pillar, arms crossed, obviously knowing what was coming next. Thatcher hated the look on the guy's face. It was like he thought of himself as above the rest of them. As if he had never partaken in any illegal activities for financial benefit.

"So, what say you?" Thatcher said. "We need a navigator."

"Jacquez Grave. Like the guy said, go southeast for two miles."

"Oh, right. I forgot there are road signs out there."

"Can't you guys use a compass?" Pedro said.

"We're talking about a specific spot. I don't know where the hell that is. Neither does Enrique."

"I guess you'll just have to wing it," Pedro said.

"I'll pay you."

"Nah. I'm good. You can sleep here tonight and tomorrow night. Then, my favor to Kris will be fulfilled."

"What's the argument *against* helping us?" Thatcher said.

"You're making a big exchange. I don't want to be seen taking part in such an operation. Simple as that. I have a good thing going here and I don't want to jeopardize it any more than I already am."

"Uh-huh." Thatcher looked up at the ceiling. "Or are you expecting a visitor?"

"I've told everyone I know that I'm busy these next couple of days."

"Right. Even that lovely chick you have in that picture frame I saw up there?"

Pedro's expression hardened. "Like I said, I have a good thing going on here that I don't want to jeopardize. You guys can find the meeting site on your own. I want you gone by Saturday."

Thatcher smiled. "Why?"

"What do you mean 'why'? That was the deal."

"Why Saturday specifically?" Thatcher said. "Got a hot date? Little missy stopping by for a little…" he clicked his tongue.

Pedro's arms slowly uncrossed. His right hand came down by his side. Thatcher knew of the pistol on the back of his waistline. Pedro wasn't going to shoot him and draw the entire neighborhood in. Not unless one of the thugs posed a threat that couldn't be stopped any other way.

Regardless, Thatcher had him on edge.

"Who knows. Maybe we'll stick around a little while longer. Stay here to enjoy a meeting with little missy."

"Dude, you're really pushing it," Pedro said. His face was turning red.

"Am I?"

"Thatcher, dial it back a bit, will ya?" Kris said.

"Fuck off, Kris," Thatcher snapped. Kris shook. Rarely did Thatcher ever raise his voice at him, even in stressful scenarios. But today, his lifelong friend looked as though he would kill him as soon as he would anyone else.

"I think I've had enough," Pedro said. "Letting you guys come here was a mistake. Time for you to leave."

"You gonna make us? How?"

"I'll shoot your asses if I have to."

"Yeah, how do you think that'll play out in the long run?" Thatcher said.

"He's got a point," Allen said. "You start shooting, the neighbors will hear it. Cops will be here long before you can come up with a bullshit explanation as to why four criminals with sleeping bags and millions of dollars of stolen cash are in your basement."

"Not to mention that'll cause them to look into your past in Texas," Kris said. Pedro looked at his friend in betrayal. How could Kris side with these guys? The answer was simple: at the end of the day, he was a wanted murderer, and while not as crazed in the head as Thatcher, he was willing to do whatever he could to survive.

"Same thing with SATURDAY!" Thatcher said with glee. "Yeah, you say you'll make us leave. And we will… if you agree to do this little assignment. Otherwise, we'll be here to greet Little Miss Sunshine. And you can do nothing to stop us without incriminating yourself. After all, you're aiding and abetting cop killers."

Pedro felt as if a fuse had been lit, leading to an explosive charge in his psyche. He knew it! He absolutely knew he should have listened to his inner voice when Kris called asking for a place to stay. He should've said he was out of town. Hell, he should've said he was dying of cancer. Anything! But no, he felt compelled to repay him for Texas.

The worst part was that Thatcher was right. The guy was actually willing to use his own predicament as leverage…and it was working! Pedro had made the mistake of revealing how happy he was living the straight life. So much so, that it was obvious he didn't want to lose it. And Thatcher was the kind of guy that would take as many people with him on a sinking ship as he could.

Pedro pointed a finger. "Saturday morning, you're gone. Sunrise."

Now, Thatcher was the one with his arms crossed and the smug look on his face. "So, we have a deal?"

"This better be quick," Pedro said. "In and out. No dawdling around."

"Ha! Don't worry about that. Roberto's not out to make friends. Just money." He moved to the sofa and plopped down, hands behind his head. "On that note, what's for dinner, Mr. Host?"

Pedro went for the stairs. *With a little luck, it'll be prison food for you in a couple of days…with a side of dick from your cell mate.*

CHAPTER 15

Six o'clock.

Denise and Cameron had been out for three hours, watching the bloated whale carcass floating behind them. Every passing moment increased the marine biologist's frustration. She had video cameras set all along the boat.

When she wasn't watching the monitors or the whale she was using as bait, she was studying the tooth. This was as pure as it got. There was no sign of permineralization. During that process, water seeps through sediments over the teeth and transports minerals into the pore spaces, which causes them to fossilize. This tooth was nothing but bone, as fresh as some of the great white samples she had in storage.

Looking at the tooth, it was nearly identical in shape to the great white's, only much larger. Most of the samples in her possession were from specimens ranging from ten to fifteen feet in length. Their inch-long teeth paled to the ferocity of the seven-inch cleaver in Denise's hand.

"We should've met with some fishermen and got chum," she said.

Cameron looked up from his magazine. "If the fish doesn't come after that whale, then it's either not hungry, or it's not here."

"Or it's occupied with something else," Denise said. "Damn. Maybe we should radio Nico."

"It'd be a waste of time."

"Cameron, I'm serious. You think it's a coincidence that a random boat accident occurs on the same day this whale beaches itself? What if the megalodon shark is the real cause of the bizarre events occurring around this island?"

"Okay, let's say you're right—what would we tell the Chief? 'Watch out, we think we've discovered an eighty-foot prehistoric shark that showed up out of nowhere?' Come on. They'll think we've gone insane unless we offer concrete evidence."

"We have the tooth. And there's other evidence we can present." Denise tilted her head to the lab storage.

"I thought you wanted to keep those samples secret until your papers were published."

"Yeah, but not at the expense of human life. A shark that size could present an extreme danger to the public. They should be warned."

"That's why we're out here. Getting *proof.* Otherwise, saying anything to the authorities will be a waste of time." Cameron returned to his magazine. "Besides, what exactly do you expect your ex-husband to do about it? Shut down the whole island? From what the officer on the beach told me, the mayor was having a fit just from having the whale on the beach."

Denise looked to the east, imagining the deep waters where that meteor struck. Scientists have been exploring the ocean for nearly a century. Yet, it was a random meteor, traveling for God knows how many eons, with no direction, just the pull of gravity to guide it, that plunged into the world where prehistoric creatures still lurked.

She never would've guessed that they would've been so relatively close to civilization. Many people speculated the deeper trenches of the Pacific Ocean would hold the key to such discoveries. However, the Atlantic waters were vast and deep enough to hide such fantastic creatures such as the megalodon. Depths that had been breached by the rock from outer space, as though God Himself had decided it was time for the world above to meet the demons He secretly kept below.

"Oh, look at that. Five burner grill on sale for two-fifty. I might have to look into that," Cameron said.

Denise shook her head. "What exactly would you do with a grill?"

"Um…cook with it!" He smirked. "It's perfectly common for people to bring grills on boats."

"Yeeeeaaah—you're not getting that."

"Oh, come on."

"You always claim to be broke, yet you're willing to throw away perfectly good money on a grill."

"I *used* to be broke. That was when I had a mortgage and a car. Now I live on this boat with you. At the moment, at least, until you move back in with your hubby."

"Oh, not this again." Denise turned around and leaned over the side.

"Yeah-yeah. You wanna warn Nico of the shark…because it'll grant you an audience with him. You can tell him about the dangerous fish *and* that you forgot how good looking he is."

"The way you say that makes it sound like YOU secretly have the hots for him."

Cameron stared into the distance, deep in thought, then nodded. "Yeah, nice try. You're not gonna turn it around on me. Don't worry, once we get footage of that big ol' shark, you'll get all kinds of grant money, and a chance to impress Nico."

"He thinks I hate him," Denise said.

"Do you?"

"I did. I guess time has offered me the ability to reflect."

"Then tell him that. Give him peace of mind, if nothing else. Quit moping. If anyone's gonna complain around here for something they apparently can't have, it's me griping about this grill."

Denise smiled. "You suck at cooking anyway."

"Says you! You should know, I make a mean steak. With some meat tenderizer, some curry powder, cayenne pepper, cumin, red pepper—" A *thump* vibrated through the hull, drawing both researchers toward the port bow. "What the hell was that?"

"I don't know." They heard another bump. This one was lighter and repetitive, concurrent with the sounds of lapping water. "Sounds like something's up against the boat."

They moved to the forward deck and looked down. Drifting along the water were floating pieces of material. Fiberglass, decking, furniture... and an unconscious man in a lifejacket.

"Holy hell! Hurry, let's get him up!"

"He's taken quite a beating. What the hell do you think happened to him?"

"I don't know, but judging by all this shit floating around him, I say he wrecked his boat."

"Another boat accident? Seems like there's a lot of that going on today," Cameron said as he snagged the man's vest with a pole.

"Well, if nothing else, you can brag that I'll get to have another meeting with Nico. We'll be giving a statement about this." They hauled the man aboard and checked his vitals. "He's still alive. Get his shirt off. I'm gonna detach the whale and get on the horn to the local hospital."

CHAPTER 16

"So much for no more craziness."

Nico watched the paramedics load the man from his ex-wife's boat to the ambulance. According to the identification on him, he was Matthew Lodes, a resident from Upper Matecumbe Key.

"Hey Chief?" Renny said through the radio.

"Go ahead."

"I'm at the spot where the professor found the wreckage. I see debris, but no sign of anyone else."

"Keep looking. Keep me informed."

"Okay, but for how long?" It was Carley Amburn this time.

"Until the sun sets or you run out of fuel. It's called mandatory overtime. Get used to the idea." He clipped the radio back to his belt and turned toward Denise. Even now, while interviewing her regarding an actual case, it was hard to look her in the eye. "He was unconscious the entire time?"

"Correct," she said.

"Has there been any missing person's reports as far as you know?" Nico asked.

"I had my dispatcher check. Nothing. Not even from Upper Matecumbe." He rubbed his hand over his sweaty forehead. "I don't understand what the hell's going on. Two boat incidents in one day? In completely separate areas, no less. It doesn't make sense."

Denise looked at Cameron, who nodded at her. *Go ahead. Tell him.* She winced, knowing how crazy she was about to sound.

"Nico?"

"Yes?"

"I have an explanation for what might be happening around here." She looked to Cameron, who handed her the tooth. She held it up to a very stunned Nico.

"What the hell is that?!"

"Are you familiar with *Carcharodon Megalodon*?"

"Uh-huh..." His eyes narrowed at the huge tooth, which looked sharp enough to pierce a man's skull like a fork through cake icing. "You've mentioned it once or twice in the past. Nothing about them still being alive." A long pause passed between them, during which both Denise and Cameron cleared their throats. Nico watched their eyes. They broke eye contact, which indicated one of two things: either they were lying, or they were telling the truth, but were nervous because of how the information might be perceived. "Okay, this isn't the time for jokes."

"We're not joking," Cameron said.

"This tooth came out of the whale," Denise said. "I think it's what caused those boat crashes."

"A shark that big has a mean appetite," Cameron said.

"Nico, I have to encourage you to get everyone out of the water," Denise said. "If I'm right, this shark could kill more people. Anyone on the water could be at risk."

"Whoa-whoa!" Nico stepped back, hands raised. He couldn't keep a straight face. These people were telling him, in all seriousness, that there was a giant megalodon swimming off his shores. "I'm at a loss."

"You should be. We are," Denise said.

"Yeah? What does your university say about this?" Nico asked. Another long pause, with her eyes breaking away again to look at the ground. "Well?"

"I haven't informed them yet."

"And why not?"

"Because... that's not important!"

Nico placed his hands on his hips. "It is to me. Let me ask you this: have you *seen* this shark?"

"Nico, speak with your mayor. You have to get everyone out of the water."

"Have. You. Seen. This. Shark?"

Denise threw her hands in the air. "No! Happy? God! I'm warning you of something serious! You saw the dead whale. Here's the tooth that came straight out of it. Here! Take it." She shoved it into his hands. "Take that to your mayor. Maybe he'll be convinced."

"Doubtful. Tell me this, *Doctor* Reta, if you found this tooth and were concerned about the threat to the public, why didn't you alert me sooner?"

"Because you never returned to the beach."

"You could've called my office."

"Alright! Truth is, I didn't think you'd believe me."

"Oh! You think?!"

"So when we hauled the whale carcass out, we were hoping to use it as bait and lure the shark close enough to get video footage of it. That's when we found the floating wreckage and Mr. Lodes. You had another set of accidents earlier. It can't be a coincidence. The megalodon is going after small vessels." She pointed at the beach where the sperm whale had lain. "When the whale came ashore, it was actively fleeing the megalodon. You realize what it takes to frighten the hell out of a mature sperm whale, *Chief* Medrano?"

Nico held a finger to the tip of the tooth. "Hard to imagine."

"Listen, if we can track this shark down, we can determine a course of action," Denise said.

Nico could feel another headache taking form. Now, he wished he went the cowardly route and let Renny or Carley meet with Denise. At worse, he expected to see her pissed-off at him regarding Donny. Not coming to him with news that a giant extinct shark was eating the island's visitors. How could he approach the island console with this? Especially with his oversight which led to Dan Huckert's death, they'd think he'd lost his mind.

Almost how he felt about Denise at this moment—a feeling that his eyes betrayed.

"Listen, we have evidence," Cameron said. His tone was more balanced than Denise—probably because he wasn't compromised with the emotion of dealing with an ex-spouse for the first time in years.

"More than a tooth, I hope," Nico said.

Now, Denise's gaze was fiery. "You think that's not real?"

"I didn't say that—"

"Why would I fake that? Why would I lie to you about all of this?"

"Well..." *Oh, damn it! Should've shrugged and maintained the poor illusion that you didn't think she was outright lying.*

Too late. Denise's jaw dropped. The gig was up. She knew beyond a doubt that he at least suspected she was lying to his face.

"Spit it out."

"No, it's nothing." Nico turned to Cameron as a passenger on the Titanic looked at a lifeboat. *Save me from this sinking ship!* "What's this evidence?"

Now, even Cameron was looking nervous. He wasn't used to seeing Denise so worked up. In addition to nervous, he felt foolish, as he egged her on all day about reconnecting with her ex. That ship went down faster than all of the boat wrecks so far today.

"Well, come aboard. We have a lab on our boat with some very interesting findings that might help you to—"

"Why would I lie to you about this?" Denise said.

Cameron swallowed. "Oh boy."

This time, Nico was the one to look away.

Denise stepped forward. "I know the thing about eye contact. I learned a thing or two about detective work from being married to you for ten years."

"Denise, can we—"

"I thought it was Doctor Reta? *Chief.*"

Cameron turned away. Any chance of this conversation turning useful was decimated by the sea of emotions on display.

Nico shrugged. "Just forget it, alright?"

"No. Spit it out. I'm dying to know."

"Fine. Look at it from my point of view. You come to me after you've received knowledge of a deadly boating incident that I'm taking frack for. You tell me it is imperative I require all boats out of the water and to possibly close the beaches. Then, you tell me to inform the island counsel that there's a prehistoric shark that's been extinct for a couple million years roaming the waters. Yeah… doesn't sound at all like you're trying to get me fired."

"What? Why would I do that?!"

"Oh, come on. You've been pissed at me ever since—"

Denise inhaled deeply, then exhaled slowly. Equally as slow were her words. "You think I'm seeking revenge on you for what happened with Don? Jesus Christ, Nico. Just as I thought I was regaining my respect for you."

She turned on her heel and marched back to the cabin, brushing by a bewildered Cameron.

With a sigh, Nico backed away. "I suppose you guys will be spending the night here?"

Cameron nodded. "As long as that's alright."

"Yeah, it's good. Just, uh…" What could he say at this point? Better to leave without doing any more damage. "It's good to see you, Cameron."

"Likewise." His tone wasn't convincing. Nico couldn't care less at this moment. He got in his interceptor and went for the office. Time to file a few reports then go home. Then the next objective would be to have a stiff drink.

All the while, the day's events rolled through his mind. He thought of the strange markings in the red jetboat. He pulled to the side and looked at the images on his phone. Zooming in, he eyed one of the incisions, then looked at the large tooth in his passenger seat.

Could such a thing really exist?

Oh, I hate that I'm even considering this. He picked up his radio. "This is the Chief. I want additional boat patrols on duty tonight. Keep a sharp watch for anything unusual in the water. Equip the boats with fishfinders."

"Fishfinders. Did I hear you right, Chief?" one of the officers said.

"Yeah, we have them installed on the boats. Just being a little extra cautious after…the whale incident." If anything went his way, that lie at least sounded believable after the incident on North Beach. "And make sure all the shark barriers are secured. Stay safe. If you see anything unusual, have dispatch ring me at home."

CHAPTER 17

Two miles north. Nothing. Ten miles west. Nothing, except a distant view of the Overseas Highway. The ocean was too big a place for only two people to conduct a search.

Renny Jackman usually loved flying the chopper. There was something about being airborne that gave him a sense of freedom. Plus it filled his ego, as he was the only officer in the Cielo Nublado Police Department that was qualified to pilot the chopper.

Today, however, he was carefully watching the fuel gauge, hoping that needle would hurry up and inch closer to the red. Aside from little bits of wreckage, there wasn't anything to be seen other than blue ocean.

In the co-pilot's seat, Carley had just about given up scanning the water. She was bored beyond belief, to the point where she wanted to take control of the joystick and steer them back home. She partially got her way—they had double-backed and were now searching two miles out from the northwest corner of the island.

"Good ol' Chief is probably halfway through a margarita right now. Meanwhile, we're up here on a wild goose chase," she said.

"Hey now. If anyone's floating around out here, we're their only chance for rescue," Renny said.

"Dude, you sounded like you were about to fall asleep midway through that sentence," Carley said.

"Probably because I was." A yawn followed that statement. "I can't take much more of this. There's nothing out here except boaters."

"And dolphins!" Carley's expression livened. She leaned against the window and watched the pod racing north. Their speed was fairly intense, lacking the grace of a family moving together. Instead, they traveled with an odd intensity, like how fish darted in the presence of a larger creature.

Carley turned to look further behind them. "What is that—HEY!!!"

"What?" Renny said as he turned to port.

"I thought I saw something."

"What? A boat?"

"No. Something under the water, going after the dolphins. Looked like a whale, but I didn't get a good enough look at it."

"We're not looking for whales. We're looking for wreckage and people in lifejackets." Renny yawned again. "If there even are any, which I'm starting to doubt."

"Just turn back around, will ya?"

"Oh, for heaven's sake." Renny swung the chopper back around. Carley eagerly searched the water. Nothing. That big shape was gone.

"Damn it. How could something that big disappear?"

"The waters are deeper around here than near the islands. This isn't a sandbar, we're a couple miles out. Bottoms out at a thousand feet in some places." He smiled. "That's assuming you even saw anything."

She sneered. "I *did* see something, thank you very much."

"Look, it's okay. You're bored to tears. Your mind's at the point where it's playing tricks on you. On top of that, you're wondering what your husband's doing at home. Don't worry, I'm sure he's not looking at porn this time."

Carley felt as though she rolled her eyes at him so much, they might actually get stuck in an odd position.

"Unlike your wife, I've got my husband well-trained."

"All guys do it. Just saying."

"All *perves* do it." She pointed at him, then resumed looking down at the dolphins. "What the—damn it, Renny!!!"

"What?! What'd I do?"

"Your stupid goofing around made us miss something." She pointed to where the pod of dolphins had been. "Look!"

Renny descended a few meters and angled the chopper for a better view. "Whoa!" In the middle of the crystal blue water was a foaming red spot. Blood, enough to fill a few trashcans. It was as though a couple of the dolphins had been put through a giant blender and instantly diced.

He looked closer. Under that big red cloud was movement. It was faint, and disappeared a moment later, but it was there.

Carley noticed it too. "You saw that, right?"

"I did," Renny said. There was no sarcasm in his voice that time. "What the hell could fuck up a dolphin that quick? Hell, even a great white would have to put serious effort into it."

"I don't know. What the hell could fuck up a sperm whale?" Carley said. She sat back in her seat. "Didn't the Chief say something about alerting him if we spotted anything out of the ordinary?"

"He did. You think this counts?"

Carley nodded. "If all the other shit hadn't occurred, I'd probably shrug it off. But something's off about all of this."

"Agreed. Still, I'm not gonna have the entire department hear my ramblings of a sea monster lurking in the Keys. I'm calling Nico directly." He dug out his phone and pointed the chopper toward home, giving one last glance at the bloodbath below. "I don't suppose a whale could do that."

"Not that I've ever heard of."

"Same." He sped the chopper within range, then scrolled down his contacts until he found the Chief's personal cell. "Hey, Chief. This might sound weird, but you did say to alert you if we spotted anything unusual…"

CHAPTER 18

"You're shitting me? How big?"

"We couldn't get a good visual. Whatever it is, it's keeping to the deeper waters. She says it was at least as big as a whale. But I've never seen a whale go to town on a pod of dolphins like this, and I've lived down here all my life."

"No, that's not common. Baleen whales aren't capable of doing such damage in the first place, and toothed whales tend to go after squid, not dolphins." Nico looked at the tooth, which rested on the arm of his recliner. "It just can't be…"

"Beg your pardon?"

"Oh! Uh, nothing. Bring it back in. I'm gonna speak with the mayor tomorrow, then I'm gonna meet with the researchers and get their take on this."

"Nico, I'm hearing it in your voice. Is this something serious?"

Nico opened his mouth to talk, but struggled to get his answer out. How could he respond without sounding like a lunatic?

"It *might* be. That's all I can say. I don't have all the answers just yet. Anyway, bring it in and go on home. There's not much daylight left anyway."

"Alright. See ya in the morning, Chief."

"Thanks for calling." Nico hung up and leaned his head back against the cushion, watching the tooth. He had been examining it for the last couple of hours. If it was a replica, it was a damn good one.

Good enough to make him search for more clues.

Propped on his lap was his computer. Through his police resources combined with a little *google* searching, he checked for any odd occurrences that had taken place around the Florida Keys since the meteor shower. He filtered through the initial reports of missing boats and people who were clearly victims of the tsunami.

It was the end of June when a sailing yacht was reported capsized thirty miles north of the Bahamas. The boat was found afloat, with a large breach in the keel. Investigators suspected the boat had either collided with another boat, or had run aground and somehow drifted away without anyone seeing. Others speculated maybe they encountered a whale and got too close.

Longshot.

Three days later, forty miles east of Key Elliot, another yacht issued a Mayday. The family aboard had anchored in a region of a hundred-feet of depth and went swimming. They reported that something snagged the anchor chain and dragged their boat backward for several yards before releasing them.

Following that incident, a researcher tracking a grey whale reported finding the animal dead with large wounds. The whale had been dead for a couple of days when he located it, leading to speculation that sharks and other smaller creatures had simply stripped the animal down.

That sounds a little too familiar.

The report that made Nico's blood run cold was only from last night, when a fishing charter from Islamorada, with two vacationers aboard, left and never returned. Spa reservations on the Key went unattended, something the owners reported unusual concerning those particular clients. Reports indicated they traveled east for marlin fishing and never returned.

Nico finished his glass and shut his eyes. Resting was no option, even with the booze in his system. All he could think of was giant sharks, and the embarrassment that he was even giving this theory any kind of credibility. Then there was the humiliation he felt from his disastrous conversation with Denise. Even if he found her theory unbelievable, he shouldn't have made such an insane speculation regarding her motive. If she was the vengeful type, she would've dragged the divorce proceedings on until the court drained him of all finances. Hell, if she really wanted to get back at him, she'd have him charged for negligence. But she didn't. She recognized the situation for what it was—an accident. A horrible accident, but an accident no less.

"Jesus, I can't believe I'm entertaining this theory," he said to himself. He picked up his phone and tried calling hers. No answer. She was probably ignoring him. "Fine. I'll just head on over."

Nico stood up, dressed himself in something presentable, then searched for his truck keys.

****

By the time he arrived at the dock, Nico was as nervous as he was when performing his first arrest warrant. Hell, considering how their last encounter went, Denise was as likely to shoot his ass as much as any wife-beater he ever arrested.

To his relief, Cameron was up on deck. He stood up as soon as he saw the Chief step out of the truck.

"Permission to come aboard."

"Sure, Chief. She's in her quarters."

Nico chuckled and boarded the vessel. "You make her sound like royalty."

"I suppose I see her that way. What brings you back?" Nico held up the tooth. Cameron swallowed. "Oh boy."

"I'm not looking to start another fight. I still find it hard to believe that one of these things could be lurking around here—let alone be alive to begin with. But I can't deny that none of the occurrences today are normal. And you did say you pulled this out of the whale."

"Well, I won't hold you up." Cameron led him through the interior of the vessel then knocked on Denise's cabin door. "Hey, Professor. You have a visitor."

"I know who it is. Tell him to stick his head back up his ass and go home."

"Already did that," Nico said. "Turns out it's hard to see while you're driving. Better to drive home, *then* stick your head up your ass."

Denise opened the door. She was staring at him with a straight face, but Nico knew her well enough to know she was suppressing a laugh.

"What are you doing back here?"

"You said you had some evidence supporting why a megalodon would be in our waters," Nico said. "I need all the information I can get in order to launch an investigation."

"Wow." Denise crossed her arms and leaned against the door frame. "My sinister plan for getting the island to fire you is really paying off."

"Look, I was speaking out of my ass. It's just hard for me to believe this is actually real."

Denise took the tooth from him and examined it. "Yeah, I guess it was a lot to take in. Though spectacular, it was easier for Cameron and I to accept as fact. Not just because of this tooth, but because of everything we've found since the meteor strike."

"Does this have anything to do with your research in the Keys?"

"It has *everything* to do with our research in the Keys. Come with me. We have something you'll find interesting."

They took a small flight of stairs to the lab area below. In the back of the lab was a freezer unit, similar to ones used for food storage, though this one appeared to be a little more high-tech.

"Let me do the honors," Cameron said. He squeezed between them and went for the unit. Cold vapor spewed from the lid as it yawned high. Once it cleared, he gestured for the Chief to take a look.

Inside was a preserved three-foot long fish. It was brown in color with stripes running down its back. Its tail was somewhat similar in shape to that of a thresher shark's, though not nearly as elongated. Even more elongated was the snout, which reminded him of that of a goblin shark. Nico didn't recognize the exact species this thing was, but there was no doubt in his mind that it was a shark.

"What's so special about this?"

"This is Scapanorhynchus, meaning 'spade snout.'"

"I've never heard of it."

"You wouldn't have, unless you were around during the Miocene Period," Denise said. Nico looked over at her. She wasn't smiling, and there was no hint of suppressed laughter. She was dead serious.

"You're suggesting this is an extinct species of shark."

"I'm not suggesting it. I'm outright telling you," Denise said. "This thing has not been seen alive until now."

"But...*how*?!"

"My suspicion is that they lived in the deeper regions of the ocean, out of sunlight, where humans don't consistently venture," she said. "There are areas between here and the Bahamas that go below six-thousand feet. These creatures could easily be lurking there, and we've simply never seen them."

"Hard to believe, with all the dives that have been made, that nobody's ever seen one," Nico said.

"When research dives are made with submersibles, they're usually checking out a specific area, such as a wreck or a vent region. And who's to say nobody's ever encountered an unknown or thought-to-be extinct species?" Denise stepped across the lab and dug a book out from the desk drawer. It was an old leather-edition journal with a cracked cover. Judging from the content Nico glimpsed from the pages his ex-wife flipped through, it was from the nineties.

Denise stopped midway through the book and held it toward him. On the page was a grainy photo taken on the ocean floor. Wherever it was, it was dark enough to be nearly pitch black, except for the lights emitting from the submersible that snapped the image.

There was something in the background. A shark of some kind, though the details were not clear.

"This was in '98," Denise said. "This was a region of deep ocean about a hundred miles north of the Bahamas. It goes about two miles down. The crew of this submersible snapped this image before losing visual of the shark." She snatched the book from Nico's hands and found another image. "Then there's this one here."

Nico raised an eyebrow at the sight of a crushed submersible lying against a bed of rocks. The quality of the image wasn't much better, making him believe it was taken in the same decade.

"The crew of this research sub claimed they spotted movement in the distance. They reportedly screamed before all communication went dead. When another submersible went down to investigate, they found the sub smashed, as you see in the photo."

"I've never heard of this incident," Nico said.

"It never made headlines," Denise said. "Probably because there weren't any real answers. Some believe it may have been a rockslide. Ohers say maybe a whale was attempting to feed and struck their vessel, hence the 'movement' they reportedly saw. Then there's some who believe underwater predators could be lurking in these regions."

Cameron approached with another set of photos. "How about some evidence from the present day?"

Nico took the photos and looked over them. The first image displayed what somewhat resembled a lionfish swimming in the shallow waters near Islamorada.

"This species is from the genus *Heterothrissa*," Denise said. "Thought to have gone extinct around the start of the Ice Age." She grabbed the next image, which displayed a two-foot long shark which resembled a dogfish. In the image was Denise, swimming alongside the small creature in her dive suit. "*Tristychius*. Originally found in Scotland. Believed to be related to the modern day dogfish. Its eyes are smaller, due to having lived in deeper waters for all its existence."

"So, this thing actually *did* come from the deep?" Nico said.

Denise smiled. "You're damn right. I've got the live specimens tagged so we can keep track of them. This specimen in the freezer had washed up ashore and was found by a pair of vacationers. It was the first indicator that the meteor had disrupted an ecosystem that we didn't even know existed."

"If these things existed in the depths, I think it's fair to assume the possibility that larger predators could have survived as well," Cameron said, pointing to the meg-tooth.

Nico gave another look at the image of the smashed sub. A hundred miles north of the Bahamas—not extremely far from Cielo Nublado. If a giant shark could wreck a steel sub like that, it could easily smash a small jetboat.

No wonder we couldn't find the other Klingberg brother. And that could explain why the other boat smashed into Dan Huckert's. They were goofing around, then the Meg attacked. They fled, accidently went on a collision course with Huckert. He thought they were attacking, so he shot at them with his shotgun. Then boom.

"You alright, Nico?"

The Chief looked at Denise, his face full of worry. "We're gonna need to do something about this."

"You're right," she said. "Unfortunately, even with these findings, the University isn't going to provide additional funding to find and isolate a giant megalodon shark until we have undeniable proof. We'll need video footage, hopefully a tracking device, all the works."

"What exactly do you hope to accomplish?" Nico asked.

"I'd like to keep the shark alive so we can study it. This creature is a scientific marvel. Killing it would be a disgrace," Denise said.

"Letting it roam freely and take human lives would be an even bigger disgrace, Denise."

"I recognize that," she said. "But we have to try, at least. We'll work out a deal. We'll make an attempt to locate the shark. If all goes well, we'll lead it out into the open ocean. Away from civilization."

"And if things *don't* go well?" Nico said.

"Then…" it was a struggle for Denise to comprehend this alternate course of action, but Nico was right about the danger the fish presented. Scientific research didn't trump human safety in her mind. "If the plan doesn't work, then we'll have to kill it. Plain and simple."

Nico was surprised to hear that direct response. Nor was he disappointed. He wasn't thrilled about the idea of killing such a unique scientific discovery. Then again, he wasn't eager to come face-to-face with it to begin with, unlike Denise, who was visibly delighted to search for it.

"That settles it," he said. "So, we'll meet in the morning and set out on your boat?"

"That'd be the best course of action," Cameron said. "Considering the size of the megalodon, we'll need the largest vessel we can obtain. Since I don't see any battleships in the area, our boat will have to do."

"Good. I'll have patrols on standby just in case. I'll also have Renny and Carley in the chopper. Eyes in the sky will come in handy if that thing gets violent." Nico clapped his hands together. "Well, I think that covers it. See you guys at oh-eight-hundred?"

"Sounds good to me, Chief," Cameron said.

Nico looked at Denise for her approval. She nodded and gave a faint, almost forced smile. There was something on her mind. Nico wasn't sure what it was, nor was he sure if he wanted to pursue it.

"I'll see you in the morning."

"Don't be late," Cameron said.

"Nah. Don't worry. This isn't your sister's birthday party," Nico said.

Cameron laughed. "Can't judge you for that. Our own mother didn't even want to show up to that goth-infested show. Goodnight!"

Nico followed the passageway up to the main deck. As he crossed over to the dock, he heard running feet behind him. He turned around and saw an eager Denise step on deck.

"Nico?"

"Yes? You alright?"

"Yeah—no… well, yes." She smiled nervously. Nico tilted his head forward. *Which is it?* The smile faded. Denise could only keep up the façade for so long. "How have you been?"

Nico shrugged. "Fine."

"Fine? You sure about that?"

"I'm pretty sure," he said.

She stepped closer, hands clasped behind her back. "Listen, I don't want to hold you up much longer—"

"I arrived without an invitation. It's alright."

"—But I'm worried about you."

"Worried about me?" Nico held his arms out to his side. "I'm living in paradise! Surrounded by ocean. Haven't had a criminal homicide since I moved out here."

"Yes, it is beautiful. But I don't think you're enjoying it to the extent that you could be."

Nico lowered his arms. He wasn't sure how to reply to that. He deserved the heaviness in his heart. If anyone needed to be checked-up on, it was Denise. Not like she let Donny drown.

"How about you? How have you been? It's been all business since you first arrived. I never really got to see how you were doing."

"Well, I've had my hands full. Been keeping busy out on the water. I feel like I've been out at sea more than I've been on land lately. It's a job most marine biologists would kill for."

"I bet it is." Nico glanced at the cockpit. "Living with Cameron, essentially. You guys getting…" He winced at the thought.

Denise did too. "Hell no. I've known him so long, that just seems weird. Plus…" She glanced back to make sure Cameron wasn't listening nearby. "He's a little hefty for my taste." The sight of mild relief in Nico's face gave her joy. "What about you? There a new 'Mrs. Medrano' here in paradise?"

"Nah."

Denise had mixed emotions from that answer. On the one hand, it was nice knowing he wasn't the type to fill the void of his marriage with a series of hookups. However, the 'why' behind his refusal to find a new love made her heart feel heavy. Nico didn't need to state it for her to know. His mind was in a constant tug-of-war between wanting happiness and feeling he didn't deserve it.

"Was there something you wanted to tell me?" Nico asked.

"Huh?"

"You ran up here pretty fast. I wasn't sure if there was something specific, or…"

"Oh! No, I just thought it'd be nice to catch up a bit." She looked away for a moment. "That's a lie. Like I said, I'm worried about you, Nico."

"I appreciate it. But I'm fine. I promise."

"Are you really?"

"Absolutely."

Denise recognized the tone. The way he said that made her think of the suspects he interrogated in Waco. He often told her the stories, specifically the more humorous ones, of suspects trying hard to paint themselves as innocent. "Absolutely! I would *never* follow that woman!" Now, it was Nico failing to sell the lie.

"Maybe it's time we talked about it," she said.

Nico cleared his throat. "I, uh, well…" At that moment, his phone rang. He quickly snatched it and accepted the call. "Chief Medrano here… Uh-huh… right. Hold on." He held the phone down and turned to look at Denise. "Sorry, there's police crap I have to deal with. We'll pick this up another time, alright?"

Denise sighed. "Alright. See you in the morning."

"Yep. Eight o'clock." Nico waved goodbye then returned to his truck. As soon as he steered the vehicle out of sight, he hung up on the telemarketer that he pretended was someone from the department.

For once, those salespeople actually came in handy. For the short term, at least.

His mind was a maelstrom of contradicting feelings. Part of him wanted to be around Denise more, to make up for lost time. But doing so would force him to face the past.

Nico's hands clutched the wheel so hard he felt it would bend. *Please, God. Tomorrow, let the focus solely be on finding an oversized shark and stopping it. And more importantly, Lord, free me of this misery!*

CHAPTER 19

The razor scraped the mirror, guiding the remainder of the precious white powder to its final destination. Thatcher's nose served as a vacuum, sucking the drugs into his respiratory system.

On his knees like a slave in ancient Rome, he leaned back and waited for the glorious high. Minutes passed and it never came. There was a slight buzz, similar to that from smoking a good joint, but not the true powerful feeling he initially got from these drugs.

Thatcher stood up in a fit of rage, swung his arm and struck the bathroom shelf, knocking its contents onto the floor. His tolerance had grown too high and the shakes were getting worse. The only solution for this problem was to suck in a higher dose.

The problem was that he had just used up the last of his drugs. The solution was that more was on the way. Ten o'clock. He had spent much of the night counting the rolls of cash. Three-point-two million—better than he expected considering the rush they were in. He could pay off Roberto and then have enough set aside to lay low for a while. And with ten kilos, he could possibly even afford to sell some of it off if things got tight. Even with the company of hookers and friends, it would be hard to use up all ten kilos. It was something Thatcher considered to be a good problem.

The *bad* problem was determining where they would go from here. He was on thin ice with Pedro as it was after their altercation last night. Maybe he could stick a knife in the guy's throat once the work was done. For all he knew, Pedro would rat them out once he cleaned out any evidence that they had been at his residence.

Someone knocked on the door.

"What's going on in there?"

Thatcher was relieved that the voice was Kris' and not Pedro's. He opened the door and found his friend staring inquiringly. "Nothing. Need to use the can?"

Kris looked past him at the cocaine setup and fallen shelf. "Christ." He pushed Thatcher aside and started cleaning up. "What are you doing? If Pedro finds out you're doing drugs in his house…"

"What's he gonna do about it?"

"You really wanna make enemies right now?" Kris said. "I don't. Not in our predicament. We still don't know where the hell we're gonna go after we're finished here with your little errand. We might have to put serious thought into leaving the U.S."

"Oh yeah? And do what? Move to Italy? Become pasta chefs?"

Kris picked up the broken shelf, then groaned as he saw the spilled shampoo splattered over the floor.

"Is this all a joke to you? You think this is some big vacation? You forget that Carl is dead?"

Thatcher got nose-to-nose with him. "You can thank *yourself* for that. You forget that you were the one who shot those people who ran out of the bank? It was those gunshots that brought the police here in full force."

"Wouldn't have happened if you didn't shoot the bank manager."

"Listen, man, you're no rookie. You know the risks this life entails. Or have you forgotten? Listening to you talk, you always make yourself sound rational minded. Like you didn't shoot two people in the back just twenty-four hours ago. Must take a special kind of psycho to do that and then act so level-headed. At least I can say I take the drugs to cloud all that heaviness." Thatcher looked down at the mess and chuckled. "You're so 'normal' that you're concerned about a simple shampoo spill. Trust me, it'll take more than that to cleanse you of the dirt you carry on your shoulders."

Thatcher tapped Kris on the arm and went for the stairs. He went up to the kitchen and saw Enrique helping himself to the coffee. He looked as apprehensive as he did before. A simple boat trip had turned into a drug deal with a notorious felon, known for putting a bullet in anyone he saw as a threat to his operation. But money had a way of dulling the nerves. There were still splinters in his fingertips from pallet assembly, something the cocaine-fueled Thatcher took notice of instantly and used to his advantage.

"Trouble downstairs?"

"No," Thatcher said. He took the freshly poured coffee from Enrique's hand. "You all set for today?"

Enrique looked at his empty hand. Now it was both a sign of his desperation and pettiness. Money was the worst drug of all. Because of it, Enrique risked arrest or even death, and on top of that, allowed himself to be Thatcher's bitch.

"Yes."

"Good." Thatcher drank from the mug. "Ahh, that's good. So, I'm thinking of moving inland. Somewhere a little less populated. You ever been to any of the flyover states?"

"Nebraska," Enrique said.

"Hmm. What's it like?"

"Not a lot of people. Don't know if you care for prairies. If you're looking to be isolated, you'll have to adapt to the lifestyle. No offense, but you don't look like a farmer to me. Then again, the central plains are somewhat hilly. Maybe you can find something there. But I don't know how you'll pull it off without a background check. That state isn't known for criminal enterprises with their claws in real estate. You've got money, but to hide, you're gonna have to find someone who's willing to accept cash under the table and forgo all the paperwork."

"You have a line on anybody?"

Enrique chuckled. "You kidding? I've been trying to stay *out* of this business. And here you come along to fuck my day up. No, I don't have any leads. And our deal remains the same. Tomorrow, I'm taking you wherever you want to go, then I'm out."

"Suit yourself. Just keep in mind, there might be a couple U.S. Marshalls waiting for you when you get back."

"What?"

"You're a known associate of mine, thanks to our previous history," Thatcher said. "They've probably already checked your residence and discovered you were missing."

Enrique's face paled. Sweat started to build along his forehead. He stared into the distance, his mind tormented by facts he failed to consider when he agreed to all of this.

Thatcher smiled briefly, then sniffled. He was undergoing his own torment—the need for more cocaine. The pressure of finding a new hiding place was only elevating his need for a proper fix.

He walked into the living room area. Further back was a hallway which led to the master bedroom. He could hear someone moving about. Couldn't be Allen—his snores still echoed from downstairs. Besides, not even this band of thugs would dare to invade the privacy of their host's private quarters.

Unless that criminal's name was Ed Thatcher.

He walked to the bedroom at the end of the hallway and pushed the door open.

"Christ!" Pedro, wearing nothing but his boxers, turned around. "What the hell, man. You trying to get yourself killed?!"

Thatcher stepped in, looking at the phone in his hand. "Making a call?"

"None of your business. Get out."

"Interesting you're hiding in here sending messages." Thatcher approached. "Planning something stupid?"

"I don't have to explain jack shit to you." Pedro pointed at the door. "You get out of my bedroom now, or I'll—"

"You'll do what? Shoot me? We had this discussion yesterday. There's no version of this where you come out on top. You can blow my brains out, but that won't stop the police from digging into the fact that you we're aiding and abetting murderers."

Fed up, Pedro held the screen up. Thatcher took it and looked over the various texts.

Hey, Carley, something came up. I can't make it to today's appointment. I'll get over there first thing Monday.

Thatcher scrolled to the next several contacts. Every conversation was the same, with Pedro explaining that he couldn't arrive to various households.

"Don't forget, I have a business here," Pedro said. "I can't just be a no-call, no-show."

"Hmm." Thatcher handed the phone back, then winced after looking at his near-nakedness. "Put something on. You look pathetic." Smiling to himself, he walked to the kitchen. He slid his mug across the counter to Enrique. "Refill."

Much to his delight, Enrique did his bidding. The statement Thatcher had made minutes ago had broken him. Enrique was as much on the run from the police as the others.

Thatcher peeked at his watch. Seven-oh-six. In a little over two hours, they would be out on the water.

Just gotta get through this exchange. Then it would be party time with ten kilos of cocaine.

CHAPTER 20

It was eight o'clock, and Nico Medrano's tolerance for bullshit was already below ground level. He started out the day with another meeting with Mayor Zahn. The result was so counter-productive, Nico genuinely wished he just closed the beaches behind his back.

"Mayor, what I'm about to tell you is unbelievable."

"Yeah? More meteors falling from the sky? Or more boat crashes? Please, for the love of God, don't tell me there have been more boat accidents."

In one sense, Nico found it hilarious that Mayor Zahn was more concerned about boat accidents than a meteor impact. It was equally frustrating, as it gave Nico an idea of how their meeting was about to go.

"No. I have reason to believe we have a shark problem."

"We have shark nets for exactly that reason."

"This might not be an ordinary shark, Mr. Mayor."

From that point on, it was downhill. Nico had debated since last night how upfront he should be about the situation, knowing that people would look at him as if he were a lunatic. That was exactly the look he was getting from the Mayor when he mentioned the word Megalodon. Ultimately, Nico believed in transparency, and wanted to express his concerns in full. The result was exactly what he feared it would be.

First, the mayor stared blankly, trying to determine whether this was a joke. Nico wasn't the type for pranks, but he did have a sense of humor. What followed were a series of laughs and questions, trying to get the Chief to break the act. That break never came, leading Zahn to realize Nico was being serious.

"We need to suspend all water activity around this island until I can confirm it is safe."

"You expect me to tell people—who've spent thousands of dollars to be here—to stay in their hotels because my Police Chief thinks a five-million year old fish is swimming out in our waters?! Nico, I don't know what's going on in that head of yours. Do you need a vacation? A girlfriend? A therapist?"

The briefing at the police station went a little bit better, though only because Nico had the advantage of rank. Because of Zahn's reaction, he was hesitant to be fully honest with his officers, but if he was going to have them patrolling the waters, he wanted them to know the full risks.

He noticed a few eyebrows stretching when he explained what a megalodon was. Like the mayor, many of the officers were trying to determine if their Chief was playing a joke on them. There were a few silent laughs disguised as coughs within the crowd, as well as some nervous grins. Even Renny and Carley were looking at Nico as though he was a dementia patient.

Nico praised himself for his high school theater classes for helping him keep a neutral tone during each meeting. He knew how he sounded, and despite his very real concerns, it was a challenge to keep a straight face. He was warning his officers about an extinct shark that had risen from the depths. Even after taking into account the bite marks on the whale, the marks on the jetboat, and other odd occurrences since the meteor crash, it was still considered fantastical.

With all that out of the way, it was time to arm himself and set out to find the damn fish.

****

Nico stepped out of his truck. In one hand he held a coffee with two sugars. In the other he held a Remington 870 pistol-grip shotgun. Slung over his back was a Colt M4 Carbine. He carried six magazines on his vest and had a belt full of shotgun shells. He wore his tactical pants and ditched the uniform shirt in favor of a black tee.

Cameron chuckled as he watched the Chief from the deck. "Damn, Nico. You sure you're not auditioning for the next big action movie franchise?" He climbed down to help load the supplies.

"Yeah, you might find it funny now, but you'll be thanking me once this megalodon decides to swallow you." Nico placed the rifle down and glanced out at the water.

Cameron looked at the shotgun. "I just hope these will be enough to stop it if it decides to get violent. These sharks were believed to have extremely tight skin."

"It damn well better be enough, because I'm in no hurry to get swallowed by a goddamn freight train with teeth," Nico said. "If it even exists in the first place."

"You still have doubts?" Cameron said.

"I'm obviously not disregarding the idea. But despite your findings, I'm gonna have to see this big ass shark in the flesh before I believe it fully."

Denise stepped out of the pilothouse and looked down at him from the fly deck. "You believe in it enough to put extra patrols out. We've seen at least three police boats pass by in the last hour."

"Good morning to you too, Denise," Nico said. "Mayor's all over my ass about it too. He's asking me why I need to have boats circling around the island like we're at war."

"Yeah? What'd you tell him?" Cameron said, waiting to laugh at the idea of Nico briefing the mayor about a giant killer shark in the ocean.

"I simply explained it's a precaution in case any large marine sea life comes too close to the beaches again. I just didn't specify what large marine animal I was concerned about."

"Any luck on closing the beaches?" Denise asked.

Nico snorted. "What do you think?"

"Yeah, sorry. Stupid question."

"I've got one for you," Nico said. "You ready to set sail?"

"Yep. Hope you don't mind the smell of fish," Denise said.

"Yeah? Why?"

"Because you'll be on chum duty."

"Oh, fabulous," Nico said. He leaned on the guardrail and shook his head. "I should've brought Carley along to handle this."

****

Thirty minutes later, they were two miles north, with three hundred feet of chum extending from the stern of the boat. So far, there was nothing on sonar except small populations of fish.

It had been seven years since Nico had put tobacco anywhere near his lips. It was his turn-to vice when dealing with stressful situations, namely complicated homicide cases. Shortness of breath, dry mouth, and various other problems gave him the willpower to quit cold-turkey. Unlike most other people who quit cigarettes, it was a simple matter for him to drop the habit. But now, with the smell of minced fish guts and oil, he was dying for a cigarette.

"Having fun down there?"

Nico turned his head just enough to see Denise in his peripheral vision. She was smiling.

"Taking delight in watching me slave away?"

"Maybe a little."

"Where's Cameron? Taking a nap?"

"He's monitoring the cameras," she said.

"And staying out of the sun," Nico said.

They heard a window slide open somewhere along the port side of the structure. "Hey, I love the sunshine, Detective," Cameron said from within the cabin.

"It's *Chief* now."

"Sorry. Force of habit. I'd offer you a beer, but it's only eight-thirty...and the Captain of this vessel doesn't allow alcohol aboard."

"Yeah, she can be a hardass," Nico said, taking delight in the shift in Denise's facial expression.

"Oh, ha-ha."

Maybe it was the need to focus on something other than the smell of chum, or the boredom of waiting for a giant shark to appear, or just the nostalgia of the good ol' banter he and Denise used to have—but he was feeling emboldened.

"You should've seen her when she went on this diet in twenty-twelve," he said. "No ice cream allowed in the house. So, you know what I did?"

"I remember. She bitched to me about it for a month straight," Cameron said. "I will say, it was a dick move to buy five tubs of ice cream."

"She had five favorite flavors. Figured it was the best way to torture her," Nico said.

"Yeah, you really were a douche," Cameron said. "Then again, who am I to talk. I would've done the exact same thing!"

The two men shared a laugh at Denise's expense.

"Yeah-yeah, laugh it up." She turned to lean on her right side, allowing her sleeveless arm to show its muscular tone. "Just so you know, I'm the fittest one on this boat."

"Right. I bet you still need someone to open a pickle jar for you."

"Hey! Some of them are screwed on really tight!" Denise said, pointing a finger. "And at least I don't put an open jar of pickles in the pantry, Mr. Attention-to-Detail."

"No, it's Mr. Nothing-is-ever-as-simple-as-it-seems. And that goes for the pickle incident. That was—" His voice trailed off. Awkward silence filled the research vessel. "That was Donny, actually."

Damn it. For a short while, I actually thought we'd make it through the day without bringing him up.

Nico resumed tossing scoopfuls of chum over the side. Cameron slid his window shut, which only added to the feeling of awkwardness. Nico felt two different waves of guilt, one for what happened with Donny, the other for the fact that his name and memory had practically become taboo.

He heard the pilothouse door shut. *Great. Now she's probably pissed at me.* Moments later, the main deck passageway opened. Nico pretended not to notice when Denise stepped beside him.

"Want me to take over?"

He shook his head. "No sense in both of us smelling like shit."

"Nothing I'm not used to," she said. She leaned back against the transom. "I have a confession."

Nico stopped and looked at her. She kept a straight face and there was no shakiness to her voice. What was she going to confess?

"Let me guess: you're seeing someone." He shrugged and resumed scooping the mixture. "Hey, I can't hold it against you. I just don't know how you can manage it with working in the field and—" Denise broke into a fit of laughter. "What?"

"I'm sorry, I had to let that play out for a moment," she said. "No, the confession is I ate some of that ice cream you and Donny brought home. A pair of jerks, you two were."

"It was good for a laugh. He was a little young to understand why I thought it was funny. 'How can ice cream be bad?' he had asked." He was shocked to be able to get this far into the conversation talking about Donny without breaking into tears. To Denise of all people, the woman whose life he felt he destroyed. Maybe talking to her about it was the right path. Maybe he'd get something out of it. Closure of some kind?

"Hey listen, uh. I was thinking…"

He stopped. What kind of closure was there? Nothing he would say would bring their son back, and it wouldn't undo the mistake he made. No, all it would do is worsen the pain.

"You were thinking…?" Denise said, waiting for him to finish his thought.

"About the megalodon—did they even live in the Atlantic Ocean? I was under the impression they lived in the Pacific." *Good segue.*

"Their teeth have been found on every continent except Antarctica," Denise said. "To be honest, this area would be perfect for a megalodon to live. We believe they adapted to sub-tropical waters. If it did surface from the depths, it probably hunted along the Keys, staying out of the shallow waters until it found a new feeding ground. Here."

"That's what I figured too. I did some reading and found a list of peculiar events. Boat wrecks, disappearances, all of which led from the initial meteor landing all the way to here," Nico said. He placed the scoop down and wiped his hands clean with a rag. "That leads me to another concern."

"Which is?"

"We were talking about leading this shark to the open ocean. How exactly are we going to do that? I don't imagine a chum trail will be enough to hold its attention."

Denise nodded toward the cabin. "Come with me."

They went inside and descended to the lower decks. Denise opened a few cabinets, revealing tightly secured vials of what looked to Nico to be medicines.

"My job occasionally requires me to do difficult tasks," she said. She pulled a metal case from the far closet and opened it, revealing a high-powered tranquilizer rifle. "Sometimes, we need to sedate animals in order to free them from traps they inadvertently wandered into, such as drift nets. My hope was to attract the megalodon with bait on a cable, draw it close enough, and inject it with enough drugs to put it to sleep. We can get it on a cable and tow it to a safer location...not before tagging it, of course. The forward motion of the boat should keep water going through the shark's gums and prevent it from suffocating."

Nico held one of the vials of tranquilizer then glanced at her. "You think this'll be enough to knock that bastard out?"

Denise sighed. "No, I can't confirm how much is needed. Best I can do is judge based on the amount we once used for a forty-three foot humpback. Of course, its size and weight were properly measured, thanks to electronic instruments provided by my university."

"And how heavy is the shark?"

"I can't say without seeing it. We estimate that the seventy-foot specimens were probably sixty tons."

"Jesus. If that's the case, how the hell would we keep it afloat?" Nico asked.

"If we sedate it, I'll make a fast dive with a propulsion vehicle and secure a cable to its mouth."

"You'd be *willing* to get close to that thing's teeth?"

"Only once I'm certain it's sedated," Denise said. "Then we'd winch it in and tow it out to sea. And thanks to the footage we'd sent to my university, they'd get a larger research boat to intercept and take over. They we'd arrange further action from there."

"Then you'd spend the next year researching the megalodon," Nico said.

"With a little luck, yeah. Who knows? Maybe I'll get on the cover of a few magazines." Denise smirked then shrugged. "Then again, I don't think *National Geographic* is quite the powerhouse it once was."

Nico placed the vial back, then looked at a brown jar with a white lid on the top shelf. "Cyanide. Oh, shit." Denise took the jar. It was only half full, having been used recently.

"Occasionally, I have to put animals down. Whales beach themselves, get infections, just like any other animal."

"You put that into your tranquilizer darts?"

"I can but I don't," she said. "If they're in the water, I get in my dive suit and use a large syringe. Or if they're on the beach, I do it on foot. Never had to put an animal down with the tranquilizer gun before."

Nico picked up one of the tranquilizer darts and held the needle close to his eye. "You guys said that the skin of these things is very tough."

"Yeah?"

"How the hell is this little needle gonna penetrate?"

"Well," she chuckled nervously. "That's the part you're not gonna like."

"Like that's a switch," Nico said. "In case you haven't noticed, I haven't enjoyed much of this trip so far. So, how's this part any different?"

"I gotta get the shark close to the boat so I can hit the soft tissue inside."

"Oh, lovely." Nico pointed at the cyanide. "Mind if I drink that? Better than being mulched."

"I would, but I don't have much on hand," Denise said. She placed it back in the cabinet, then moved for the steps. "Come on. Don't want that chum line to run thin."

CHAPTER 21

"Come on! Come on! Let's go!" Thatcher shouted from the flybridge, pointing to his watch with a shaky hand.

Kris approached from Pedro's front doorstep, his eyes wide with alarm. Was Thatcher's brain already fried from the drug use? Or was his need for a fix so damn bad that he forgot the concept of keeping a low profile? Either way, it wasn't good.

"Dude. Shhh!" He glanced about to check if any neighbors were around. At the moment, there was nobody standing in the yard, but that didn't mean the houses weren't occupied.

"Then hurry it up, Kris," Thatcher said.

"Don't—" Kris bit his lip, refraining from demanding that names not be used in the open. That very sentence would be just as damning to their predicament should it be overheard. He turned toward Allen and Enrique. Pedro was still inside. "Hey, Pedro? Where'd you go."

There was no answer. Kris clenched a fist. If this guy caused a delay and got Thatcher worked up, Kris would probably go mad. Between the unbearable snoring and dreaded sense of anticipation, Kris found it almost impossible to sleep last night. This drug deal felt like an unnecessary risk, and an even more unnecessary loss of funds. They were risking both arrest as well as a potential violent encounter with Roberto. The stress and exhaustion were like two sides of a vice, pressing hard on his psyche.

At this point, there was no stopping the exchange. All Kris could ask for was to get it over with as quickly as possible.

His patience drained away. Kris marched into the house and spotted his former associate stepping out of the bathroom. "What's the holdup, Pedro?"

"Sorry. Just had to clear myself out," Pedro said.

"Right." It actually made sense. The anxiety made Kris' own bowels threaten to unload. "Let's get this over with."

The two men stepped outside and approached the boat. Enrique was up on the flybridge, and Allen was hiding down below as usual. The guy was practically a fifth wheel at this point, offering no skills except for his trigger finger.

"You guys sure you want to do this?" Pedro said.

"Yes. We do," Thatcher said.

Kris leaned toward his friend and whispered, "Bud, he's gone crazy. Best thing to do right now is to get through this as smoothly as possible."

Pedro sneered at him. "Listen, *Kris*, we're not buds. Not anymore. Yeah, I appreciate you watching my back and all, but the way you've screwed me today—you're as much of a piece of shit as your boss."

Kris' temper was rising like hot lava. So far, *nothing* was going as smoothly as he hoped. And they hadn't even made it out of the dock yet.

"You guys gonna continue flirting or get aboard this damn ship?!" Thatcher said.

"Ship?" Enrique said. "It's not a cruise liner. You make it sound like we're hauling two-hundred thousand tons of cargo."

Thatcher smacked him on the back of the head. "Will you shut up?"

Kris boarded the boat. Luckily, Pedro was right behind him. Had he taken his sweet time, Kris' attitude would've rivaled Thatcher's, and his mind wasn't even compromised by addiction. Just stress.

Enrique started the engine and backed the cruiser from the dock. "Which way are we going?"

"Roberto said it was southeast of here," Thatcher said. He pointed to the right. "So, that way."

"Uh, hey genius? We're *on* the southeast side of the island," Pedro said. "Just turn around and go straight out."

"Easy enough," Enrique said. His voice was filled with defeat. He felt as though he had sold himself into slavery. While he didn't particularly enjoy the life he was living, at least it wasn't prison. And he couldn't shake the feeling that the road he was on was eventually going to lead him there. He remembered that first day in the joint. From the moment he stepped inside, the inmates were eyeballing him, determining what use they could get, whether it'd be manipulation, or *other* needs. Nothing was worse than that first night. The inmates howled endlessly, the sealed cell doors made of steel failing to muffle their voices.

Then, of course, there was the shower rooms. And laundry duty. Enrique's fingers tightened as his mind involuntarily recalled the feeling of being ramrodded. It was never just one or two guys like they portrayed in older movies. No, it was four at minimum, depending on the victim. For larger, more violent men, there'd be a gang of at least ten. And the rapists were always undefeated.

Not being a particularly great fighter, Enrique was easy prey. Perhaps that was the punishment for the life of crime he had chosen. That contemplation was enough to make him choose the straight life. Until yesterday, when the need for cash blinded his good judgement. Wealth—it was almost just as bad and addicting as the drugs Thatcher was on.

As the boss said, the cops had probably checked his residence out already and found out he was missing. Considering his previous association with Thatcher, they probably considered him a suspect already. Enrique was on the run now, as though he was there at that bank. Going home was risking prison, and there was no way in hell he was going back. Not to those rapists. Not to the thugs in the yard. Not to the beatings, sexual assault, and claustrophobia of tight spaces.

Nebraska would have to work out.

"Two miles out, right?"

"That's right," Thatcher said.

Pedro climbed to the flybridge and pointed to the horizon. "To get to the Grave, you'll want to find the maintenance buoy. It's a marker for reef divers, about a mile out. Then, you'll want to turn ten degrees starboard and go straight on."

"Wow. That's simple. Why'd we even bring you in the first place?" Enrique said.

"I don't know. Could it be because I was blackmailed?" Pedro said, glaring at Thatcher.

The gang leader didn't take notice. Instead, his attention was on the other boats on the water. Pedro saw one coming in from the south. He noticed Thatcher's hand moving toward the gun tucked under his shirt. "Don't."

"What are they doing here?" Thatcher whispered. He looked at his navigator. "You set us up, didn't you? I should kill you right here."

"Shh! Keep your fucking voice down, will you?" Pedro said. "They're a few hundred yards away. Just get below and keep out of sight."

"There's another one," Enrique said.

"Yeah, no shit," Pedro said. "I saw it on the local news. The Police Chief had a press conference last night. There was an incident on the north beach and a couple of boating accidents yesterday. My guess is he's feeling extra paranoid this morning. It has nothing to do with us. Not at the moment, at least. That can change if you idiots don't stop acting like... idiots! Now, get below."

Thatcher stared him in the eye. The debate going on in his mind whether he should lash out at Pedro was so evident that it may as well been spoken out loud. To Pedro's amazement, the thug climbed down and disappeared into the cabin. Kris followed him in. What followed were a series of muffled voices, each one more agitated than the last.

Pedro's heart raced as he watched the police boats. There were two men on each one.

"Another," Enrique said. Pedro spun back and saw the vessel coming from the north. His hand started to quiver, something that caught Enrique's attention.

"They really are out in full force."

Enrique watched his hand, then his face. "You fucked us over, didn't you?"

"No, I did not. I already told you, the cops are increasing their patrols. The Chief of Police is doing some kind of work with a marine research vessel. What exactly they're looking for, I have no clue. Just keep going forward."

Begrudgingly, Enrique stayed the course. What else could he do at this point other than take Pedro's word for it. He took the boat out to sea, cautiously watching the three vessels. After a couple of minutes, they were behind him. They maintained course, keeping a couple of hundred feet out from the shoreline.

Enrique breathed a sigh of relief. "Alright, sorry. Looks like you were right."

"Yep." Pedro leaned against the guardrail, equally relieved. "Just a bunch of patrols. As long as we are out of sight, we should be fine."

Thatcher was back on deck. "Clear?"

"Yes. Clear."

"I guess I misjudged you, Pedro."

"Yes." Pedro glanced at his phone, then tucked it back into his pocket. "Yes you did."

CHAPTER 22

When Francesca Pascal woke up, she thought she'd be spending the morning having breakfast with her boyfriend, then spending the day while he was at work enjoying the beach and attempting to write some short stories. Being the wannabe author, she needed to get over the reality that she had to put actual work into getting the words on the page. For some reason, she was feeling good when she got out of bed. It was a long weekend for her, with the boss being on the mainland for the next few days. Maybe the stars had aligned. Maybe *today* she'd have the focus and drive to pursue her ambition.

That inspiration lasted about five minutes. When she got the text from her boyfriend, the next ten minutes were spent pacing around the house freaking out. The following half hour, she'd be crouched by the toilet, losing what little was in her stomach.

It wasn't everyday someone received a text from her boyfriend stating: *Babe, I'm alright. At nine-thirty, alert the police. Tell them that the men from that bank robbery in Miami are holding me hostage, and that they'll be performing a drug deal near Jaquez Grave at ten-o'clock. They'll be on board a cruiser. Four-man crew, five counting me.*

Tell the cops that I was forced to house these men during the night. The cops will find their personal belongings in my basement. They fled the mainland and came to my house, because one of the men knew me in the past and thought I would help him. When it didn't go their way, they forced their way in at gunpoint.

I AM NOT PART OF THE CREW. Make sure the cops know that. These men are armed and dangerous.

Do not text back. Do not call. They've got a close eye on me. I'm deleting this text as soon as I send it so they don't find it. Also, before you call, take a snapshot of this text, attach it to an email, then send it to the cops. Then call to make sure they look at it immediately and are able to intercept these guys at the right moment.

Do not screw this up. Nine-thirty.

Sorry to get you involved in this, but I need your help.

It was nine-twenty-seven. Francesca could not comprehend what was so special about nine-thirty. Why not alert the cops right away and have them go to his house? How did he know this criminal in the past? There was too much to comprehend. Her mind was stuck at the fact that her boyfriend was being held at gunpoint and taken along to a drug deal.

Nine-twenty-eight. She thought she would pass out. Her heart wouldn't stop beating. By now, there was nothing left in her digestive tract. Her hair was sticking to her sweaty face, her eyes were glazed over, and her skin was pasty white. She normally had gorgeous tan skin, but if one saw her for the first time today, they wouldn't know it.

The last two minutes were so excruciating that by the time nine-thirty came by, she could barely type in the digits in the phone. She sent the email with the attached message, then called the dispatch office.

"9-1-1. State your location please."

"Listen, this is an emergency. Check the department email. I just sent an important message from my boyfriend. He's being held captive on a boat."

"Did you say held captive?"

"Yes. By those men in Florida. The ones who robbed the bank. They've been hiding out on our island and now they're off to do a drug deal. My boyfriend's name is Pedro Contreras. He says they're going to Jaquez Grave right now to do the deal. The arrangement is for ten o'clock."

CHAPTER 23

"Whoa! Holy shit, Chief? What's with all the blood?"

Nico groaned. This was the fifth boater to come by their operation in the last hour. It was after nine-thirty in the morning and the ocean was alive with people jetting, sailing, parasailing, swimming, and fishing.

"I'm helping these people catch a shark that's in the area," Nico said.

The college-age couple on the dinghy perked up with interest.

"Is it dangerous?" the woman asked.

As with the previous four encounters, Nico hesitated, unsure of how truthful to be. And as with each exchange, he went with the blunt truth.

"Yes. It is dangerous. That's why there's a heavier police presence in the water today."

"Has it killed anyone on the beach?" the young man asked.

"Well, no, but…"

"What kind of shark is it? A great white? A hammerhead?"

"I—" Nico swallowed. "Oh, what the hell. We think it's a prehistoric species. A megalodon. We have reason to believe—"

Both of the couples broke into laughter—just as the four other groups he encountered did. Both Nico and Denise shut their eyes and looked away.

The woman wiped her eyes. "Oh man, Chief. You're funny. That's why we love having you here."

Nico held his hand out. "Look guys, I'm being dead serious."

"I'm sure you are!" the young man said. "I'll keep an eye out for any seven-foot dorsal fins!"

"Please, guys. I'm a marine biologist," Denise said. "Everything the Chief is saying is true."

"Oh, I'm sure it is, ma'am. You guys play this act so well, you ought to go on stage."

The girlfriend laughed. "Hell, I'd say their chemistry is so good, they should think about becoming a couple!"

"Sounds good to me. Thanks for the laugh, Chief. We'll warn the island about the super-shark." They laughed as they took their boat to the southwest.

Nico itched his neck, and watched bitterly as the boat shrank in the distance. Denise put an arm on his shoulder.

"I've been meaning to ask how your meeting with the mayor went this morning. Somehow, I think I already know the answer."

"Your intuition is unmatched," Nico said. "The guy literally thought I was playing a big joke on him. Then he thought, not even exaggeratingly, that I was losing my mind." He snickered. "That remark I said yesterday about you trying to get me fired by bringing this issue to him and the island counsel—damn, it would've worked out had that been your motive."

"Well, if you ever piss me off, I'll know what to do then," Denise said with a laugh.

Nico smirked. "Who knows? Maybe he's right. After all, we've been chumming for two hours and there's no sign of the bastard. I figure this was his hunting ground. Unless it moved on elsewhere."

"We've still got three quarters of the surrounding waters to check," Denise said.

"Yeah, I know. I'm just afraid someone like that young couple will encounter it first," Nico said.

"Which young couple? The ones we saw a half-hour ago that said you were losing your mind?" Denise said.

Nico soured. That was the fourth boat they encountered. The punk on the helm, wearing a mohawk that made him look like a stereotypical 80's crime henchman, had a few choice words for the Chief. Probably one of those 'screw-the-police' types and just wanted to feel like a tough guy in his own mind.

"Nah, I probably wouldn't take too much issue with that one getting eaten."

"Ah." Denise leaned on the guardrail next to him. "You mean the ones who said we'd make a great couple?"

He snorted. "Goes to show they have idiotic judgement."

"Oh, come on. It wasn't all *that* bad, was it?"

He looked over at her. "You were the one who served papers. Not that I hold it against you, though."

"Look, hon. I'm just gonna say what's on my mind…"

"Oh boy. Here we go. I thought we were hunting oversized extinct sharks? Not plunging into my mind."

"Joke all you want, Nico. But I want you to know something that's really important—You can't bring Donny back. That much is certain. But you look at yourself like you do the murderers you used to arrest. You see yourself as absolute scum of the earth, and you're not."

"You're being way too kind."

"It's that intuition you mentioned," Denise said. "The point is, the way I handled the situation probably wasn't the correct way."

"Oh, Jesus, Denise—"

"Listen, Nico. I ran off too. One of the first things I did was move out. Got a lawyer shortly after."

"I got off easy."

"No you didn't. You lost a son, just like me. We never really talked about this, and I think it's time. Why do you think Cameron's hiding in the cabin? You think he's *really* watching the monitors? Well, the sonar, yes. But that can also be done in the pilothouse."

"Or he could be on the can. I could smell the breakfast burritos this morning."

Denise shuddered. "Story of my life. At least you don't have to live with it. But let's not change the subject."

"No. Let's." Nico stepped away.

"Nico, I'm giving you permission to forgive yourself. You're not a murderer. You're not a monster. You're a good man and a good father—"

"Good fath—" Nico spun to face her. "I got him *killed*. I'm not even close to being a good father."

"You loved him and he loved you. It was an accident, and I recognize that. You wouldn't do anything to hurt Donny. I miss him and I know you do too. Yes, there's a hole in both our hearts that can't be filled. But, the more I think about it, the more I realize I handled it wrong. Fact is, by leaving, I made a second gap in my heart—and yours. All night, I was wondering if it was possible that second gap could be patched."

The two stood silently, staring at each other. Nico's heart thumped so hard it was making him shake.

Is she serious? Who am I kidding? Of course she's serious.

Nico was speechless. How could he respond to this? He never really considered what she was suggesting a possibility. Right away, his guard went up. He turned away and watched the water.

No. It can't work. I want it to, but I screwed up too badly. And if I lose her again, I don't know if I'd be able to handle it.

Like a crack of thunder, Suzie's voice blared through the radio.

"Chief?! Come in. I just got an urgent message."

Nico fumbled for his radio. "Yeah, go ahead."

"Sir, we just got a tip regarding the band of murderers who robbed a bank in Miami yesterday. They're near this island."

"OUR island? Where'd the tip come from?"

"Somebody says her boyfriend is being held captive by the gang and are using his property as a hideout. We got a call and an email from this individual, and she states that these men are en-route right now to Jaquez Grave to perform a drug deal. The time of the deal is ten-o'clock."

"Ten o'clock?" Nico checked his watch. Nine-thirty-six. "If we got this message now, it means they're trying to get us to catch them in the act. Alert the Coast Guard and give them the same info you gave me. Then alert Miami PD, let them know we might have a line on the people who killed their officers."

"Copy that, Chief."

Nico took another glance at his watch. "Damn it." He looked at Denise and Cameron, who had arrived on deck. "This is a time sensitive matter. We need to get to the southeast end of the island to group with the others. You guys alright with this?"

"How dangerous are these guys?" Cameron asked.

"They've killed too cops, put one other in critical condition. On top of that, they killed three people yesterday during a robbery. They're allegedly making a deal near a wreck site roughly two miles southeast of the island."

"A drug deal? All the way out there?" Denise said.

"My guess is that they're either meeting someone by boat, or someone's flying in from the Bahamas by plane. There's been an increase in drug trafficking there in recent years," Nico said.

"Well, shit. Let's go stop them," Denise said.

"Wait." Nico held his hands up. "This could go sour. These guys probably won't want to be taken alive."

"We'll be fine," Cameron said. "I'll stay at the helm. Denise can stay below deck."

"Yeah right!" Denise smacked him upside the head. "*I'll* be at the helm. You're the bigger target anyway, so *you* can hide below deck. Besides, I'm better at driving the boat anyway."

"Says you!" Cameron said.

"Alright, if you're not gonna wait ashore, then let's settle this debate *on the way* to the drug deal," Nico said. Both Denise and Cameron raced up to the pilothouse. The engine started up and the boat turned starboard. A moment later, Cameron appeared on the fly deck. "Nico? We going straight to the wreck?"

"Not yet. There's a beach on the west side. Take us there and stop a couple hundred feet from the shark nets, will ya?"

"You got it."

Nico pulled his radio out. The traffic was full of transmissions from the other officers asking him for the course of action.

"This is the Chief. I need all boat units to meet me near west beach. I want every officer equipped with rifles. Make sure each one has the safety off—there's a chance that this is gonna get ugly. Jackson, I need you up in the chopper. Auburn, you feel comfortable with that sniper rifle?"

"Damn right, Chief," Carley said.

"Good, because you guys are taking point. Get in the air immediately. Everyone else, assemble at west beach. I'll be in the research boat, *Manta Ray*, so keep an eye out for that."

"Boat Three copies."

"Boat Six copies."

"Boat Two copies."

"Boat Four copies."

"Boat One copies."

"Boat Five copies."

"Boat Seven Copies."

Seven patrol boats, each carrying two police officers. That was over a third of his entire police force right there. Nico hated the thought of putting them in harm's way, but this was what they were trained to do.

"Son of a bitch. Even after two decades of law enforcement, it still never ceases to amaze me how life can go from zero to a hundred." He picked up his carbine and made sure it was primed and ready.

He figured he'd use it to kill a giant extinct shark. Instead, he was going to war against some bank robbers. In a way, that was worse. At least the shark didn't kill for the sake of greed.

****

Renny Jackson strapped himself into the cockpit and started the rotors. "So much for the quiet life."

The fuselage door slid open. Carley climbed aboard, sniper rifle in hand. She was a mixed bag of emotions. For one, she was inexperienced in major drug bust operations. Everything she and Renny had done up to this moment was small potatoes compared to this. They had searched boats, hotel rooms, and houses for drugs, had a few scuffles now and then. Never in her life, however, did she consider that they'd go up against actual cop-killers. On that note, she was eager to see some real action. She never desired to point a gun at another human being, but if such an event was meant to occur, Ed Thatcher and his murderous gang were the way to go.

"You ready for this?" Renny said.

Carley chambered a round. "Ready as I'll ever be." She checked the time. Nine-fifty-three. "Do we know who this drug dealer is that they're meeting with?"

"Not sure, but I'll say this: if they're doing business with *those* guys, then I guarantee they're just as dangerous." Renny initiated ascent. "Too bad the Coast Guard's not here to help us deal with this shit."

CHAPTER 24

Thatcher tapped his feet, eagerly watching the southeast skies. It was a clear blue day with a few scattered clouds. Though ninety-two degrees and sunny, he was clattering his teeth as though it was January in New Jersey. The addiction was wreaking havoc on his senses. Every so often, he'd lick his lips, his nerves tricking him into thinking he had a little powder left over from this morning's bump. If he could even call it a bump. He may as well have taken nothing.

Allen Lo stood in the cabin with his submachine gun, the same one he used during the robbery. He was just as jittery as his boss, though only due to his nerves. Roberto Rosing was not a force to be reckoned with. The guy was certainly going to be packing heat, and would have at least four men with him, all armed with high-powered automatic rifles. Allen had heard that the guy knifed three men in a room one time during a deal gone wrong. They tried to take his supply without paying. Clearly, Roberto didn't take too kindly to that. He killed the buyers and took their money, then had a new deal arranged later that same day. Double-dipping. Some say he liked it when things went wrong. Some wondered if he orchestrated such things. All Allen knew was that this was Thatcher's second time buying from him. If he did it once and came out okay, then maybe the same would happen today.

Then again, Roberto hadn't dealt with an antsy, addiction-fueled Thatcher that first time. When Allen first met Thatcher, he had the essence of a man in control. Compared to what he had become, he was a well-spoken individual who exhibited good judgement overall. He knew when arrangements carried too much heat. He had a good eye on the police activity in the area. Then came the drug addiction. And with it came a temper which steadily grew worse over the months.

Thatcher looked up at Pedro, who stood next to Enrique on the flybridge. "You *sure* this is the right place?"

"Yes." Pedro looked at his watch. "Just relax. You've got a few minutes before your guy shows up. You said yourself, he's very precise."

"We'd better be in the right spot. If you've fucked us over, man—" It was as though Thatcher didn't hear a word Pedro had said. The addict held his pistol in hand, waving it around like he was directing traffic with it.

"Here he comes," Enrique said, pointing to the horizon. Thatcher climbed to the flybridge for a better look, shoving the operator aside upon arrival. The plane appeared like a small mosquito in the sky at first. As it drew closer, their eyes took in the details of its structure. It was a seaplane, perfectly capable of landing in the water next to their boat.

Thatcher grinned. "Finally. Kris! Get the money."

"Uh, Thatcher?" Kris pointed at the pistol in his hand. "You might wanna tuck that away. Not sure if Roberto's gonna take kindly to that."

Thatcher looked at the weapon, then back at him. His eyes expressed the desire to argue, however, his rotten brain still retained a small hint of common sense. He tucked the pistol in his pants and covered it with his shirt. Yeah, Roberto wasn't stupid. He would know it was there, but as long as it wasn't in hand, he wouldn't care.

The plane decreased altitude and moved in for the landing. Water sprayed to each side as the floats touched down. The plane settled to a stop a few hundred feet from the cruiser. Enrique brought the boat closer, settling within fifty feet of the fuselage.

The fuselage door slid open. Two men stood there, both armed with H&K submachine guns. They wore white shirts, khaki pants, sunglasses, and blank facial expressions. The overall demeanor gave them the impression of secret service agents protecting a political figure.

One checked out the nearby area, then looked back into the fuselage. "All clear."

He stepped aside, making way for his employer, a forty-five year old man with a balding scalp, a crooked jaw, and a face wrinkled by stress. It was hard to imagine Roberto as anxious. Then again, if the man was always on the lookout for police and rival gangs, as well as traitors in his own organization, that might take a strain on one's health.

"You have the money?" He spoke in a high voice, which differed from his physical appearance. It went to show that Roberto didn't achieve respect through superficial facades, but from his reputation. He stared Thatcher down with cold, deathly eyes as he awaited an answer.

Thatcher looked down at Kris, who had stuffed the money into a large briefcase, courtesy of Pedro.

"Right here. One-point-three million."

Roberto nodded at his men, who then prepared a small inflatable craft. They set it out on the water, then lowered their boss onto it. After joining him, they moved the short distance to the cruiser. Two other gunmen stood at the fuselage door, ready to cover their boss in case anything went wrong.

In the raft was a briefcase of their own, which held Thatcher's attention. It was so intoxicating that the gang leader almost didn't hear Roberto when he demanded the money.

"Hand it to my men!" Roberto made it clear he was not interested in wasting time. He wanted this transaction done asap.

"The package," Thatcher said. Roberto's gaze narrowed. The two men in the raft lifted their gun muzzles slightly. A show of force, but not enough to escalate conflict. They knew the crew aboard this cruiser were armed. Worse, they were cop-killers. Sloppy, but distinctly willing to engage in conflict to get their way.

Kris stood ready with the briefcase in one hand, and the other at his hip, ready to spring for a shotgun which was propped less than a meter away. It was pumped and ready to go. He may not have agreed to this transaction, but now that they were here, it would be a cold day in hell before he was gonna let himself or his group get screwed over. Not even by Roberto Rosing.

Too much was sacrificed for this money. No way in hell was he going to stand for a third of it being wasted on fake drugs.

"A sample," Kris said. Roberto looked over at him. Though his face remained hardened, a minor relaxation in his posture indicated he had more respect for Kris than Thatcher. Probably because he didn't have the desperation that the addict exhibited.

Roberto looked at one of his men, then nodded. The gunman opened the case, then handed his employer a kilo of cocaine. Roberto tossed it to Thatcher.

"Test it, and let's wrap this up."

Thatcher fumbled with the small package, his trembling hand going for his knife. He gently pierced the plastic and scooped out a gram of the stuff, which disappeared up his nose.

"Ahhh!" He took another bump, groaned pleasurably again, then went for another.

"Hey?!" Roberto said. "You gonna have a party right here?! Or are you going to pay up?"

Thatcher nodded, then waved at Kris. "This is good shit. He's good. Give him the money. Give him the money." His head wobbled as though he was a human bobblehead.

Kris groaned, embarrassed at his partner's pathetic behavior. Self-respect was completely out the window. He wondered how this transaction would have gone had a more stable person like himself not been present.

"Here." He leaned over the side and handed the briefcase to Roberto's henchman. They opened it, proceeded to look over the cash in search of any phony bills or tracking devices.

"All three million. It's all there," Thatcher said. He took another hit of the cocaine and leaned back against the helm, staring at the sky. The shakes were gone, replaced by a feeling of great reward. He felt as though he just won a dozen Olympic gold medals.

With this blissful sensation came a change in demeanor. He was confident now, though he moved as though he was on speed. The glint coming off his brow intensified as more sweat beaded from his hairline.

"Like I said, the money's all there. Now, if I may have the rest of the package?" He snapped his fingers twice, something Roberto didn't take kindly to.

"Watch yourself. Those drugs are giving you a false sense of confidence."

"Duly noted," Kris said. "That said, mind if we wrap this up? You yourself said you didn't want to drag this out."

"That is correct," Roberto said. Kris noticed a faint smile on the drug dealer's face. It was the kind of grin a man had when he felt respect for a business associate. It was only a minor respect. At the end of the day, Kris was as sloppy as Thatcher, despite his confident image.

Roberto closed the money case, then took the drug case. He clipped it shut, then began to reach for Kris.

With sudden haste, he withdrew and looked to the northwest.

Kris' heart started racing. "What's the problem?" As soon as he spoke, he heard the rotors of a passing helicopter.

The gang all looked in unison, seeing the lone police helicopter moving in close. The fuselage door was open, with a sniper peering down at them through the scope of an M24 sniper rifle.

"Sorry to intrude, but you're all under arrest. Place your weapons down and put your hands in the air. The Coast Guard has been notified, and more police units are on the way. You are outnumbered and outgunned."

Roberto's stony face transformed into a barbaric mess. He looked at the equally flabbergasted Thatcher, back at the choppers, then back at him.

"YOU! You set us up!"

Thatcher's eyes widened. "What?! No we didn't."

"We ought to kill you right now!" Roberto said, his hand creeping to a pistol tucked in the back of his pants.

"We didn't bring them. How did they even know—" Thatcher paused, turned around and gazed at Pedro. "You!"

Pedro backed away. "No. I didn't know..."

Thatcher grabbed him by the shirt. "You think I'm stupid?! You tipped them off!" With strength doubled by rage and drugs, he threw the navigator down to the main deck, where he landed by Kris' feet.

Pedro groaned and looked at his friend as though seeking help.

Kris looked at him in stunned silence. "You piece of shit."

"I didn't—"

"Cut the bullshit. These guys wouldn't do this. We're all wanted for murder. Enrique has a past connection with us, so they think he was in on the bank run. The only one bitching and moaning about living the straight life is *you*! You sold us out, you fuck."

Pedro shed the mercy-seeking look, and stood up, staring Kris down like he was about to brawl. "*You* did this! I agreed to let you hide out! Not get me involved in this bullshit. And your pal decides to threaten my girl..." He stood up and held his hands high, mimicking the role of a hostage for the cops. Kris may be a murderer, but he wouldn't shoot someone right in front of police witnesses. No way. That'd be a guaranteed life sentence. "So, I had her tell the cops you took me at gunpoint, forced your way into my home, and made me bring you here. As far as they're concerned, I'm a helpless victim."

"Yeah, definitely helpless," Kris said. He grabbed the shotgun and blew a hole in Pedro's chest, the force sending his bloody corpse flinging over the guardrail.

Pedro bobbed with the waves, his face not expressing pain, but astonishment. He didn't think Kris would actually do it. Thatcher, maybe. But not Kris.

As though to punish him further, Kris aimed over the guardrail. This time, the iron sights were centered on Pedro's head, which ruptured like fruit when the buckshot struck.

****

"Hooooly shit!" Renny said. "Chief? We've got druggies killing their own. I think they realized their hostage tipped us off."

"They shot him?" Nico asked.

"Oh yeah! Point blank with a twelve-gauge. He's in the water. There's movement on the boat."

"Raft's going for the plane," Carley said.

"Don't take chances with these guys. Shoot the wing engines. Don't let them take off. Keep your distance—and open fire on the suspects if necessary. We're coming in. Boats One, Two, and Three, circle behind

and cut them off. Four and Five, take the south. Six, cover the north. Seven and I will block the west. Get them completely surrounded."

Carley lifted her hand from her rifle, steadied herself, then took aim. Renny positioned the chopper west of the exchange, giving her a clear view of the plane rotors.

"Man, as if they weren't pissed off enough," she said.

"Hey, usually I'm the target of your sniping," Renny quipped.

Carley smiled. She appreciated that despite the intensity of the situation, they managed to keep the banter going. It had a way of calming her down and helping her focus.

"The day's still young."

****

"Get us back on the plane!" Roberto shouted to his men. One of them started the small motor and sped back to the fuselage door, where the other two men awaited.

Thatcher leaned over the guardrail. "Hey! Give me my shit!"

Roberto flipped him off. "What good will it do you?! Look what's coming!" He pointed at the small fleet of police boats speeding toward them. The line had broken, with several of the crafts moving around the cruiser in an obvious attempt to cut them off.

The drug dealer climbed aboard his plane, then gave one last glance at his buyers. "Don't bend over for the soap!"

Thatcher drew his pistol and fired several wild shots, striking the fuselage. The henchmen returned fire, causing all four gang members to dive for cover. The pilot started up the engines and began moving the plane forward, intending to circle back.

Another gunshot rang out, this one coming from the sky. The port engine clunked and sputtered, with metal spitting from the fan. The sniper had fired a round straight into the compressor and damaged the turbine. Right as Roberto and his men realized what happened, another shot rang out, producing the same result in the starboard engine.

****

"Well done. They're not going anywhere," Nico said. He stood at the starboard side rail of the *Manta Ray's* fly deck. Denise was at the helm, awaiting his commands through an open window. The police boats moved to their top speeds, their flashers blinking across the ocean. Moving up to fifty miles per hour, they made wide arcs around the damaged plane.

"Keep a distance. They just exchanged gunfire. Suzie, any word from the Coast Guard?"

"They're sending a cutter from Key West, but they've got chopper units en-route and response vessels coming in from the Miami Sector."

The choppers would arrive soon, but not soon enough. For now, Nico and his cops were on their own. They just needed to maintain this standoff long enough for more air support to arrive.

"Chief. It looks like the pilot's still attempting to take off," Renny said.

Nico could hear the dying engines from where he stood. Smoke was billowing from the rear nozzle. He estimated that both engines had damaged combustion chambers and compressors. The turbines were functional, though sluggish due to obstacles in the system.

The cruiser was starting to turn around. Angry shouts filled the air. The suspects were arguing amongst themselves.

"Renny?"

"Yeah?"

"Go ahead and let them know they're better off surrendering peacefully. Make sure your partner has her crosshairs set on them. If it looks like they're about to shoot, take 'em out."

"Noted. Standby."

****

"What are you doing?! Get us in the air now!" Roberto smacked his pilot on the head.

"I—I can't, boss! They shot out the engines. I can't get enough power to get us airborne. We're fucked."

Roberto smacked him again then moved back into the fuselage. He couldn't believe it. He should have trusted his instincts than to do business with a high-profile suspect.

His four guards stood by the windows, watching the police boats.

"What would you like us to do?" one asked.

Roberto took a breath and regained his composure. "Nothing. Right now, we're just facing a drug trafficking charge. It's *those* guys that have more to worry about. Let me make a quick call. I can get the DEA off our back, send some funds to the judge, and get our bail set." He got on his phone.

"So…*surrender*?"

"Yes. They shot out our engines, moron. You think we're gonna shoot our way out of this and take the raft to Andros Town? Do it!"

****

Thatcher lunged for the helm, ripping Enrique's arms from it.

"What are you doing, man? We need to get out of here!"

"Thatcher, stop it!" Kris said.

"The hell with that! My shit's in that plane," Thatcher said.

"We're surrounded by cops and you're worried about cocaine?!" Enrique said. "Fuck you! I'm not staying around for this shit." He grabbed the helm again, ignoring the warnings from the chopper's microphone.

"Yeah you are," Thatcher said.

"No, I'm not. I'm *not* going back to prison."

The two men wrestled for control of the helm. Fueled by his cocaine high, Thatcher easily ripped Enrique away from the console a second time, then threw him against the rail. He spun the boat toward the plane, ignoring the police presence around him.

"If you think you can outshoot Roberto AND flee the cops, you're insane!" Enrique said.

"Shut up."

Enrique stood up and grabbed the kilo from the console, then held it over the water. White powder fell from the slit in the bag—the *one* thing that managed to halt Thatcher's actions.

"Give that back."

"You crazy fucks! I never should've helped you in the first place!"

"Hand it back!"

"Only if you get us out of here."

Thatcher lunged at him. His intention was to grab Enrique by the shirt and beat him to a pulp. Instead, he accidentally shoved him—and the kilo—over the guardrail into the water. Thatcher beat the dashboard and shouted incoherently, his glorious high descending into a vicious adrenaline burst. He proceeded to kick the dashboard and curse.

Enrique floundered, the drugs claimed by the ocean. He surfaced, only to sink right away. He was never a great swimmer. In his youth he joked he sank like a stone. That joke wasn't funny anymore, as it was true.

For a split-second, he was able to get his head above water.

"Help me!"

Allen Lo, overwhelmed by his friends' stupid, impractical actions, was the only one to admit true defeat. Letting Enrique die was only going to worsen his predicament.

I technically didn't kill anybody. If I can somehow prove that, maybe I can get a lesser sentence.

He dropped his weapon, hurried out on deck, and reached for Enrique's hand. "Swim over here. Grab my hand!"

Enrique couldn't hear him over the sound of splashing and his own gasps of struggle. Allen leaned halfway off the boat, his arm hyperextended so far he felt it would shoot out of his shoulder. Finally, Enrique spotted him, and with all his might, closed the distance.

"Almost there! Come on!"

Meanwhile, the police boats completed their circle. They were surrounded. Thatcher was cursing, Kris held his shotgun—whether he was going to fight, Allen had no clue. And Roberto's crew, he had no idea what they were doing. But if the cops witnessed him saving his companion, maybe that'd win him some sympathy in the court.

Allen watched Enrique close the distance. He reached again, and this time, they grasped hands.

The relief in Enrique's voice was instantaneous. The terror of drowning was horrifying. Only when truly faced with it did Enrique realize that, as much as he hated prison, death was worse.

"Oh, God! Thanks, man. Pull me up will ya?" he said.

Allen froze. He *didn't* pull Enrique up. His eyes were fixed, not on the water, but something *beneath* the water. A shape, like a glacier moving beneath the waves, came into view. With its ascent came visible details. It was grey in color, the eyes pale white as though they belonged to an undead ghoul. Then came the opening of an enormous mouth lined with seven-inch incisors.

He screamed, releasing his grip on Enrique to save his own skin. The floundering criminal sank…only to rise suddenly. Only when he saw the world of teeth around him did he realize Allen's reason for abandoning him.

The fish broke the surface, spraying the cruiser and its occupants—first with water, then with the blood of their companion after its jaws clamped down. Enrique's head and shoulders popped off the rest of his body, the arms flopping midair like bird wings until he plopped onto the deck.

Right at Allen's feet.

The shark swallowed, then crashed back down, pushing the plane and cruiser further apart.

****

"Holy CHRIST!" Denise said.

Nico peeked through the window. "Looks like we found our shark."

CHAPTER 25

The dorsal fin coursed around the two criminal groups, following an invisible trail between them and the police barrier. Its caudal fin was shaped like the blade of a karambit knife, and appeared equally ready to slash anything foolish enough to come near it.

For the first time in his professional career, Nico felt frozen by alarm. The mere sight of this creature was enough for him to know his officers were outmatched. Measuring the tip of the dorsal to the tip of the tail, it had to be *at least* forty feet. That alone was twice as long as the biggest great white he had ever seen.

It continued to circle the bank robbers and drug traffickers. Either it was curious as to which it should attack first, or it was put on guard by the presence of the police vessels. It probably hadn't been in the proximity of so many boats at the same time.

"Alllllrighty then, Chief. Maybe you're not as crazy as everyone thought."

"Jesus," Nico muttered. Even now, Renny's sense of humor couldn't be suppressed.

Cameron joined him on the fly deck. He had to see it for himself: a true megalodon shark. Thought to be extinct after two million years, it had survived. Thanks to the calamity from beyond the stars, the apex predator has emerged from the depths to reclaim the world it once dominated.

"You alright?" Nico said.

Cameron shook his head. "I'm honestly not sure if I'm fascinated, or about to shit my pants."

"Sir... what should we do?" Renny said.

Nico studied the situation. This creature had already wrecked a few boats along the Keys during its trip to this island, all of which were roughly the same size as the police cruisers. If provoked, the fish would have no qualms about going after his officers. There was no way of telling how effective their rifles would be against its thick skin.

Not without trial and error, at least.

"Break off," he said.

"Sir?" one of the other officers said.

"You heard me. Break off, get back to the island. To anyone patrolling the beach, get everyone out of the water immediately. Dispatch, radio the

Coast Guard again. Tell them to double-time it, because we have an eighty-foot shark in our waters. If they don't believe you, tell them we have police footage from our copter."

"I suppose you want us to remain in the air," Renny said.

"Affirmative. We need constant eyes on this damn thing."

"Sir, what about the ARMED robbers?" Carley said.

"Keep an eye on them as long as possible, but the greater focus is the megalodon," Nico said.

The police cruisers to the east broke ranks, going wide of the standoff. Meanwhile, the fish continued its circle, slowing as it detected the movements of the boats.

"It's on edge," Denise said. "There's probably too much stimulation in the water."

"Good. Hopefully it'll stay that way until the freaking Guard gets here," Nico said.

"What about those guys in the plane?" Cameron asked.

"They better sit tight and not do anything to piss that fish off." He looked at his carbine, which now seemed incredibly puny compared to the monstrosity he intended to use it against.

Denise leaned out the window. "Nico? What if we hit the shark with a tracking device? I've got a speargun that we can use to tag it, like we were originally going to. That way, we can at least track its movements."

"What about your push to study the thing?" Nico said.

Denise shook her head. "It just killed a person. Scumbag or not, it doesn't matter. It has a taste for human flesh now, which means it has to be destroyed."

"Damn it." Cameron looked down, defeated by the truth. He hated the idea of killing such a magnificent animal, but Denise was right. "It's not a complete loss. Where there's one, there's others. There's the chance we can study one in its natural habitat. Unfortunately for this one, there's no way around it—this fish needs to be put down."

"Agreed, though I'm not willing to get close enough to that thing to tag it." Nico looked up at the chopper and clicked his radio transmitter. "Carley, you got the fish in your sights?"

"Affirmative."

"Wait for our people to set a distance of five hundred yards. Once I give you the signal, put as many rounds in its head as possible. Kill it."

"Aye-aye, Chief."

Nico watched the other boats break formation and speed to the northwest. "Let's see if we can end this here and now. As long as those crooks don't do anything to screw this up."

****

The last time Roberto Rosing felt his bowels threaten to let loose in front of others was at the age of fifteen when he was held at gunpoint. It was his third drug deal and the first to go wrong. The Cartel had executed his friend, after removing a few fingers with a cigar cutter. They weren't torturing him for information, they were just having some sick fun. It was thanks to that very torture that Roberto managed to escape. Since then, it took a great deal to strike intense fear into his soul.

For the megalodon, however, it took minimal effort. All it had to do was make its presence known.

It took Roberto a whole minute to convince himself he wasn't seeing things. He sold the drugs, but never took them. Addicts usually made for poor leaders. But after witnessing that huge mouth chomp down on Thatcher's man, Roberto figured he *had* to be hallucinating. But he wasn't. The beast was there, circling his plane and Thatcher's boat.

"We need to get out of here," he said.

"But... you said you wanted us to wait," one of his henchmen replied.

"Yeah, that was *before* the GIANT SHARK arrived," he said. He looked out the starboard window and pointed. "Look! Even the cops are running! They don't give two shits about us. Let's get out of here."

"We can't take off," the pilot said. "There's no way we're flying out of here, sir."

Roberto grabbed one of the H&Ks. "I'm not waiting for this thing to take us under."

One of his guards placed a hand on his shoulder. "Boss, it might not come after us."

Roberto ripped his hand away. "You see what it did to that guy? You want to be next? You said it *might* not come after us, but I say, if we kill it, it *certainly won't* come after us. Now, open the damn door."

With a yielding nod, the guard nodded to another who stood by the fuselage door. The man pulled it open, revealing the open sea. The shark was passing by the nose of the plane and turning left. Large swells rolled toward the floats as the fish passed between them and Thatcher's boat.

Three of Roberto's gunmen took position at the doorway. They aimed several feet ahead of the fin at the large grey shape that was the shark's head.

"This is our chance. Shoot! Now!" he snapped. Like a firing squad executing a prisoner, the men unleashed a hail of bullets at the fish.

The swells tripled in size and intensity. The caudal fin lashed, the shark zipping forward at a speed matching a jetboat. The plane rocked with the waves, the men staggering around the fuselage in an attempt to keep their balance.

"It's behind us," one of them cried.

"Keep shooting!" Roberto said. "Break the windows if you have to. Just kill the damn thing!"

One of the men leaned out the doorway and fired a few more rounds, only to freeze as the dorsal fin turned. The pointed snout emerged from the water, the pasty eyes rolling back. In the blink of an eye, the fish closed over three hundred feet of distance.

Their attempt to kill it only served to spur it on.

The other gunmen punched their gun muzzles through the windows and fired unanimously at the oncoming fish. Bullets scraped its snout, leaving nothing but faint scratches on its skin.

With a mighty *crash* the fish collided with the plane. The portside hull imploded, bending the tail to the left. The nose dipped, water surging against the windshield. The pilot screamed as he watched millions of gallons of ocean rage on the other side of the glass. Then the inevitable cracks appeared. By the time the pilot finally rose from his seat, the ocean broke through, sweeping through the cockpit and into the fuselage.

Roberto didn't even see the water coming. He just felt a sense of wetness and weightlessness all at once.

The megalodon released its grip on the plane and went for the wing, breaking it off the craft with ease. Spitting the inedible material out, it went for the fuselage again. This time, it didn't bother parting its jaws. It had learned that these non-living bodies could not withstand a blow from its snout. Like an enraged bull, it struck the plane straight on.

Cockpit and tail parted ways and drifted in different directions. Men and equipment fell into the void between them. Among them were two briefcases, which quickly followed the wreckage to the depths.

It took several moments for Roberto to surface. When the front of the plane sank, it created a vacuum that sucked him down for several meters. After taking a breath, he heard pistol shots, followed by the sound of screaming over to his left. One of his men was clinging to the raft, emptying his magazine into an oncoming shark. The jaws parted and shut, engulfing him completely. Blood spurted through the shark's gills as it turned for its next victim.

It found the pilot and quickly snatched him up, the teeth popping his torso like a balloon. One by one, it tracked down the remaining three henchmen. One didn't even see it coming until he looked over his shoulder and saw the cave entrance lined with teeth.

His scream was as brief as the rest of his life.

Finally, the shark came at Roberto. Powered by an intensified heartbeat, he stroked and kicked, barely gaining a yard of distance before the fish closed in.

"Shit! SHIIIIIIT!"

The jaws parted. He shut his eyes and awaited the swift pain from dozens of teeth hacking his body. Instead, he felt a rush of water. Then a sudden heat. Severe heat, as though the water he was in had been cranked to a boil. He opened his eyes, yet the world was as dark as when they were shut. It was a world without air and blistering fluid.

The shark had swallowed him whole.

Those teeth which he feared so much, he was now longing for. Now, he was doomed to slowly suffocate and melt.

"NO—" his scream was cut short as his vocals were burned away by stomach acid.

****

"Shit! Holy shit Al'mighty!" Thatcher shouted as he watched the remains of the plane—along with his cocaine and cash—disappear beneath the waves.

Kris wasn't sure what was more shocking: the presence of a giant shark, the fact that Thatcher was more concerned about his lost drugs than his life, or whatever it was he was trying to say. One thing he was sure of was his determination to get the hell out of here. Had anyone other than Thatcher been at the helm, they would've been a mile away already. Instead, the idiot kept them close to the mayhem.

He ascended the ladder and grabbed the helm. "We're getting out of here."

"But the briefcases…"

Kris slapped him across the face. "Dude, snap out of it! If we make it out of here, I'm gonna make you fucking detox. That thing just broke the plane, sank everything in it, and you still think you have a shot of collecting your shit. You don't even have diving gear." He pointed the boat northwest and throttled.

His timing was perfect. The cruiser jetted forward right as the megalodon rose to seize it. Its teeth snapped shut on nothing but ocean mist. Wasting no time, it turned and proceeded to chase the white boat.

"Shoot it," Kris said.

"I'm the one who calls the shots," Thatcher said, prodding himself with his thumb.

Kris looked back at him. "Are you SERIOUSLY dick measuring right now?!" He stomped down on the deck to get Allen's attention. "Lo! Get your ass out there and shoot the bastard."

After a short hesitation, the third remaining thug arrived on deck. He was nearly hyperventilating, the gun shaking in his grip.

The fish was directly behind the boat, its snout roughly fifty feet away. It was keeping pace.

How in the hell can something that big move so damn fast?

He emptied his submachine gun into the beast. The fish jolted its head, obviously feeling the sting of the projectiles, though there was no blood.

Finally, some degree of sense crept into Thatcher's mind. He joined Allen down below, grabbed the shotgun, and blasted the megalodon's face.

"Eat that, you prick. Come on! Get some of this!"

As if directly replying to that last remark, the meg increased speed. Fifty feet became thirty.

"Oh, shit! It's not stopping!" Allen said.

"Hold on," Kris said. His eye wasn't on the fish, but the group of police boats straight ahead. "Let's give it something else to chew on."

****

"No, no, no! Damn it!"

Every part of Nico's plan had gone to hell. The drug shippers in the plane had to shoot at the thing and drive it into a frenzy before Carley could snipe it. Not that it made much difference, as the fish showed no signs of injury. If anything, he felt validated in his decision to pull back his police force.

However, even that aspect of the plan was ruined, as the bank robbers were leading the shark right to them. The cruiser hooked to the left and closed in on Boat Seven. The officer on deck raised his carbine and fired a few shots, striking the hull of the oncoming boat, failing to hit the suspects.

The boat sped past, scraping the side of his. The damage to the paint job was the least of the officer's worry.

As it neared Boat Seven, the megalodon found easier prey. It shifted course slightly to the left and rammed the keel with an impact that launched the boat clear off the water.

Nico could do nothing but watch as two of his officers were flung from the boat. One was snatched before he hit the water, the other bouncing along the surface like a skipping stone.

The fish made a sharp turn, smacking the second officer with its caudal fin. Right away, he was airborne again, soaring straight for the chopper. Renny tried to veer, but was too late. The officer bounced along the windshield and skidded up to the rotors. A thick red cloud spewed like a demonic lawn sprinkler, two hundred feet in the air.

The megalodon did not stop. It went straight for the nearest police boat like a World War 2 torpedo. The rifleman aboard Boat Five unleashed the fury of his M4 Carbine.

Bullets struck the meg's snout but failed to hinder its advance. The fish dove, only to rise again. It breached the water as though posing for a *National Geographic* documentary. Its immense bulk crashed down on the police boat, crushing it and its two occupants.

"Christ alive!" Nico said, watching debris flying from the explosive impact. Already, Boat Six and Four were closing in. "Disengage. I repeat, disengage," Nico ordered through his radio. "All units, get to shore. You can't stop it."

Boat Six doubled back. Four never had the chance. The megalodon had no sooner hit the water when it swam toward the cruiser. This time, both officers were firing at it, one with a rifle, the other with a shotgun. They aimed for the eyes, landing shots all around its face.

One shot landed in its mouth, tearing the soft flesh inside. The fish jerked to the right. For the briefest of moments, it looked to be fleeing. Then its tail swung high and smacked the rifleman off the deck like a golf ball from its tee. The fin had struck with such force that all the blood was forced from every orifice, creating a red trail which made the victim appear like a shooting star straight out of hell.

The helmsman continued squeezing the trigger, even after all his shells were spent. After a few moments, he dropped the weapon and drew his Glock, unloading it onto the horrific shape moving beneath the water. That shape passed under his boat and angled up.

The boat exploded as though hit with c4. Through the debris emerged the shark, leaping for the second time. It appeared to hover for a moment before crashing down in the wreckage. It found the body of the helmsman and bit down, creating another dark blood cloud.

"My God," Denise said. She felt nauseas. For most of her life, as many scientists did, she had always hoped that such a creature could maybe exist in the present day. Now, she understood she was a fool for wishing that. Maybe there was a reason God decided to banish these creatures to the depths before Man's arrival. Who knows? Maybe they were puppets of the devil himself.

She had read that Satan corrupts what is beautiful, and there was nothing more beautiful than the ocean. But today, it was now red with carnage, blanketed with wreckage, and exuded death and destruction.

A bloodbath.

It was only going to get worse. The megalodon was already going after Boat Six. Despite the officer pushing the vessel to its maximum speed, the shark was still closing in. Rifle rounds failed to deter it. It was worse—the fish had learned that the weapons the humans used could not hurt it.

All caution was gone. Only bloodlust remained.

She watched as the dorsal fin gradually closed in on Boat Six. The sound of collision was like thunder echoing under the water. The megalodon struck the keel, rearing the boat up like a seesaw. The bow dipped, the ocean racing around the cockpit.

The megalodon surfaced again, this time with intent to bite. Teeth pierced the transom. Now the bow was teetering up, and the stern dipping under the water as the shark began to pull. The rifleman aboard screamed for dear life, the helmsman not daring to step away from the wheel.

"Damn it! God damn it!" Nico shouted. With his carbine in hand, he popped off rounds at the shark's head. It continued to pull the boat under, unfazed by the assault.

Denise couldn't stand by and simply watch. She hated herself for the crazy thing she was contemplating, but doing nothing was worse. Gunning the throttle, she raced the *Manta Ray* at the shark. Her ex-husband, realizing they were getting closer, peeked through the window.

"What are you doing?"

"Something stupid," she said. "But it might save your men." Nico didn't argue. Part of her wished he would, because the second thoughts she was having were getting worse with each yard.

The fish was too fixated with its prize to notice the oncoming boat. Its head was still above water, its caudal fin slashing eighty feet behind it.

Five yards. Four. Three. Two. One.

Denise ducked her head down.

Crash!

The impact rocked both machine and fish, knocking the former away from its prize. The police boat was flung forward as though propelled by spring-loaded action. The megalodon rolled along the surface, revealing its pale belly for a moment before submerging.

Nico and Cameron hurried to the starboard rail on the main deck. The officers aboard the police boat were unharmed, though their vessel was dead in the water. So would *they* be if they weren't hauled to safety in the next sixty seconds.

Denise steered the *Manta Ray* alongside theirs. Her ex-husband and assistant reached across to haul the two officers up.

Sudden impact shook the boat, the resulting tremor threatening to knock her to her knees.

The megalodon had struck, its tail smacking the underside as it passed underneath. When Denise stood up, she saw the dorsal fin emerge. The shark was circling back. Another good hit and it would breach the hull. The fish seemed to have no regards for any damage its own body took from such jarring impacts. Perhaps its brain was protected by some kind of jell casing which acted as an airbag in such moments. Seeing as the megalodon didn't even appear the least bit sluggish, it was possible that was the case.

Their troubles were mounting. The engine had stalled and the police boat was knocked away from the impact. With increasing speed, the fish approached, intent on plowing through her boat like a bulldozer through concrete. Nico started shooting at it. Cameron joined in too, using the Remington. Neither did any damage.

A shadow took form, accompanied by a heavy downdraft. Sniper rounds filled the air as Carley blasted the fish from above. Like the other firearms, they had no effect. Yet, the pilot had a special trick up his sleeve.

The chopper passed over the shark, scraping the snout with its skids. That got its attention. The fish turned and went after the chopper, which proceeded to lead it north, away from the two boats.

"Jesus, Renny, you crazy son of a bitch," Nico said.

"*Crazy? How about 'nice one, Jackson! You just earned yourself a raise. And a promotion. And a medal'...oh shit!*" He ascended briefly to avoid the shark's snapping jaws. Its attempt to snatch the chopper failed, and it crashed down into the water. The chopper, still covered in the blood of the officer diced in the rotors, continued to lure it north, with Carley popping off rounds at its face.

"First, focus on not earning yourself a gravestone," Nico said.

"*Will do.*"

****

"Jesus, it's not stopping," Carley said. She loaded five fresh rounds into her rifle and resumed shooting. Not one bullet managed to pierce the skin.

"Aim for its mouth," Renny said.

"I can't."

"You can't?! Thing's as big as the broad side of a barn."

"It's under the water, dipshit," Carley said. Her voice trembled. Her nerves were still fried from witnessing the aftermath of her fellow officer shredded in the rotors. His blood was on the edge of the fuselage door along with a few ribbons of clothing.

The next five rounds were driven by vengeance. None of them fulfilled their purpose, as the fish continued advancing on them. Renny recognized the signs of another breach. The fish submerged several yards, angled its body up, and shot out of the water. Renny had already ascended, and was grateful at his good judgement of going an extra ten feet, as it literally made all the difference. He didn't expect such a heavy organism to leap thirty feet clear out of the water, but the damn thing did it.

Walls of ocean lifted upon its return, as they did when Moses parted the sea.

Renny lowered the chopper, watching the water in case the meg wanted to make another attempt. After a few moments it appeared again. It was moving east, away from them.

"Aw, what's the matter, sharky? Give up? Going for easier prey?"

Carley followed the shark's trajectory with her eyes. "Yes, actually."

Renny turned the chopper for a better look. "Oh, great." A few hundred feet in its path was a small sailing yacht.

There was no time to warn them. The megalodon sped toward the boat as though it held a personal grudge. From afar, they watched pieces of the boat fly in opposite directions. The megalodon passed through it, doubling back to munch on the stranded couple huddled on the flybridge.

Both officers felt their hearts sink with the wreckage. This fish was truly evil. It was as though it took genuine pleasure in wreaking havoc on anything weaker than itself. It couldn't seem to get enough, either. Already, it was darting further north.

Renny followed the fish for a few hundred yards, then realized it was moving in on a fishing striker. The man on board had something on the line. The rod was bent and the line taut. The fisherman was too wrapped up in the moment to realize the seven foot dorsal fin closing in on him.

Pushing the chopper to its maximum speed of two-hundred miles-per-hour, Renny hovered the chopper over the deck. The fisherman looked up, his cap swept from his brow by the draft.

"Hey?! What's the deal?" he shouted.

"Sir, you're in danger. We're sending a ladder down to you," Renny said through the speaker.

"What?! Danger?! I'm fine. Go away! Can't you see I'm in the middle of something?!"

Carley threw the ladder down. The man brushed it away. "What's with this harassment?"

"It's not harassment! There's a shark coming right for you, dude! It's already killed several people!" Carley shouted. She pointed a finger to the southwest.

The man looked. There was nothing there.

"You guys are crazy! I have a marlin on the line. First one in ten years. I'm not letting you screw this up—WHOA!" The pole was nearly yanked from his grasp, the rod threatening to snap. Several tense jolts followed, then the line went slack.

The man reeled it in and found that the wire had broken. He looked up at the chopper. "You assholes! See what you did?!"

"For the love of God, man! Climb the damn ladder!" Renny said.

"Are you cops so bored that you feel the need to prank people?" He threw his rod on the deck. "You think I'm so stupid to believe that there's a giant shark coming at me?"

A fountain of ocean sprayed the deck. The man looked in awe as the megalodon appeared alongside the stern. In its jaws was his marlin, its bill sticking out of the left side of its mouth like a cigarette. The shark raised its head high, not wanting to lose its human prey even while its jaws were occupied with the billfish.

With a swing of its head, the shark smacked the boat. In doing so, the marlin's bill, still protruding from the side of its mouth, skewered the fisherman. Like a sausage embedded on a toothpick, he was lifted off the deck. He dangled along the side of the meg's jaws before finally it swallowed him and his prized marlin.

For good measure, the megalodon struck the boat once more, caving in the starboard side. Water rushed into the breach and finished the job.

Now, the shark was heading west. Renny followed its trajectory. "Chief? It's heading for North Beach. It's gone nuts. Going after anything on the water."

****

"Chief? Do you copy?"

After checking over his officers, one of which had taken a hit to the head during the assault, Nico yanked his radio from his belt. "I copy. Patrols, how's the evacuation going?"

"There's still people in the water, Chief," one of the shore patrols said. *"We're doing the best we can, but there's only a handful of us and a lot of these people are pretty far out. We can't get word to them."*

"Damn it to hell," Nico said. He looked to Denise, who stood on the fly bridge. "Take us north."

"You got it."

"Dispatch, what's the ETA on the Coast Guard?"

"Chopper's on approach on max speed," Suzie replied. *"Should arrive any minute. Cutter's been updated on the situation. Its commanding officer is being flown in for a briefing."*

"Very comforting," Nico muttered.

****

Despite the police presence, North Beach was as packed as it always was. Several people went all the way out to the shark nets. Beyond them were people on rubber rafts, small sailboats, paddleboats, and parasailers.

Many of those in the shallows responded to the officers' demands to vacate the water, while those further out failed to comply. Even with the use of bullhorns, many remained a couple hundred feet out.

When Renny and Carley arrived, they went right to work on alerting all of the vessels in the immediate area. The first two, both sailboats, complied without offering resistance. They moved for the docks on the northeast shore.

The next vessel they approached was a yacht hauling a parasailer. Despite a police chopper in front of them and the echo of the microphone, they continued to go about their activities as though nothing was wrong.

"You'd think these people would get the hint," Renny said. He approached the yacht, saw a pair of guys standing near the helm with beers in their hands. Not even eleven in the morning and they were already started on the suds. The sight of alcohol and the lack of urgency at a police chopper in front of them made it clear this was not going to be a simple venture. Still, he had to try. "I need you guys to dock your boat at once. There's an immediate threat in the water."

One of the guys raised his beer as though to toast the officers. He pointed to the open fuselage door. "Hey, babe! You're smoking hot for a police chick!"

Any other time, Carley would've been flattered, even despite the fact that the compliment came from a drunken idiot. This time, she didn't even take in the words. Her eyes were on the east.

The fish was moving in fast. Its dorsal fin emerged first. Then, forty feet ahead of it, the snout appeared. The eyes were rolling back, the lips parting to reveal red gums lined with white teeth. The woman on the parasail saw the fish and screamed.

When the two dudes finally looked, they descended into simultaneous panic. The shark was fifty feet out and lifting its head to bite a chunk out of the boat. One of them grabbed the throttle and shifted it to full speed. Their boat sped underneath the chopper, the wind draft causing the parasail to drop closer to the water—and right into the path of the shark.

Like a bird snapping a bug out of midair, the fish plucked the woman and dove, taking the cord with it.

The two guys felt the quick jolt reverberate through the deck as the cord snapped. When they looked behind them, the woman and the parasail were gone. Moments later, bits of red fabric floated to the surface, each one arriving closer to the fast moving boat.

Renny followed them, watching the shape slowly closing in. He wished he had a grenade or a depth charge to drop on the damn thing. A bazooka would definitely come in handy. Hell, he'd take a cherry bomb at this point. Anything, as long as it got the shark's attention off the civilians. They were idiots, sure, but they didn't deserve *this*.

Bits of nylon broke away from its jaws as the teeth shredded the parachute. By the time the fish reached the boat, the only bits left were those caught in its teeth.

A single impact toppled the boat end over end. Both men were in the water now, landing within ten feet of each other.

The shark closed in on one, snatched him in his jaws, then whipped its tail as it darted away. Its caudal fin struck the other with the force of a monorail. As opposed to the officer, who was launched out of the water, this victim simply exploded on impact. Limbs and guts drifted apart in the cloud of blood.

Finally, the fish moved in toward the abundance of vibration coming from the shallower areas.

Carley emptied her final five rounds into the creature's back as it closed in on the nets.

Now, the people who had ignored the police instructions understood the cause for alarm. The megalodon started by going after the small boats outside the nets. It attacked with such precision that it almost appeared systematic. It grabbed a sailboat in its jaws and crunched it like a pretzel, sending wood and limbs sprinkling to the water like crumbs.

Rubber rafts, and the people they carried, popped effortlessly between its teeth. Dinghies snapped like toothpicks.

Emboldened by the sense of superiority, the megalodon moved in for the nets. For the second time in twenty-four hours, they failed to prevent an outside force from entering the swim zone. It took little effort for the megalodon to shred a wide enough hole in the material for its body to pass through.

For a thousand square feet of space, there was not a single inch of still water. Between the hyperviolent movements by the shark and those of the hundreds trying to flee, the water looked as though it was boiling.

It took in mouthfuls at a time. The shark didn't even have to focus on any individual target. It simply moved in toward a group, opened its mouth, and when it closed its jaw, there were writhing victims between its teeth. The smacking of its caudal fin sent others hurtling through the air like meteors. Some splattered on the beach like upside down pizzas, while others simply landed in impossible, inhuman shapes.

The officers on the beach did their best to shoot the fish, but with the abundance of panicking people, even a target as large as the meg was difficult to hit. Not that it mattered anyway. The few shots that found their way to its flesh simply skidded off.

Such puny weapons weren't going to drive the creature away. The meg had literally found a buffet. The only thing that could stop its massacre was the presence of a true challenger.

The megalodon halted, its lateral line detecting movement from a large object approaching from the east. The object was roughly the same size as itself and moving toward the shallows. There was a smell of diesel that only the man-made things above produced.

This incoming craft wasn't just any boat. It was the one that had rammed it earlier.

Being the master of this territory, the megalodon could not let any challenge go unanswered. It plowed through the net a second time on its way out, then darted for its enemy.

"Where's it going—oh, shit..." Renny saw the *Manta Ray* speeding from the southeast. "Chief, it's coming right at you."

"I know. We gotta get it away from the beach. You guys focus on getting any stragglers out of the water."

"What about you, Chief?" Carley said.

"Don't worry about us."

"Damn you, Nico," Carley said. How many more cops had to be sacrificed today?

****

The sound of the boat horn did the trick. Denise sounded it off a second time, while watching the distant fin draw nearer. Now that she had successfully driven the shark away from the beach, the tight sensation in her stomach set in.

What have I done? It was a thought based solely on self-preservation. She reminded herself that she could have docked the boat and stayed inland if she wanted to.

Outside, one of the officers from Boat Six was standing ready with his Glock. The other was below, barely conscious after hitting his head. Nico stood ready with his rifle.

"Cameron, where are you?"

Right then, he arrived in the pilothouse. In his hand was the tranquilizer gun and a case with the cyanide. "Got the stuff you asked me to get."

She took it from him and went outside. "Take the wheel." She joined her ex-husband down on the main deck and started loading the dart with the cyanide.

"I hope this plan of yours works," Nico said.

"Well, if you didn't, I'd be questioning why you brought us over here," she said.

Fair enough. "I see you still enjoy your fair share of sarcasm."

"I was married to you for nearly a decade. Sarcasm was how I survived," she said.

"Lovely," Nico said. He watched as the swells grew larger as the shark cut along the surface. "Hey?"

"Yeah?"

"Tell you what. If we survive this, maybe we'll have that talk."

"Really?" she said.

"Yes, really." He looked at the tranquilizer dart. "Then again, with that little needle, it's not looking good for us, is it?"

Denise looked at the dart. The needle was three inches long, suitable for most creatures including whales. But whales weren't also bulletproof, unlike this shark.

"The only way for this to work is to get a dart in its mouth."

"Yeah... I'm not sure if you've noticed, but the only time that thing opens its mouth is to chomp down on somebody," Nico said. He shrugged and took the rifle from her. "Well, we didn't come this way for nothing. Come on, fishy!"

Just a couple hundred feet to go. Five seconds to impact. He kept the scope on the bastard's nose, hoping it'd rise out of the water and expose that toothy smile.

"Look!" the officer called out. His voice was drowned out by the sound of twin T700-GE-401C gas turbine engines. Like an angel sent from heaven, the HH-60J Jayhawk flew in from the north and hovered a few hundred feet to the east. The fuselage door was open. Inside, one of the crew was taking aim with the Barret M82 anti-material precision rifle.

Unlike anything the police force carried, the 50. caliber rounds fired from that weapon managed to get the meg's attention. Two rounds struck near its left pectoral fin, drawing blood. The fish jerked to its right and sped past the stern of the *Manta Ray*.

The chopper continued pursuit, the gunman firing several more shots at the fish.

"This is CG-Four calling the Cielo Nublado Police Department."

"This is the Chief. Thanks for the save."

"No problem, sir. I'd recommend you dock that boat right away. We've lost visual of the fish. I suspect it went deep. Unfortunately, we don't have a way of tracking it."

"Copy that." Nico lowered his radio. "Damn. If only we managed to get the tag on the thing."

Denise put a hand on his arm. "At least we'll live to fight another day." She looked up at the pilothouse. "Cameron? Take us in, will ya?"

"No argument there!" he replied.

Nico watched the chaos ensue on the beach as emergency personnel attempted to assist the many injured. Panicked civilians ram amongst them, many searching for loved ones throughout the chaos.

He imagined Rob the Mayor having a heart attack. Tourism on this island would be dead for the next several years at least. North Beach would forever be known as 'Blood Beach.' And despite the heavy sacrifices, the police department would still probably receive the brunt of the blame—because that's how people seem to operate in today's society.

One thing was for certain—this island would never be the same again.

CHAPTER 26

The engine sputtered. It was leaking oil into the water below thanks to the bullet holes placed by the police officer the thugs had sacrificed to the shark. To make matters worse, they were noticing increased air traffic. News media was flying to the island in droves. They hadn't stuck around to witness it, but it was clear that things went from bad to worse with the giant shark.

Kris turned the boat northward then watched the island to his right.

"We need to get out of here," Allen said.

"Yeah, no shit. Let's head back to Pedro's house and grab our money!" Thatcher said.

"If we leave, we might as well blow our own brains out," Kris said. "Enrique's boat is about to die. We need to head inland."

"Oh, right. Sure!" Thatcher said. "Because it's not like the entire world doesn't know we were hiding out on this island by now."

"He's right," Allen said. "They're probably looking for us. They know we were hiding out in Pedro's house. So we can't go back there."

"Wait," Thatcher waved a finger, his face ghostly white, including his eyes. "We *have* to go back to his place. The rest of our cash is stashed there."

"Yeah, sure. Because the cops aren't investigating that as we speak..." Kris said.

"They're busy with the shark," Thatcher said.

"If you don't think they have *at least* one patrol unit checking out Pedro's residence, then the drugs truly have fried your neurons, friend!" Kris said. "Don't forget, we're still some of the most wanted men in the east coast right now. A giant shark doesn't change that."

"Plus, we can guarantee neighboring police departments are sending aid to Cielo Nublado as we speak," Allen said.

Thatcher shook his head. "No. NO! We can't come out of this empty-handed. We just can't!"

"If you weren't such a junkie, and insisted on making a deal with Roberto, then we wouldn't be in this mess," Kris said.

"Oh yeah? If you didn't shoot those people in the parking lot, the cops wouldn't have been alerted so quickly," Thatcher said. "And we wouldn't have been identified."

"Are we seriously doing this dance again?" Allen said. "Guys, we need to figure out what to do. I mean, right this moment! In case you haven't noticed, we're sticking out like a sore thumb right now."

Kris leaned forward and placed his forehead on the dashboard, mimicking the motion of bashing his own skull in. He was somewhat tempted to. What Allen said was correct. The odds were not in their favor. Then add the stress of their stolen loot no longer being in their possession, meaning everything they'd endured had been for nothing.

"Okay, let's look at this with level heads. We can't stay adrift, and we can't flee. This boat's not gonna last. We're lucky we've made it this far. Our only chance is to go back."

Thatcher crossed his arms. "Might as well stick our head in a hornets' nest."

"Chill out. At the moment, I'm certain they're distracted with the shark phenomenon…"

"Yeah—is nobody going to mention that?!" Allen said. "Holy shit, that freaking shark. It was as big as a—"

"Dude, didn't you just say we need to figure out a solution? Now, all of a sudden, you want to go on about mutant sharks?"

Allen stepped back. "Right."

"Anyway," Kris said, "If we go back now, we can blend in. We just need to stay away from police presence. And the media presence if we can help it."

"Where do we stay? We can't just be wandering the streets all night," Thatcher said.

For once, the druggie had a point. Kris pondered all the options. Hotels were a no-go. Returning to Pedro's house was suicide. They didn't know anybody else. They couldn't hang around outdoors, considering an increased police and military presence would guarantee they'd be spotted. The only viable option would be to use force to obtain a hideout. Considering how things had gone thus far, such an action would almost guarantee more collateral damage.

To make matters worse, it wasn't as simple as kicking in a door and forcing the homeowner to let them stay. They needed to know something about the home they'd be invading. How many residents were there? Did they own firearms? Were they expecting anyone to be coming over, such as a spouse that worked late? Worse: would that place be related to anyone in the police department? That'd be unlikely, but then again, 'unlikely' apparently was their thing recently. It had gone to the max today with the UNLIKELY appearance of a giant shark.

"There's only one viable option I can think of at the top of my head," Kris said. "That boat leading the police charge—that *wasn't* a police boat."

"Yeah? So what?" Thatcher said. "The cops were still using it."

"You remember what Pedro said? He had heard from the news that the Police Chief was teaming up with a researcher to investigate some recent accidents. *That* boat was the research vessel he was using."

Thatcher shrugged. "Your point?"

"That researcher, to my knowledge, isn't from here. If we can overtake that boat, we can use it to slip away. You saw as well as I there was only a couple of people on it. We can overtake it."

"I'm starting to feel like a pirate," Thatcher said. "The Coast Guard won't search that vessel. The only thing we might have to worry about is the Chief himself stopping by for a visit."

"Then we'll plan for that," Kris said.

Thatcher rubbed his bristly chin. "You know, you might be on to something, Kris. If the scientist on that boat is a marine biologist, they might know how to dive."

"Yeah, possibly." Kris wasn't sure he liked where this was going.

"Maybe with a little incentive, we can put that fella to use. We know where the plane went down. More importantly, its *cargo*."

Kris nearly facepalmed his forehead. "You seriously want to go after the sunken drugs and money?"

Thatcher shrugged. "You yourself said that recovering the money at Pedro's house was suicide. Right now, we're flat broke, and on the run. We get the money we paid Roberto, as well as the cocaine, we can make do just fine for a while."

Allen raised a hand. "I'm with Thatcher on this one."

Thatcher hit him with an intimidating stare. "On this one? When were you *not* with me?"

"I—you know what I mean," Allen said. He turned to face Kris, deliberately avoiding Thatcher's piercing gaze. "He is right, though. We *need* that money. It's a million, three. Might only be a third of what we hauled from the bank, but it's better than nothing."

Kris thought about the long-term. In order to hide, they'd have to travel to a different state, preferably on the other side of the country. Such an endeavor would be impossible without funds.

"I suppose you're right."

"Good." Thatcher checked the ammo in his pistol magazine. "Any thoughts on where that lady's boat is docked?"

"Dunno. We'll have to check the piers." Kris checked his watch. "If we're gonna follow this course of action, we need to start now, while the cops are occupied. Let's dock this boat somewhere and hope nobody notices until we're gone."

CHAPTER 27

Usually when Nico felt this physically exhausted, he was many days into a dreary investigation that involved piecing together many details. Today, it only took a few hours.

Shortly after the attack, a second Coast Guard chopper arrived. Both birds spent the next hour patrolling the air, and finding any stray boaters that were unaware of the situation. By twelve-thirty, the Sentinel-Class Cutter *Harlin* arrived on the north side of the island. Its captain, Samuel Grade was immediately brought to shore by the rigid-hulled cutter boat.

Captain Grade was an inch taller than Nico and roughly the same age. In their first meeting at twelve-thirty, he seemed skeptical about the existence of a megalodon shark, despite the reports from the helicopter crews. The meeting was brief, with him setting up a small basecamp on North Beach while he communicated with the chopper units and coordinated emergency efforts here on shore.

One useful thing he accomplished was getting emergency medical flights near the island. Despite the increased number of personnel, the workload was still overwhelming.

Even by mid-afternoon, the beach was still in chaos. The carnage was abundant. With the vast body-count, it was impossible to get a handle on the number of people who were missing. The dispatch office was flooded with phone calls. Every resident or visitor who couldn't get in touch with a friend or loved one were ringing the telephone line. In some of these cases, it was a simple matter of a missed call or appointment, followed by nerves gone haywire.

To make matters worse, Captain Grade demanded that all boats remain docked. The ocean was being treated as molten lava. Anyone that dared to pass over it was risking death. Nobody was allowed to leave the island unless it was by flight, and all private chopper and seaplane pilots were contracted by the island counsel. As far as the general population was concerned, they were trapped there until told otherwise.

It was four o'clock when Nico's police force successfully got everybody off North Beach. The carnage itself had yet to be cleared. Ambulances were moving like busses, carrying dead and wounded to the hospital and returning for more. Then there were the pesky reporters, all of whom had an ounce of integrity between them. On multiple occasions, they felt the need to stick a microphone in Nico's face as he was hauling a twisted body out of the water.

He thought he had seen it all in his days as a detective. The worst thing about working in that field was learning all the unique ways a person could die. He'd seen people stabbed, shot, mutilated, tortured, decomposed, and much more. Young and old, evil knew no bounds. But until now, he never knew mass death.

A month ago, he was praised for preventing such a disaster. While not the deadliest tsunami ever recorded, it was still a force of nature that resulted in serious damage. Nico had taken great pride in the fact that there wasn't a single fatality, despite having almost no time to prepare.

Today, it was as though nature was laughing in his face. He thwarted its plans once, so it sent its demon from the black abyss, driven out by the same meteor that launched the great wave.

Nico knelt down on one knee, submerging himself up to his shoulders in water. "Found another one."

Paramedics waded in, followed by Renny and Carley. Both were shaken by their failed attempt to stop the beast, and the carnage they had to witness. But sitting in the office and doing nothing did nothing to calm their nerves. They needed to work, even if it meant subjecting themselves to more horrors brought by the shark.

They each lowered themselves into the water and found something to grab on to. At a count of three, they lifted the body out. It was shrunken, the face and torso caved in. Bones stuck out of the chest cavity like thorns.

Carley felt her grasp starting to slip. She maintained control long enough to help carry the body to shore. Once there, she sprinted away and dry heaved. Nico went to check on her, but Renny got there first.

"Well, I know one good thing that resulted from today," Renny said.

Carley accepted the water bottle he offered her, took a small sip, then stood straight. "Yeah? What's that?"

"Considering all the first responder work we're doing, I can say I've earned the right to sleep in my own bed instead of the couch."

"That's what you think," Carley said. She dug her phone out and started texting.

"What do you think you're doing?"

"It's been a shitty day. I need to do something to make me laugh." Carley sent the text, then showed it to him.

Hey! Just letting you know, your husband's making fun at me for dry heaving.

"What?! That's a lie!"

The response came in. *That bastard. You'd think he'd know better. I'll take care of him when he gets home.*

"Great." Renny reread the reply, then grinned. "Then again, by 'take care of me' she could've meant—" Carley yanked the phone away and sent another text. Renny cleared his throat. "You're telling her what I just said, aren't you?"

"Like I said, I need *something* amusing to happen. Torturing you always lifts my spirits."

A moment later, Renny's phone buzzed. He glanced at the screen, which showed a snapshot of his wife's text conversation with Carley, and her reply: *Yeah, buddy. Keep dreaming.*

"Even after blowing up my phone for two hours and being all worried about me, she goes right back to being mad at me on a dime," he said.

"Just her?" Nico said. The two officers glanced back at him, then simultaneously laughed. It was a much needed moment of levity, especially considering the day's work wasn't yet finished. Nico put a hand on their shoulders. "In all seriousness, you guys kicked ass out there. Saved my ass, and I appreciate that."

"Well, we all owe you an apology for, well, making faces when you first said there was a giant shark during briefing."

Nico looked down the beach, where his ex-wife and her assistant were standing. They were in conversation with Captain Grade, who was likely requesting intel about the creature.

"I can't say I acted much better when the situation was first brought to my attention," he said. "Even with a dead whale with bite wounds as big as Rhode Island, it was hard to believe."

"I just hope the Coast Guard kills it," Carley said. She watched the beach, and the first responders dredging the waters for remains. "Hell, I might consider transferring after this. It'll be hard to look at this place the same way."

"This place will be dead for five years at minimum," Renny said. "The missus has brought up the desire to move. She's been craving a change of scenery."

"Yeah? Where'd you guys go?"

"We don't have definite plans, but at the moment, I'm thinking somewhere with woods." He smiled at the Chief. "You should come too! We'd make quite the team. You'd be the small town sheriff. I'll be the deputy. We'd patrol the woods, not worrying about giant sharks."

"Nope. Just Bigfoot," Carley said.

"At this point, I wouldn't be surprised," Nico said. For the first few moments, the thought of moving into the Midwest and policing a small country town sounded appealing. He loved nature, and thick woods was something he hadn't gotten to experience much. Staying on this island long term no longer sounded appealing.

There was one issue surrounding the idea of moving inland—there was no ocean. With no ocean, there would be no Denise.

"Oh, JEEZ! Go and kiss her already! This is worse than high school," Carley said.

"Huh? What?"

"Oh, don't start with that," Carley said. "You're watching your ex more intently than Renny watches topless sunbathers on the beach. Except with you, there's a little sparkle in your eye. It's cute."

"There's no sparkle—"

Renny shook his head. "I gotta agree with her, Chief. Not on the 'cute' thing, though."

"I appreciate you clearing that up." For the second time, Nico placed a hand on their shoulders. "You guys go back to the office and get in some dry clothes. I wish I could send you home, but unfortunately, we're now short-staffed."

"How's Benny?" Renny asked.

"He'll be spending the night in the hospital. Maybe two, but he'll be fine. Craig's in shock, though. Guy deserves a medal for keeping it together while we led the thing away from the beach." The moment of levity had passed. Multiple cops were dead, two more were out of commission. Many others would probably have to seek therapy for PTSD.

Before anything could be done, that shark needed to be killed.

"See you guys later," he said. As he walked away, he looked back one last time. "Carley, be nice to Renny. Let the memory foam on his couch forget about him."

She responded with an exaggerated sigh. "If you say so, Chief."

When Nico approached the Coast Guard Captain, it was evident that the operation to hunt the shark was about to begin. The two choppers had landed for refuel and the cruiser was being prepped to return him to the cutter.

The *USCG Omega Fury* was a forty-one meter Sentinel-Class Cutter, with a crew of twenty-two. Its armament consisted of four .50 caliber machine guns and a M242 Bushmaster autocannon.

He had seen the Coast Guard sniper rifle successfully break its skin, so there was no doubt that the Bushmaster was more than enough to get the job done. And the shark would have a field day trying to break the reinforced steel hull of a cutter. It might rock the boat and nauseate the crew, but breaching? It would implode its own head before sinking that vessel.

Among it were three medium-sized response boats. Each had a three man crew and were armed with fifty-caliber machine guns. Unlike the cutter, those boats were vulnerable to the megalodon's attacks.

Captain Grade turned to face Nico after seeing him approach. "Ah, Chief. Good you're here. We're about to get started."

"What's the plan, Captain?"

"There's not much to it, Chief. It's big, but at the end of the day, it's just a fish. We're gonna lure it within range and blow the hell out of it with the Bushmaster. Already got my one-liner picked out. As my drill instructor used to say, 'sucks to be you!'" He chuckled. "Just have a little patience. This island will be yours again by sunset."

"I'm looking forward to it," Nico said. He pointed to the smaller vessels cruising near the *Omega Fury*. "Listen, you might be better off simply using the choppers and the cutter. Those response boats won't stand a chance against the megalodon."

He noticed a slight smirk and head shake from the Captain. Nico didn't know much about this man personally, but he knew those gestures. His concerns were being brushed away like pests from a picnic table. On top of that, Grade didn't think he'd notice, or the motions would have been more pronounced.

"Don't worry, Chief," he said. "Our men are expert seamen. They know how to read sonar and maneuver a boat. Plus, those Brownings mounted on their deck pack a real punch. The shark will wish the meteor killed it."

"You said you were going to bait it?" Denise said.

"Yes, with good ol' fashioned chum. That's pretty standard for searching for sharks."

"Yes, I know. I'm just informing you, I'm not sure how quickly the meg will respond. It's already fed heavily today, and I'm not sure how fast its digestive system works."

"But we do know one thing," Nico said. "This fish responds quickly to threats. It might come at you, not for hunger, but for territorial reasons. It was fast to abandon an abundance of food at the beach to attack Denise's boat. Because of the size, I think it saw us as a challenger."

Captain Grade chuckled. "Then it's gonna be in for a shock when it tries to go after my ship."

"Captain, I'm just saying—"

"Chief, with all due respect, this is my operation. I know what I'm doing. You just worry about keeping everyone else out of the water. Nobody leaves this island, except by air." Captain Grade didn't bother waiting for an acknowledgement. He marched to his boat, boarded it, and started barking commands on his radio as the ensign on board started the engine.

Nico looked at Denise. "How are you holding up? You alright?"

"Can't say this has been a particularly glorious day," she said. "Overall, though, I'm doing alright. What about you?"

"Hasn't been my favorite day on the job," he said. "We're still recovering bodies. To make matters worse, we'll be spending the next several days nonstop trying to sort out all the victims' identities. Considering several of them were swallowed whole, or killed out at sea, that's going to be a real pain. Plus, people are already getting restless. Many of them want to leave and now my police force has to act like Soviet Russia and keep them here. Add the fact that I had to visit six households today to inform the families of the men I lost… I think you get the idea of what kind of day I'm having."

"I'm sorry. Is there anything I can do?"

"The only thing that can lift my spirits right now is chicken and rice."

"Beg your pardon?"

"You remember? You used to bake a chicken and rice recipe. I'd be taking bites out of it, scalding hot, as you'd take it out of the oven because it was so freaking good."

It took Denise a moment to remember, after which, she felt foolish. How could she have forgotten? In their ten years of marriage, he craved that recipe practically every week. So much energy had been spent trying to forget it all, but now that the memories had been unlocked, she couldn't help but smile.

"I am a kickass cook."

"Nobody ever denied that," Nico said. "Then again, for all I know, you've probably lost your touch. You've been on the water constantly for the last three years. Can't imagine you do much cooking on that boat."

"Hey now!" Denise said. "For one, we actually do have a small stove and oven in the galley. Considering we're a small crew, it's suitable. Though a nice household stove is preferable—which leads me to my second point. No way in hell have I lost my touch, mister."

"People so confident don't feel the need to be so defensive," Nico said, unable to hide his mischievous smile.

"Oh really? Why don't I prove it to you?"

"Fine. My place at eight. I'll pick you up. Unless you don't think you're up to it."

She scoffed. "I'll be there."

"Good." They shared a laugh. It was short lived, thanks to a new radio transmission.

"Dispatch to any available units, we have reports of a brawl over at the west pier. Someone's trying to take their boat out."

Nico threw his head back in frustration. "Ohhhh, Jesus... won't the craziness ever end. Sorry, I have to run."

"No problem. You sure you won't be too busy with everything going on?"

"Monroe County is sending some Deputies to assist and a Lieutenant to assist," Nico said. "They'll be landing in a half hour or so. I'm gonna have to sleep sometime." He hurried to his truck, then pointed at her as he got in. "Eight o'clock!"

"Eight o'clock," she replied with a thumbs up. Nico started the flashers and sped off to the other side of the island.

Denise felt her spirits lift. After a dark day such as this, it was comforting to have something good occur. First, she would have to make a stop at the local grocery store.

CHAPTER 28

The grocery store was packed. Denise found it simultaneously remarkable and sad how a shark attack triggered a wave of panic buying. People were stuffing their carts and baskets with pasta, bread, and yes—toilet paper.

You'd think they were condemned to stay on this island for a lifetime. What should've been a quick fifteen minute trip took over an hour, mainly because of the long lines. Luckily, she had no problem getting the chicken breasts. Apparently, poultry wasn't a delicacy in the apocalypse. The rice, on the other hand, was almost out. She had to reach in-between a horde of customers to get the last couple of boxes. After getting her soup mix and other ingredients, she waited in line, which took up the bulk of that hour at the store.

"Jesus, fighting the megalodon was more pleasant," she said to herself as she walked out, items in hand. It was five-thirty now. She heard a news report through somebody's car radio as she passed by, the reporter stating that the Coast Guard was commencing their operation on the south side of the island. They were following the shark's last known trajectory.

The walk back to the northeast dock was relatively quiet. Most of the crowds were over at the western docks, where the ferries usually arrived. Those who weren't making life harder for the police were either spending their afternoons in their hotels or at the bar.

The section of beach near the docks was quiet, as the attack happened further west. From three hundred meters away, she could still see the recovery efforts. Boats kept to the shallows, dredging the bottom for remains. The shark nets had been removed to allow them easy access to the shore in case of another attack. The adjacent areas of the beach were vacant, as though the sand itself was haunted.

"Looks like I've got a couple of hours to kill." She boarded the vessel and went inside. Surprisingly, Cameron was nowhere to be seen. "Hey, big guy! Where are ya?" Still no answer.

If he was in his cabin, he would've heard her. Denise went through the passageway into the galley. The groceries dropped from her hand as she saw her assistant sprawled out on the deck. His face was bloodied, his left eye swollen, his shirt stained red.

Then came the feeling of a pistol placed against her temple. "Ah-ha!" Two other men stepped in from the next entryway. The crooks from the bank.

Denise slowly raised her hands. "What do you want?"

The thug with the gun pressed to her head was already eyeballing her figure. "Well…"

"Thatcher!" the thug with the tan skin and dark hair said. He seemed slightly more in control than the man to her right. The third one, a short man with a hint of Asian in his ethnicity among a mix of others, stepped over and reached for her pants. Denise wheezed, assuming the worst.

"Oh, knock it off. He's just taking your phone," the second one said. He looked over to the one named Thatcher. "Quit eye-fucking her."

"Stop telling me what to do, asshole." He tilted his head to examine her neckline. "Gotta say, she looks better up close than she did from afar."

"You didn't even see her. You were too fixed on getting your cocaine and getting us killed in the process."

"Kris, I've had just about enough of you. I'm in charge of this gig!"

"Seriously?!" the man named Kris said. "That thing you have in mind—get it *out* of your mind. We need her. You said so yourself."

Begrudgingly, Thatcher removed the pistol from her temple. "I suppose you're right this time."

Cameron gritted his teeth as he started to pick himself up off the floor. Thatcher immediately kicked him in the ribs.

"Don't move."

"Suck my nuts," Cameron snarled.

"Oh yeah?" Thatcher knelt down and pressed the pistol to his mouth. "Open up. See if you like sucking on *this*."

Kris grabbed him by the shoulder and forced him back. "Snap out of it. You're not helping this situation." He turned to look at the third member. "Allen, find something to tie this guy's wrists behind his back."

Denise felt her nerves going haywire. These guys were openly using their names in front of witnesses. Either they were extremely sloppy, or they had plans to dispose of them after they got whatever use they apparently needed. And once disposable, Thatcher would probably have free rein to fulfill his sick fantasies.

Kris' eyes turned toward her. "What's your name?"

"Why are you here?" she said.

"Don't make me ask you again," he said. His voice was more intense this time, making Denise realize that behind that 'calm' demeanor was an extremely violent man. Considering the kind of company he kept, he had no qualms about killing.

"Denise."

"Denise, where's the Police Chief?" he asked. "I know he was on your boat. I saw you back at the exchange. Considering you were working with the cops..."

"We were looking for the shark," she said. "Then the call came in...."

"Yeah-yeah, we get it," Allen said.

"Where is the shark?" Thatcher said.

"I have no idea. The Coast Guard's looking for it right now," she said. "No boats are allowed on the water until they've confirmed it's dead."

"Perfect!" Thatcher said. "Then we won't have to worry about anyone interfering."

"Except the Coast Guard themselves," Allen said.

"Interfering? With what?" Denise said.

Thatcher leaned in close. So close, that she could smell his stale breath and see the mild signs of decay in his lower incisors.

"You're going to pay us back for the merchandise that you lost."

"I didn't lose anything," Denise said.

Thatcher grabbed her by the jaw. "Oh, yeah you did. You helped the cops. You played a huge role in what happened. And now you're going to help us get our supplies back."

Denise yanked her head away from his grasp. "How?"

"You're a marine biologist, are you not?" Kris said.

"Yes..."

"That means you can dive, correct?"

No, actually a good number of us don't dive. Fortunately, or unfortunately, I do.

Knowing it was best not to overcomplicate things, she simply nodded.

"Good! Here's the plan: We're gonna head back to the site where we made our drug deal. You're going to dive and recover two briefcases. One has over a million dollars in cash. The other has ten kilos of cocaine."

"Nine," Thatcher said.

"Nine, whatever. *You* are going to recover it. Then you're gonna take us wherever we tell you to go."

"That's over two hundred feet deep," Denise said.

"You saying you can't dive two hundred feet?" Thatcher said.

"It's going to be very difficult to find your supplies down there in that darkness. And what if we run into the shark?"

"You said the Coast Guard is hunting it. We can monitor their frequencies," Allen said.

"No we can't! We're not the CIA. They don't use open frequencies to communicate," Denise said.

Kris broke eye contact, realizing she had a point. His expression livened, and he turned back toward her. "No, but they will keep constant communication with the local police department. Who, in turn, will keep the local news updated. And you know them. The minute they hear that the Coast Guard finds the thing, they'll blast it all over the radio."

"Possibly."

"And *then* we'll go out and do what we need to do," Thatcher said.

Allen leaned against the refrigerator and scratched his head. "Assuming they don't engage the shark close by."

"The wreck is southeast of us. As long as they state their general location when they announce they've found the shark—and it's far enough away—then we'll be good to go," Kris said.

Thatcher put his boot into Cameron's ribs, then pointed a finger at Denise. "You *will* dive. If you refuse, I'll pop a hole in the side of your buddy's head. Then, I'll deal with you. Believe me, it won't be as quick. Not even Kris will do anything to stop it at that point."

It took every ounce of strength for Denise not to scream and run. Such situations were seen in the movies, but rarely did anybody actually experience such a thing.

First I nearly get devoured. Now, I'm being held at gunpoint and forced to recover lost drugs.

She looked down at Cameron. He was barely conscious, the skin around his wrist already red from the tight bindings. They had probably forced their way in and put a gun in his face, then beat the hell out of him for the fun of it. Or maybe it was to bloody him up and reinforce the threat of killing him unless she did as instructed.

One thing was for sure: they had no qualms about killing.

"Okay. Just don't hit him anymore."

"Fine. Just don't do anything dumb," Kris said. He knelt down and grabbed Cameron by the arm. "On your feet, Mash Potato. We're heading up to the wheelhouse. Gotta keep an eye on that radio."

CHAPTER 29

Almost twenty years in the United States Coast Guard, having just signed papers for another six-year term, Captain Grade thought he had seen it all. He had been part of missions to the Antarctic, intercepted Columbian drug dealers in the Gulf Coast, and performed several rescue missions in hurricane season. He had seen his fair share of death, especially in the aftermath of Hurricane Katrina in 2004. That was his first true wake-up call regarding nature's wrath.

He always hoped he wouldn't see such a horrific disaster again. In the event of the meteor tsunami, he was relieved that the casualties were fairly low along the Bahamas and the Florida Keys. There were still repairs needed to be done, but the damage was minimal overall. Grade remembered feeling relieved. Maybe that would be the year's worst event.

Then came the emergency notification that a giant shark was attacking Cielo Nublado.

He didn't often question orders, it wasn't proper. The Coast Guard wasn't necessarily known for its high-ranking officers playing pranks. But a giant shark attacking an island? No, it *had* to be a joke. Even as he left Key West, he was wondering what he was truly heading into. Only after seeing the aftermath and various footage of the event was he finally convinced.

The Captain stood in the bridge, watching the chopper units pepper the surrounding water with dead shark. In the ninety minutes they had been hunting, there was no sign of the target. Either it was actively avoiding them, or was simply hunting on another part of the island.

"Perhaps we should've taken that marine biologist along as a consultant," he said.

The Chief Petty Officer turned away from the sonar operator. "Pardon me, Captain, but what use would she be? Yeah, it's a dangerous animal, but at the end of the day, it's nothing more than a big fish. There's not much to it."

"A big fish that we didn't know existed until today," Grade said.

"This is Chopper Four to Omega Fury."

The officers turned to the radioman to watch as he took the call. "Fury here."

"I've got something. About a click north of our position. Moving fast."

Grade looked to the sonar operator. "Any readings?"

The guardsman nodded. "Aye-aye, sir. Large submarine object, moving at five miles per hour. Moving toward the bait."

"That's gotta be it." Grade switched on his own radio. "Chopper Four, move in for a visual. Boats Forty-five, Forty-four, and Forty-three, close in on their position. Lure the bastard to the surface so we can get a clear shot at it." The boat operators replied with *"Aye-aye, sir."*

The Captain turned to the radioman. "Alert the local PD. Inform them that we've located the shark and are about to initiate our attack. They'll have their beaches back by tomorrow."

"Aye-aye, Captain." The radioman switched channels to nine. "This is the United States Coast Guard *Omega Fury* calling Cielo Nublado Police Department…"

****

"Right? Good. I appreciate you keeping me informed. Kill that thing," Nico said. Professional? Not really. Did he care? Definitely not.

The news that they had located the shark came at the perfect time. It was a couple of minutes to eight, following an exhausting afternoon of deescalating the crisis on the island. Around six, his reinforcements arrived and went straight to work policing the island. Renny and Carley, among many other officers, volunteered to stay late and show them the ropes.

In that time, the uneasy population began to settle down. Word that the Coast Guard was hunting the fish seemed to ease the panic. At around seven, attempts to leave the island by boat finally ceased. Nico had to endure a little name-calling that he wasn't used to. Typically, he was called a fascist, pig, skinhead—despite being Latino *and* having a head full of hair—bully, power-hungry, and right wing. Of course, anything to the right of Lenin was considered right wing to some of these clowns. Today, however, he was called the opposite. Totalitarian. Oppressor. Typical of some of the college-age talking points, except this time he felt it might have been somewhat true. He wasn't used to this martial law method of policing, and frankly, he didn't like it.

These were the days when police could not win. Throughout his career, Nico had experienced his fair share of criticism, but nothing compared to today. The media was already reporting that he knew of the shark's existence, yet allowed people in the water anyway. So far, the good ol' mayor didn't do anything to counter these reports. Robert Zahn was a good guy, until his own reputation was threatened. In such a case, he would use anyone he could as a human shield against negative press. He was on his second and final term as mayor for Cielo Nublado. A community with many immigrants from Cuba, they understood the importance of term limits, no matter what office. With his mind on expanding his political career, Robert would not want to leave this island bearing responsibility for a massive death toll.

No Kevlar was strong enough to protect against the onslaught of media bullets. He was surprised they left him alone to focus on the issues at hand. Tomorrow, once the shark was dead, it would be a different story. He would tell the truth, that he alerted the Island Counsel and they dismissed his claims, and they would fire back. Probably with a character assassination.

The thing Nico feared most was the lengths they possibly would go. Robert Zahn knew of the circumstances why he left Texas, and was very sympathetic about it. Still, his own skin was what mattered most to him. If he used the accident as a sign of Nico's 'bad judgement', Nico would find himself facing the inside of his own jail cell—because, at minimum, he would beat Robert to a pulp.

Maybe this was fate. While Nico truly believed this island to be beautiful, he wasn't here out of a love for paradise. It was the first escape route. Surrounding oneself with gorgeous scenery sometimes was enough to obscure the demons that clawed at his psyche. But that scenery had been tattered by death, and the island's natural beauty no longer served as a mental shield. The only way to defeat those demons was to face them directly.

Twenty-four hours ago, the thought of meeting with Denise made him so anxious, he almost felt nauseated. Now, in spite of everything that occurred today, he was feeling the opposite. She was the one he'd turn to when a day on the job was rough. Whenever he needed to open up after seeing a human being reduced to puss after being left in a basement for a month, she'd be the one he would talk to. Seeing the *Manta Ray* up ahead lifted his spirits in the same way as when he saw her car in his driveway back in Waco.

He pulled up to the pier and waited. A few minutes went by and she didn't show. The lights were on in the pilothouse and quarters. She was definitely there. Perhaps she lost track of the time.

Nico called her cell phone. It rang five times before going to voicemail. He sent a text. *Hey, I'm out here by the dock.*

No reply.

"Probably got lost in paperwork or something research-y." Not a big deal. Going up and knocking on the door took him back to their first date.

He was patrol sergeant at that time, and she was living at home completing her doctorate. The fact that he was an officer meant nothing to her father. He looked at Nico with the same suspicion as he would some alley cat sniffing for some tail. A father always protected his child, no matter their age. That first meeting made Nico feel like a teenager again, especially after getting the look from Mr. Reta. It was one of those 'don't do anything stupid or I'll beat your face in' looks. Nico knew when a guy meant it, and Mr. Reta was not the type to kid around. It took a few visits for him to warm up to Nico. Still, that threat of an ass-kicking lingered all the way up to their wedding.

Nico boarded the vessel and knocked on the aft passageway entrance. Part of him almost anticipated someone like her father to be on the other side of that door, ready to deck him. After a minute he knocked again. He heard footsteps on the other side, but nobody opened the door.

"Denise? Hello?" He tried the handle. It was unlocked. He opened the door and peeked inside. "Hey, it's me. Where you at—"

His life flashed before his eyes as a fist struck his jaw. Instinct kicked in. Nico threw back, hitting the assailant in the nose and knocking him back. Before he could draw his pistol, he was struck in the temple by the butt of a shotgun. He hit the deck, then curled his hands and knees as a series of kicks pummeled him. The muzzle of that shotgun was pressed to his temple, halting any desire to continue fighting.

It took a second for his vision to clear. When he looked up, he recognized the three men standing above him. The one with the shotgun was Kris Hebron. Standing beside him was Allen Lo and Ed Thatcher, the latter of which was kneeling to remove his Glock and radio.

"Thanks for sending that text," he said. "Came in handy for us to know you were coming."

"On your feet," Kris said.

Slowly, Nico stood up. He kept a straight posture, despite the urge to hunch over. He took a few good kicks to the gut, and everything inside felt like mush. All three men had weapons trained on him. If he had learned anything from the previous encounter as well as their criminal history, it was that these guys were trigger happy.

"What are you doing here? Where's Denise and Cameron?"

"They're fine," Kris said. "Whether they stay that way depends on how well you all cooperate."

"Cooperate? What's the big idea?" Nico said.

"We're going to retrieve our lost merchandise," Kris said. "You and your lady friend are going to help us do that."

Nico watched the guns they pointed at him, partially to make sure their itchy trigger fingers didn't look like they would accidently discharge them. If those bastards didn't have those guns, he'd take all three of them on right now. Nico was no stranger to brawling. In fact, he enjoyed a good fight. If only these assholes didn't have Denise hostage...

"Where are they?" he asked.

"They're fine," Kris said.

"Yeah? Prove it, because your word's worth nothing to me," Nico said.

Thatcher laughed, then raised his pistol to eye level. "Forget it. We don't even need this guy."

Kris grabbed him by the wrist, forcing the gun away. "Yes we do. He's leverage."

"Leverage? What exactly is your plan?"

"Your lady friend is going to retrieve two briefcases from the area the plane went down," Kris said. "Now that we have you, she'll have a little extra incentive."

"Yeah? So, why the delay? Waiting for me?"

"No, actually. She cleverly left out the fact that you were coming," Kris said. "You might've had the drop on us had you not texted her." He held up Denise's iPhone. In the middle of the screen was Nico's recent text.

Allen Lo stepped behind the Chief and pushed him forward. They went up the steps and entered the pilothouse. Seated on the deck beside the console were Denise and Cameron. Both had their hands tied behind their backs and duct tape over their mouths.

Denise didn't appear to be injured. Cameron, though, looked as if he'd gone toe-to-toe with Mike Tyson. His face was swollen and bruised, and by the way he was hunched, he had taken several hits to the midsection, possibly resulting in cracked ribs.

He looked at his attackers. "You bastards."

Thatcher shoved him forward. "Get in there."

Nico stepped by his ex-wife. "You alright?" She nodded, unable to speak. He looked at them again. "Is the gagging necessary?"

"I'll take it off once we're out of here," Kris said. He looked at Allen, then cocked his head at the Chief. Allen approached with a roll of duct tape, yanked Nico's hands behind his back, then wrapped the tape around his wrists. It was a humiliating feeling. Nico had more than his fair share of encounters with criminals, but never had he been a hostage. To think of how easily they overpowered him made him angrier.

At that moment, the evening dispatcher's voice came through the radio. *"We've got Coast Guard choppers moving to the north. They're in pursuit of the megalodon."*

The criminals looked at each other and smiled.

"Well, would you look at that!" Thatcher said. "We don't need to hope for a media broadcast!"

"No, I suppose we don't," Kris said. He looked at Nico. "You coming here proved more useful than we ever could have hoped for. Now, we can finally get started." He nodded at Allen, who knelt behind Denise and cut the tape from her wrists. She yanked the tape from her mouth and threw it at Kris. She knew he wouldn't shoot her. Can't dispose of his only chance of regaining the drugs and cash.

However, they had a couple of other people they could use to make their point. Thatcher made Nico an example by striking him across the temple, knocking him to his side.

"Take us out," he said. "If your hand goes anywhere near that radio, you'll get a free course in neurology. We'll show you parts of the human brain piece by piece. At least, we'll do our best—it'll be hard to decipher after the shotgun blows his fucking head off."

Denise looked at Nico, then at Kris. "Don't hit them anymore. We'll get you your shit, and you go off on your way. You can even have the boat."

"We'll negotiate all that after. Start the engine."

Nico rolled back to a seated position, then nodded at Denise. "Just do as they say."

Begrudgingly, Denise approached the helm. She hated relenting to the will of these killers. But doing nothing would guarantee further harm to Nico and Cameron.

On the other hand, she understood Nico's tone. The gears in his head were turning. He was already figuring out a plan. She just needed to have faith that he could come up with something fast enough, and that he could pull it off. In the meantime, she would just have to obey the gang's demands.

She started the boat up and throttled it southeast for *Jaquez Grave*.

CHAPTER 30

"*Chopper Four in position. Gunner is ready to turn the thing to sushi.*"

"Leave that to the Bushmaster," Grade said.

All units were in position. The *Omega Fury's* bow was pointed at the incoming shark. Boats Forty-four and Forty-five were two hundred off meters off the starboard bow, and Forty-three several hundred left of them. Their goal was to shepherd the fish into the kill zone in case it tried to divert. It was still running deep, out of sight except for the choppers. Even they could only see the faint silhouette, like an ominous shadow moving under the surface. With the light dwindling, they would soon lose all visual unless the creature came up to the surface.

"The problem with our bait is that it sinks," Grade said. An idea came to mind. It was risky—though not much riskier than what they were already attempting. "Chopper Five. Decrease altitude to two meters. Draw the bastard up. We'll monitor its position. When is ascends, haul ass."

"*Aye-aye, Captain.*"

Captain Grade watched from the bridge as the orange and white chopper moved east, then settled in the megalodon's path. The setting sun reflected off its hull, making the aircraft appear like a star glistening above the ocean.

"Biologic increasing speed. Moving toward Five at twelve mph," the sonar operator said.

That was more than double the previous speed. The plan was working. In a few moments, the Captain would be able to brag that he led the only operation that successfully killed a megalodon shark.

He stood by the sonar operator and watched the screen. "Chopper Five, prepare to ascend. In five, four, three—"

"Sir, bogey's changing course," the operator said. "Going due-west. Twenty-knots."

"What the—" Grade watched the blip on the screen move to the left. "Chopper Five, do you have visual?"

"*Negative, sir. Lost it as soon as it changed course.*"

"Why the hell would it retreat?" the Petty Officer said.

"I don't know. Maybe it saw the ship and thought it was a bigger fish. I don't know," Grade said. He allowed a split-second groan. For a moment, it looked like the job was going to be easy, literally as simple as drawing the fish in and blasting it to oblivion. As luck would have it, it *had* to retreat. "Let's go after it. Chopper units, I want you to pursue. Draw it back up. According to the Police Chief, it had no qualms about going after helicopters. Use your sniper rifles if you have to."

"Four copies."

"Five copies. Moving west."

"I still don't get it," the Chief Petty officer said. "It should've detected us much sooner. I don't get why it decided to run all of a sudden."

Grade took a sip from his coffee thermos. The flavor was the only thing going in his favor so far today. "Well, it's a fish. I guess it got scared. What's got you so worried? You think it's strategically luring us away?"

The officer laughed. "No, Captain. I just find it odd that it would suddenly go *that* way. It's not even going west. It's going southwest. If it was running from us, wouldn't it go north?"

"You're thinking about this too hard. Let's just kill the bastard and get this over with." He turned to the radio operator. "I want all units pursuing the target. Gunners remain on standby."

CHAPTER 31

"I repeat, Cielo Nublado PD, we are still pursuing target. It is westbound, heading for the Keys."

The dispatcher's voice followed the Coast Guard's transmission. *"We copy. Keep us informed."*

Nico noticed Thatcher rubbing his hands together in satisfaction. As luck would have it, the Coast Guard was practically *helping* them at this point. Both the shark and the only authorities that could stop them were going in the opposite direction. As far as the police were concerned, Nico was at home on his couch. Nobody, not even Renny had the guts to pay him a personal visit if he didn't answer.

The sight of Kris' shotgun to Denise's back was infuriating. His heart raced as though he had swallowed a half-dozen sugar pills. He'd seen people held at gunpoint, negotiated his way through more than his fair share of hostage situations. Never, though, had he experienced the angst of having someone close to him as the victim. On one occasion, he led an operation to deescalate a hostage situation involving a bitter ex-boyfriend who held his former flame at gunpoint. That situation ended favorably, with the guy coming to his senses and surrendering. When leading the cuffed suspect to the squad car, Nico had to fend off a vehemently angry father. It took three cops to keep him off the suspect.

Back then, Nico understood how he felt. Any man with the slightest sense of empathy would. Now, he *really* understood how he felt. That anger only intensified when he looked over at Cameron. The research assistant's left eye was nearly swollen shut at this point. He was still hunched over in pain. Cameron was no pushover. He enjoyed a good fight. In his Marine days, he probably could've taken all three of these thugs. If he was this subdued, it meant two things—he was in significant pain, and he didn't want to risk Denise's safety.

"We're here," Denise said.

"Good." Kris turned to Allen. "Go out and drop the anchor." The timid thug had a little more spring in his step as he went out the door. The news of the Coast Guard chasing the megalodon to the west had eased his concerns about getting caught.

"Time for you to get changed, missy," Thatcher said. Another sadistic smile creased his face. "Unless you'd prefer to dive in your birthday suit."

Denise ignored the statement. She looked past Thatcher at Kris. Hot tempered and murderous, he was clearly the more level-headed one of the group. In this case, that was like saying she'd rather get covered in bird shit than pig shit.

"Uncover their mouths," she said, pointing at the two hostages.

Kris put his finger to her face. "Listen, lady. *I'm* the one who gives the orders around here."

"Don't forget who's the head of this group," Thatcher muttered.

"Shut the fuck up, you stupid junkie. If not for your issues, we wouldn't be in this mess," Kris said. He turned back to Denise, who stood arms crossed and tilting her head toward the men. Muttering a few curse words under his breath, he tore the tape from their mouths.

"Yow!" Cameron exclaimed.

"Get over it," Kris said. "On your feet. You're coming outside with us. It'll be best for Ms. Scientist to be able to see you when she surfaces. I don't want to waste time with her worrying about your well-being."

Nico stood up quick. Cameron was struggling, his face radiating pain. Had his hands not been bound behind his back, Nico would assist him. All he had was the goodwill of those around him. Too bad he was surrounded by murderers.

"Help him," he said.

"Why? He having trouble?" Thatcher said.

"Yes, actually. No thanks to you guys," Nico said. "He didn't do anything to you. He never crossed you. You broke in."

"And kicked his ass," Thatcher said. He laughed like a cartoon villain. Maybe it was the drugs he was taking that forged such a delusion of grandeur. Nico had put away enough drug addicts to know what one looked like. The constant sniffling, the enlarged pupils, the aggressive behavior—unlike Kris, who was using aggression to maintain control, Thatcher seemed violent just for the sake of it.

"Christ..." Kris grabbed Cameron by the arm and lifted him to his feet.

"How you feeling, man?" Nico said.

Cameron spat blood onto the floor then looked at him. "Like a big fat pinata."

"You probably are full of candy, considering..." Thatcher prodded his belly, then laughed.

Cameron shook his head. "Boy, if you and I were on the streets and you didn't have that gun—"

Thatcher thrust the pistol against his face. "You'd do what?"

"I'd give you three hundred pounds of ass-whooping. You'd look like a mashed potato after I was through with you."

Thatcher mimicked fright, dropping his jaw and bringing his hands to his face. "Oh my! Ohhhh! Ahhhh!"

"I'm losing my patience," Kris said, waving his hand toward the door. "Out on deck. I'm not gonna tell you again."

Cameron eyed the drug addict. *Yeah, take a step closer. I dare you.* Then he looked at Denise, remembered what was at stake, then dialed his aggression back. With enough time, maybe he'd get a shot at some payback. Just the thought of it gave him a hit of dopamine which dulled the pain from his cracked ribs. He could only imagine how good it'd feel to actually follow through.

Until then, he would have to comply.

The group descended to the main deck. Allen stood ready, holding a submachine gun in hand. He looked at the setting sun. Its golden rays were blinding, forcing everyone to face the opposite direction.

"How long should this take? It'll be dark soon," he said.

"I can get down there faster with my diver propulsion vehicle," Denise said. "You'll have to allow me time to surface. I'll have to make several safety stops."

"Won't it be too dark down there?" Nico said.

"Not with a good flashlight," Kris said. "A diver like her probably has a hundred. Right?"

"Well, not a hundred. But yes, I do have a light."

"You expect her to swim all the way up with two briefcases?" Cameron said. "That's nonsense!"

"We'll send a line down with her," Kris said. "She can attach them to the briefcases and we can pull them up so she doesn't have to. We'll even attach some light sticks to the end of the ropes so she can easily locate them."

"How considerate of you," Denise said. A blow to the face caught her off guard. The world spun. Everything was bright, as though the sun was shining from all directions.

"Goddamnit, Thatcher!" Kris said.

"You son of a bitch!"

Kris saw Nico stepping forward, and immediately hit him in the forehead with the butt of his shotgun. This time, it was the Chief's world that was spinning. He stumbled back and hit the guardrail, blood trickling from his brow.

When his vision cleared, he saw Thatcher standing over his ex-wife.

"Shut your mouth, bitch. If you wanna open it again, I can think of something it can be used for." He undid the button of his jeans.

This time, it was Cameron who snapped. For a hefty guy with cracked ribs, he was spry. Enough so that Kris couldn't catch him. He body-slammed Thatcher, knocking him to the gunwale.

"Leave her alone!"

A single crack echoed through the evening air. Before the sound faded, it was followed by the dull thud from Cameron's body hitting the deck. Denise scurried back, her eyes locked on the bullet hole in her friend's forehead.

"Goddamnit, Thatcher!" Kris said.

"You saw it!" Thatcher shouted back.

Nico was on his feet again, his senses back in full force, the sight of Cameron's death sparking a burst of adrenaline that almost made it impossible to control himself.

Noticing this, Kris was fast to turn his shotgun on him. "Don't try it, Chief, or you're next."

"Oh! So you can shoot him, but it's bad if *I* do it," Thatcher said.

"Dude, will you... Shut. The. Fuck. Up?" Kris pushed him aside and approached the body. One less hostage, thus less leverage to use against Denise. Now all they had was the Chief. If any good came from this, it was that she now knew beyond a shadow of a doubt that they weren't bluffing.

He could tell she was on the verge of an outburst. If so, it would lead to defiance, unless they motivated her to keep her eyes on the prize.

Kris looked at Allen, then tilted his head to the Chief. "Rough him up a tad."

Allen approached Nico, only to hesitate when met with a sneering expression of a man who could easily break every bone in his body. The fact that his hands were bound made no difference.

"What a pussy," Thatcher said. He took the initiative, strutting across the deck, and hit Nico in the face. Multiple blows to the midsection followed. Once again, Nico was crouched in a fetal position as he absorbed the abuse.

"Okay! Alright! Stop!" Denise said.

Kris grabbed Thatcher by the collar and pulled him backward, not bothering to waste time with verbal commands. As far as Thatcher was concerned, he was still the leader of this gang.

"Go get in your suit," Kris said.

"I'll go down with her and make sure she doesn't try anything stupid," Thatcher said.

"Yeeeeeah, no. You've already proven you've got more on the brain than drugs and cash," Kris said. "I'll keep an eye on her. You and Allen, get rid of that." He pointed at Cameron's body. He helped Denise to her feet, then goaded her to the lower decks.

CHAPTER 32

"Christ, is this guy trying to swim right into the sun?" U.S.C.G. Coast Guard sniper Craig Bryan said. His thick aviator sunglasses could only partially hinder the direct rays of the setting sun. He could only imagine how his pilots felt, being as they had to stare directly into it. The target had angled to its right, leading them directly west.

"There is good news," the pilot Jack Cordle said. "The fish is slowing down."

"Good. Maybe I can get another shot at the prick," Bryan said. He was still buzzing from the previous encounter with the shark, and craving a second shot at it. The Captain's plan to hit it with the *Omega Fury's* autocannon was a disappointment to him. Bryan wanted another crack at killing the thing himself.

Captain Grade's voice boomed through their headsets. *"Target slowing down. Turning southeast again. Get ahead of it and draw it up."*

"We'll do our best, Captain," Cordle said. He looked over at the co-pilot, Mark Evans. "Ready to risk our asses again?"

"Do we have a choice?"

"We can ask five to do it," Bryan said.

"You just wanna shoot the thing," Evans said.

"What's the problem with that?"

"Nothing, except that's not our orders," Evans said. "Last time you shot it, the thing ran. The point is to keep the thing *from* running."

Cordle wasn't in the mood for banter. He flicked a few switches on the instrument panel. "Deploying HELRAS."

The sonar dipped into the water.

"It's up ahead, ten degrees to port. It's continuing south," Evans said.

"Bryan, hang ready with that rifle. You might get your precious opportunity if that thing tries to take a bite out of us," Cordle said.

Bryan already had the weapon positioned. The pilots rotated the chopper, facing his rifle out in the shark's direction. In doing so, the co-pilot checked the status of the other units.

Chopper Five was circling high, while the three response boats were forming another spread, like a football defense team ready to intercept the shark. Each gunner was in position, each one as eager as Bryan to carve the fish like a pumpkin with .50 caliber rounds.

Fifteen-hundred feet back was the *Omega Fury*, its engines pushing it at full speed. The American flag waved proudly behind the bridge. In front of it, the Bushmaster rotated to port. Unfortunately for the response boat gunners, the twenty-five millimeter gun would get first dibs.

Ensign Bryan blew raspberries like a grumpy toddler. He was proud to serve in the Coast Guard and had every intention to re-enlist at the end of his four years. The only drawback were the remarks from ignorant civilians, who never served a day in their life. Most respected the service, but there were those who'd joke that people join the Coast Guard because they couldn't handle the "real military". Once, he heard that from someone in the Florida National Guard. A weekend warrior with no self-awareness. Then there were asshats from the Army and Marines. When most of them joked, it was friendly fun. All the branches talked shit about the other. But, like with all groups, there were jerks that actually felt the Coast Guard was useless and that Bryan should've joined an actual infantry unit.

If he could kill that damn shark himself, that would shut up any naysayers. Already, he was practicing his in-your-face victory speech. "What asshole in the Army, Marines, or Navy can say they killed an eighty-foot killer shark? Nobody, that's who? Took a Coast Guard sniper to do it!" It would make a better headline than if the Cutter did the job. A steel ship against a fish half its size. It'd be a unique headline, though it wouldn't impress the naysayers.

"It's turning around," Evans said. "Increasing speed. Ascending rapidly."

"Coming right at us?" Bryan said.

"Negative," Evans said. "It's going for—Forty-three, it's heading right toward you guys."

As he spoke, the dorsal fin made its appearance. Behind it was a swift caudal fin, kicking water with each rapid movement. The shark was over four hundred feet to Chopper Four's portside, closing on its target.

Boat Forty-three was turning to port. Its gunner spotted the oncoming fin and began firing. Bullets plunged into the water, drawing blood from the shark's back. By the looks of it, the damage they caused only seemed to motivate the shark further.

Bryan's hand quivered. He tried to center the fish in his crosshairs, nearly succeeding until the pilots decided to elevate the chopper. "Damn it!" He put his eye back to the scope, then found the fish a second time.

By then, it was too late.

The shark dipped, arched under the water, then ascended underneath the vessel. Boat Forty-three looked as weightless as a toy model as it was flung into the air. The shark followed it, spitting out chunks of hull midflight. Gravity brought both of them back down.

What followed were a series of thrashing motions as the shark proceeded to seek out the fallen guardsmen.

Through the scope, Bryan watched three separate blood clouds appear around the wreckage.

Forty-four and Forty-five closed in on the beast, splitting in opposite directions to create a crossfire.

"Bogey's moving north. Forty-five, it's going for you next."

"Where? We don't see anything—OH MY GOD!"

The crash could be heard through the receiver and across the ocean. Boat Forty-five exploded as though a bomb had been planted underneath it. Through the cloud of wreckage emerged the fish. In its jaws were two crewmen, both impaled on its lower jaw and writhing in agony. The shark closed its mouth, instantly reducing them to pulp.

It took Bryan a moment to identify the position of the helmsman. Even if he was dead, he would still be floating due to wearing a lifejacket. To his great surprise, he spotted the man alive and conscious roughly fifteen feet to the right. Despite the trauma of the explosive impact that ravaged his boat, he was vigorously swimming away from the wreckage. The will to survive was strong enough to overpower haziness and pain, but not strong enough to grant him the strength to outswim a killer shark.

The fish had detected his movements and began to pursue, traveling along the surface.

"Do not fire, Omega Fury. I repeat, do not fire. We have a man in the kill zone." Chopper Five's pilot announced.

"Standby," Bryan said into his microphone. "I have a shot." He didn't wait for orders from his commanding officer. He adjusted the scope for distance and windspeed, followed the dorsal fin and aimed thirty feet ahead of it. He fired three times, the weapon kicking back against his shoulder with each discharge.

The meg had opened its mouth, its snout towering above its next snack, when the bullets struck near its right eye. Spurting blood, the fish dove again, the resulting waves pushing the guardsman further to the south.

"Nice shot. You hit it, Four," Chopper Five's pilot said.

"Gotta give Bryan credit for that one," Cordle said.

"Damn right," Bryan said.

"Now is not the time to break out the champagne," Captain Grade said. "Chopper Five, move down and get the ensign. On the double!" The Captain didn't bother hiding his frustration. He had openly stated he expected this to be a smooth operation, and it turned out to be anything but.

Five men had just died under his command. Certainly, he was going to face reprimand by his Commander over in Mayport. There would be a hearing and maybe even a demotion. He would express how he was facing unprecedented circumstances.

Deep down, Bryan hoped they would still ding him for using small response boats despite receiving reports from the local police that the shark had sunk several boats of similar size. The only one that could withstand a hit from the fish was the *Omega Fury*.

Bait. The bastard had used them as bait, and was naïve enough to think he would be able to gun the fish down before suffering any casualties.

Chopper Five was hovering fifteen feet above the swimmer. He was passed out now, bobbing in the water like a fishing lure. With no hopes of the man putting the quick strop around himself, one of the crewmembers dove into the water.

"Hustle it up," Grade said.

The rescue swimmer grabbed ahold of his fellow guardsman, looped the quick strop under his arms, then signaled to the other crewmembers to hoist him up.

Bryan watched as the chopper crew lifted the two men out of the water. Then, as though determined not to let them out of its reach, the ocean lashed out with a claw-like wave. From underneath that wave came the megalodon. As quickly as it appeared, the two dangling men vanished. Closing its jaws, the meg returned to the water, cable in tow.

Chopper Five's engines stalled as it was dragged down by the immense force.

"Mayday! We are going down!"

Rhetorical, as anyone with two eyes could see the aircraft make its plunge. The spiraling rotors snapped after slicing the water, sending huge slivers of metal skidding over the ocean. The tail broke, snapping like a twig, the windshield imploding into shards which lacerated the pilots. If the smell of fuel and water distortion from the craft's weight wasn't already enough to draw the shark back, the smell of their blood sealed their fate.

The megalodon struck from underneath. For a moment, the chopper was airborne again. The shark drove its snout into the fuselage, folding the steel frame inward. It bit on the deck and shook the fuselage left and right, literally trying to shake the humans out.

Two more shots rang out from Bryan's rifle. They struck the fish along its head, drawing blood, but not repelling it from its evil deed.

Boat Forty-four moved in from the south. *"The fuselage is in the way. We can't get a shot!"*

"Maintain your distance," Grade said.

"But sir..."

"You want that thing to come at you? Hold your damn distance!"

The megalodon proceeded to ravage the chopper. Bryan could imagine the men inside bouncing off the walls like ping pong balls. Their only hope, if they were still alive, was him.

He loaded a fresh magazine. Five bullets. Just *one* of them needed to hit the shark's brain. And judging by the way it took the last two shots, it was too preoccupied to worry about the injuries it sustained from the rifle. Maybe it didn't feel them that time, maybe it was focused on attacking the chopper, or maybe it believed they didn't do much damage. How smart was a giant shark? Did it understand injuries? Or was it just so determined to kill that it didn't give a damn?

The sniper lined his muzzle with the shark's head. Up and down, left and right, the target was in constant motion. Constant, but persistent. Maybe the creature was more mechanically minded than it led him to believe.

Up. Down.

Left. Right.

Bryan squeezed the trigger. His first shot hit the fish in the snout. The second struck two feet to the left. The third hit the lower jaw, sending a tooth rocketing away like a NASA shuttle. The fourth shot landed near the edge of its mouth.

It was the fifth bullet that grabbed the shark's attention. What was once the shark's right eye was now a mangled heap of flesh that resembled a crushed grape. It spat out the helicopter and raced along the ocean, thrashing its head and tail. Bryan smiled, so pleased with his marksmanship that he nearly forgot that seven guardsmen were dead.

He watched the shark as he reloaded his weapon. The way it moved reminded him of an earthworm he used as bait when fishing as a child. It was a struggle to get the little invertebrate on a hook because it was writhing so much. No matter how hard it tried, he always overpowered it.

As far as he was concerned, no matter how hard the fish moved, it would not escape the wrath of his weapon. Unless it dived, of course. Bryan wasn't concerned of that happening, because it was now moving right toward *them*. Blood gushing from the hole where its eye had been, it sliced through the ocean, its teeth sparkling against the sunlight. Bryan wondered if it knew the shot came from his chopper.

Fine with me. Makes for an easy shot.

As though reading his mind, the pilots elevated the chopper. Perfect. Bryan now could plant all five rounds straight down into the shark's head. A good tight grouping would land one of those bullets in or near its brain. He figured it had to be a somewhat easy target to hit. Such a big head meant a large brain.

He centered the crosshairs between the eyes, then launched all five rounds in quick succession. Blood jetted from the shark's head as though blown out by a hose. The fish lurched, and like the worm on Bryan's fishing hook, it thrashed both head and tail. The ocean churned from nonstop coiling.

It wasn't dead, but there was certainly significant damage done to its neuro-cortex. It rolled as a crocodile did when killing a victim. In this case, the fish *was* the victim.

Finally, it had a taste of its own medicine. After all the death and destruction it had caused, it now was getting what it deserved.

Better yet, Bryan's ego never felt more inflated. All those people who talked down to him about not being a 'real' soldier would shut their pie-holes from now on. Nobody would talk trash to a guy who singlehandedly killed a giant shark responsible for the deaths of dozens of people.

Another full magazine found its way into the rifle frame. As he did when the shark was shaking the fuselage, he timed its movements. He needed to plant more bullets straight down on the top of its head. Right into the brain cavity.

This was it. Final victory and certain promotion. And an 'in your face' to all the jackasses who talked shit to him.

Bryan timed the creature's movements, placed his finger on the trigger, then started to squeeze.

In rapid succession, blood spurted from the shark's body. From head to tail, its body opened up as though an invisible chainsaw was cutting through it. The echo of heavy gunshots reached his ears.

The *Omega Fury* had opened fire with its autocannon. The shark reared its head up, blood raining freely from its jaw and gills. More bullets punched through its head, ravaging its remaining eye. Chunks of meat erupted from its head as the autocannon continued its bombardment. In moments, the shark's entire face was reduced to minced meat.

The Captain wasn't taking any chances. The gun continued blasting away, the shark dancing in place as though being zapped by a giant surge of electricity. It took several excruciating moments for Grade to finally cease fire. When that time finally came, there was little to identify the creature as a predator. The snout was unrecognizable. The Bushmaster had acted as a giant blender, leaving behind a giant heap of shredded flesh and cartilage which looked as mushy as wet newspaper. The lower jaw hung slack, held intact only by a few strands of flesh. Almost all the teeth had been knocked free.

By the time its head smacked into the water, the megalodon was dead.

"Chopper Four, this is the Captain. Confirm target is dead."

"Chopper Four confirms, sir. Target is—" Cordle gazed at the body as it drifted in the blood-filled waves before sinking. "Yeah, it's dead. It's deader than dead."

"Excellent job everybody," the Captain said. *"Boat Forty-four, move in on the wreckage and see if there are any survivors. We'll be notifying the island police."*

Both Cordle and Evans breathed a collective sigh of relief.

"Finally!" the former said.

"Think we're gonna get interviewed by the press?" Evans asked.

"Not so much by the press, but by the brass over in Mayport. They're gonna want an explanation as to why this went so wrong," Cordle said. He covered his microphone to make absolutely sure that his words weren't accidently being broadcasted across the *Omega Fury's* frequency. "Grade's not gonna have a good day."

"No, I don't think so," Evans said. "What do you think, Bryan?"

Ensign Craig Bryan didn't hear the question. He stared down at the water, an embittered man watching his trophy's lifeless corpse sink beyond view. A kill that nearly was *his*. That rightfully should have been his.

Instead, Captain Grade would receive credit for killing the fish. Bryan's role would be reduced to a footnote in the report, the evidence of his marksmanship destroyed by the Bushmaster.

"Bryan? Everything alright back there?"

The sniper continued watching the red froth. "Just dandy."

CHAPTER 33

Renny Jackson was ready to call it a night. He had been on the job for over thirteen hours and was barely keeping his eyes open. It wasn't the longest shift he had ever worked, but it was by far the busiest. Double shifts usually entailed the typical patrolling, disorderly conducts, kicking people out of bars, and getting guests quiet in hotels. Not settling near-riots after nearly getting killed by a supposedly-extinct shark.

Each of the public beaches were patrolled by at least six county deputies and state troopers. Same with the docks. Nobody was allowed on the water, including the police themselves, unless someone left the island on a boat. There was a question of whether anyone would bother chasing after anyone who departed. By now, the footage was all over the internet. Nobody in their right mind wanted to be anywhere near the water, knowing that the predator lurking below had a head like a battering ram.

The last hour had been spent at a tiki bar in the west side. Earlier, a few traumatized people had gotten themselves drunk. Booze and shock didn't mix well, and in this case, it led to them getting aggressive with other patrons. Prior to that, he and Carley had to assist in breaking up a fight at a hotel bar on Seventh Street. Working an evening filled with altercation after altercation, Renny felt as though the public was trying to up the casualty rates.

Confident that things were settling down, Renny returned to the station. As usual, Carley hitched a ride with him. During the night, they had to endure a few remarks from assisting officers, telling them how cute they looked together. Most of them were flabbergasted to learn they were married to other people. Naturally, that led to speculation that they were hooking up in secret. Nothing of the sort was explicitly said, but Renny and Carley knew the human condition. Gossip was like a cancer on the human mind and it metastasized very quickly.

Renny got out of the patrol car and stretched. "Oh, man! Normally, I'd ask if you wanted to go out for a drink. But considering the company we'd keep…"

"Right? Though a shot of whiskey does sound appealing," she said. They entered the station through the back. There were a couple of officers in the briefing lobby taking a breather from monitoring the jail. Both of them were already exhausted and miserable. To make matters worse, they were midnighters called to work afternoons. The misery was only just starting for them.

"How are the prisoners?" Carley said.

"Ugh," one exclaimed. "Whole place smells like barf. Most of these idiots have filled themselves to the eyeballs with beer. Now they're paying the price."

Renny patted him on the shoulder. "Get used to it. There's bound to be more while everyone's crammed on this island."

The other officer stood up and went for the coffee pot. "Actually, you might be wrong. Didn't you hear?"

"Hear what?"

Both officers glared at them.

"Your radios not on?" the first one said.

"Switched them off when we left Ramos' Tiki Bar," Renny said. "I'm ready to go home. Didn't want a call coming in to draw me back to town."

"What's the news?" Carley said.

"The Coast Guard just radioed in," the officer with the mug said. "They killed the megalodon. They're sending divers down to retrieve the body."

"We've been ordered to sound the all-clear," the other said. "People can take their boats back to the mainland now. No more fuss. More importantly, no more drunken brawls."

Renny put a hand over his heart. "Thank god. I was ready for this shit to be over before it even started. Any word from the Chief?"

The midnighters shook their heads. "Nothing. Dispatch has been trying to get ahold of him, but he hasn't been responding."

Renny and Carley looked at one another. Nico never ignored calls from the office. He always made it clear he was available twenty-four-seven. It was part of his role as Chief. With his professionalism, there was no way he'd ignore a call from the Coast Guard.

Both of them walked through the hallway which led to the dispatch office. Suzie was standing up and gathering her belongings. Like them, she had worked about fourteen hours and was ready to head home.

"Has Nico gotten back with you?" Renny said.

Suzie shook her head. "I tried his cell. I tried his radio. I don't know what's going on, but he hasn't replied." Her tone expressed the same concern they felt. "You know where he lives, right?"

"I do," Renny said.

"It's not for me to ask, but… would you consider checking in on him? He hasn't responded in the last hour or so, and I'm feeling a little nervous."

"Yeah, we'll do that," Carley said. She looked at Renny. "You're driving."

"When is it ever your turn?" he replied.

****

The first and most obvious clue that Nico wasn't home was the absence of his truck. The lights were out and the porch light was on. Still, just so he could say he tried, Renny knocked on the door. No answer.

"Okay, this is getting weirder," Carley said. "Where could he be?"

"He could be anywhere. It's not like the guy doesn't have a personal life just because he's Chief."

"Give me a break," Carley said. "You know just as well as I do that he wouldn't ignore dispatch. Especially not the Guard."

Renny dug out his smartphone. "Fine. I'll try his cell."

"Dispatch said they already tried," Carley said.

"Maybe he'll answer if he sees my contact name?"

"Yeah? What does he have you listed under? Dipshit?"

"Oh, you're hilarious!" Renny held the phone to his ear and listened to the ringtone. Ten seconds later, it went to voicemail. "Damn! He's not picking up."

Carley shrugged. "Maybe he saw your name and thought 'hell no! I'm definitely not answering this idiot.'"

"You're just on a roll today, aren't you?" Renny said. "Maybe you should give him a call since you're so worried about him."

Carley was already dialing. Her attempt was as futile as Renny's. The call went to voicemail. "Hey, Chief. This is Carley Auburn. Dispatch is trying to get ahold of you. I don't know if you're aware, but the Coast Guard has killed the megalodon. Call them back. Or call Renny, whichever you prefer. We can't seem to locate you. Hope everything's alright. Bye." She clipped her phone back to her belt. "Gosh! Where the hell could he be?"

"How should I know?" Renny said. "I should be snuggling up on my couch right now. Instead, I'm checking in on my boss. It's like I'm a young secretary trying to advance her career."

Carley looked at him with disgust. "You know, women do have other methods of getting ahead in life."

"Sure they do!" Renny said. "Doesn't mean some of them don't take shortcuts."

Carley went back to her side of the car. "I'd text your wife, but since you're sleeping on the couch again, I guess I'll save it for later."

"Oh, thanks!" Renny said. "I guess I ought to invest in memory foam cushions. Makes sleeping on that thing a lot more comfortable."

"Ha! Quit being so dramatic. I'm not dumb. I know she doesn't literally make you sleep on the couch," Carley said.

"Once in a while she does," Renny said. "No thanks to you."

"You know me. I'm the relationship guru. I figure a little time spent apart will make you appreciate your time together all the more."

"Right. Relationship guru." Renny laughed. "I guess it makes sense. Hell, you were even trying to get the Chief to hook back up with his ex."

"I think they're good together."

"Right! You're just a hopeless romantic."

Carley slammed her door shut and crossed her arms over the car frame. "I beg your pardon? I happen to remember you agreeing with me."

"I was just trying to help the Chief get a little... you know." He winked. As he predicted, Carley gave him a scolding look. "Hey, you can't blame me. For all I know, he's probably over at her boat wetting his whistle, if you know what I mean."

"I *always* know what you mean. I'm sure—" She stared off into the distance. A lightbulb switched on in her mind.

"Hey, if you prefer, there's other naughty nautical phrases. 'Sticking his oar in the water.' Or maybe, 'making a deep dive.'"

"The *Manta Ray*."

"Manta ray? Sorry? I'm not quite catching on to the phrase. They just glide through the water... oh! Gliding? Maybe you mean the Chief is 'gliding' in his familiar—" A pebble struck him in the forehead. "OW!"

"Serves you right, idiot. No, I'm referring to Dr. Reta's *boat!*"

Renny rubbed his brow. "How the hell was I supposed to know?"

"Probably because we were there when she arrived yesterday? Do you not pay attention to anything except sunbathers on the beach?"

"Yes, but only because you make me. You think he's over there?" Renny asked.

"It's worth a look. Let's go check."

"Yeah... I'm not one to walk in on the Chief while he's in the middle of—"

"Will you shut up and drive?!"

Renny groaned as he sank into the driver's seat. "If he sees us and gets pissed off, the official story is that *you* made us go over there."

"Fine. Not like you don't blame me for everything else anyway," Carley said. "Listen, if his truck is there, we can assume he's... 'spending time' with the doctor."

"Why can't you just say 'banging'?" Renny said.

"Because I'm not a fifteen-year old boy! Anyhow, if he's there, then we'll leave him alone. Not like we won't see him in the morning."

"And if he's not there?"

"Then there's cause for concern."

CHAPTER 34

The air smelled different when Denise returned to the deck. Before, it consisted of the typical salty ocean mist. Now, there was a hint of staleness, metal, and gunpowder. Maybe it was just her state of mind altering her senses. A numbness had crept over her after seeing Cameron die in front of her.

His body had been removed. Nico was seated once again, held at gunpoint by both Thatcher and Allen.

"Finally. I was starting to think you were having a special date down there," the former said.

Denise nearly shuttered. Of course changing clothes took forever. No woman wanted to strip down in front of a piece of garbage like Kris Hebron. The initial hesitation was out of concern regarding his ability to restrain himself. The fact that he openly stated that nothing 'like that' would happen to her meant nothing to Denise. He was still a violent thug who gave in to his impulses. To her relief, such a thing didn't occur while she changed into her diving gear. What would happen after she completed the task and they no longer needed her was unclear.

Nico stood up when he saw her. "You alright, Denise?"

Thatcher pushed him back. Nico stood firm, his feet seemingly locked to the deck.

"I'd get back down if I were you. Unless you'd like to end up like your pudgy friend."

"Dude, just shut up," Nico said. He walked past him toward Denise.

"Hey! HEY! Stop right there!"

"If you're gonna shoot me, just do it," Nico said. Part of him wished he would. Without any hostages to use as leverage, Denise could easily escape while supposedly diving for the merchandise. As a matter of fact, she could do that anyway. She would require convincing, but it was a doable option. She could swim underwater, undetectable by the thugs, and make her way back to the island. It would be a strenuous journey, but a worthwhile one made possible by the air cannister.

"That's close enough," Kris said.

"I'm checking on her." Nico turned to show his bound wrists. "Exactly what are you so concerned about?"

Kris looked at the duct tape numbing the Chief's wrists. Satisfied there were no tricks up his sleeve, he waved a hand toward Denise. "Hurry up with your reunion. We've got work to do."

Nico didn't wait for permission. It was awkward to comfort her with his hands behind his back. Normally, he'd offer a hug. To his surprise, it was Denise who embraced him. She wrapped her arms tight around his shoulders and held him close. A few tears slipped out and wet his collar.

"I'm afraid they're gonna kill you," she said.

"They won't," he said loudly. His next statement was spoken in a whisper. "When you dive, don't worry about me. Just get the hell out of here. Swim for the island. Stay underwater so they can't see you."

"I'm not leaving you," she whispered back.

Now, Kris was getting suspicious. "Let's hurry it up, kiddos! Bell's about to ring. Better get to your assignment."

Denise saw him approach. She had maybe five seconds before she'd be yanked away. "I'm not leaving. Don't ask me to."

"They'll kill us both. If I can at least save you, that'd be worth something."

"Maybe it's time someone saved *you*," Denise said. Kris pulled her by the arm.

"Alright, get to work."

"Okay! Fine! Give me a sec. I need to get my light ready. I'm not gonna be able to see shit down there."

"You have any underwater flares?" Nico asked.

"I do."

"Oh no! Nice try!" Kris said.

"What?" Nico said.

"Don't play stupid. Like we're gonna give you guys a flare gun that you can..." he placed a finger on his chin as if in thought, "oh, let's see—use to shoot at us!"

"Or signal the Coast Guard," Thatcher said.

"The Coast Guard's on the other side of the island," Denise said. "You don't have to worry about them."

"Only for so long," Thatcher said. He held up Nico's police radio. "Thanks to this, we've been able to keep tabs on everything that's been going on. They just reported that they've killed the shark."

"Which means you need to hurry the hell up." Kris lightly pushed Denise to the diving ramp.

"Hang on," Thatcher said. "Where's the flare gun? Don't make me ask twice."

Nico nodded at the pilothouse. "Most seafaring crafts keep a flare gun in the cockpit in case of emergencies."

Kris looked up, then back at the Chief. With him down on the main deck, there was no threat of him obtaining the flare. "Fine. Now, sit."

Nico gazed at Denise. "Be careful."

"I will."

"For fucksake," Thatcher said. "It's not like there's a giant shark down there that'll gobble you up. Go on! Move!"

Denise stepped onto the dive deck, positioned her goggles and rebreather in the proper place, then picked up her diver propulsion vehicle. Gently, she lowered herself into the water. Allen began lowering the two ropes into the water. At their ends were light sticks, glowing bright green, a small lead weight, and a clip for securing the briefcase.

"When you secure the cases, give the ropes a tug so we know to pull them up," Kris said. Denise nodded, while resisting the temptation to flip him the bird.

Denise began her descent. The first fifty feet was well lit by the sun's rays and the boat's exterior lights. Beyond that, she needed her flashlight to guide the way. It was a dark world. A sharp contrast to the golden one she passed through. She had never scuba dived at night before. Even in daylight, she rarely went this deep without a submersible. It was simply easier to do the work that needed to be done without having to worry about nitrogen narcosis.

At seventy-feet she was in pure darkness. The reach of her flashlight ended a hundred and forty-feet down, where the seafloor waited. If there was any good fortune, it was the fact that there wasn't any coral or batches of seaweed in this area. Fewer places for the briefcases to hide.

Still, it'd be a long and tedious search that would test her spirits, as well as the patience of the drug dealers above.

CHAPTER 35

"Ooookay... Houston, we have a problem."

Carley swallowed. "Yes, I am inclined to agree." How could she not. She was looking at an empty dock where the *Manta Ray* had previously been moored. It would have been possible they were at the wrong dock or that Denise had moved it somewhere else, had it not been for the presence of Nico's truck parked nearby.

He was gone, as was the boat—at a time when no boats were allowed to leave and they needed him most.

"I'm gonna state the obvious and say something's off about this," Renny said.

Once again, Carley was inclined to agree. "I don't get it. Why would they take off?"

"Maybe the Chief said 'to hell with this. I'm outta here.'"

"You know he wouldn't do that!"

Renny raised his hands in terms of surrender. "Hey, I'm just reading the terrain. It's not like him to not answer his radio or cell phone either. And his ol' lady's boat is gone. With him aboard, by the looks of it."

"You think they could've left to meet with the Coast Guard?" Carley asked.

Renny shook his head. "Doesn't explain why he won't answer the radio. And he would've said something to dispatch."

"Good point," Carley said. "What should we do? Drive around?"

"Drive where?" Renny said. "This is our only clue to his whereabouts. He could be anywhere on this island."

"Unit Nine to Cielo Nublado dispatch." It was one of the County deputies.

"This is Dispatch. Go ahead."

"We're on the west side of the island. We got flagged down by a resident who claims someone illegally docked their boat at his pier. We did a quick inspection, and we think this is the boat used by the bank robbery suspects."

"Unit Nine? Was this a cruiser? Thirty-two footer?" Renny said.

"Affirmative."

"Stand by. I'm heading over there."

****

Two other squad cars were already at the scene by the time Renny and Carley arrived. Every officer, rightfully so, had a hand resting on their sidearm. Some stood near their vehicles with rifles in hand. The gang's reputation preceded them. The State and County had been given instructions to shoot on sight unless the suspects immediately surrendered.

At first glance, Carley recognized the cruiser. There was no doubt it was the one she had in her crosshairs earlier that day. If it wasn't clear enough already, the sight of bullet holes along its hull would have erased any doubt.

Renny approached the deputy on scene. "Hi. Give me the scoop."

"We were patrolling around this street. Long story short, the homeowner here came out and flagged us down. Told us some punk parked his boat on his property. He had assumed it was some tourist or something like that. He didn't realize the thing was riddled with bullet holes. When we went to investigate, well... it was easy to put two-and-two together."

"It sucks that we have to deal with that shark. Now we have to worry about these assholes running loose on the island," another deputy said.

"What about the property they were hiding out in? Has anyone checked that?"

"We've had officers stationed there since the attack," Renny said. "Found some of the money they stole and some weapons. I have a feeling those guys, though sloppy, are smart enough not to return there."

"It looks to me like they had no choice but to return to the island," Carley said. "Some of those bullet holes look like they might've hit the engine."

"I think so too," the first deputy said. He looked at the night sky as though resenting it. "Such is our luck that this guy worked late. Otherwise, we would've found this thing while it was still daylight. With the cover of darkness, it'll be harder to track the suspects down."

"We can't let them run loose, that's for damn sure," another officer said. "They could kill someone else. Or take them hostage."

"That's assuming they're hiding out at all. You'd think somebody might've seen them," the deputy said. "They could've taken a boat and fled this island for all we know."

The pieces came together. The Chief not responding; the *Manta Ray* being gone; these criminals nowhere to be found.

The two partners didn't bother strapping themselves in before speeding off, leaving the deputies confused.

"Oh my god," Carley said. "You think those guys hijacked Denise's boat?"

"Everything's pointing at that possibility," Renny said.

"Where do we look? They could be anywhere," Carley said.

"Going back to the mainland would be suicide," Renny said. "Same with the Keys. If they went west, they would've been intercepted by the Coast Guard. Unless they were going southeast."

"Making a run to the Bahamas? Does that make sense? How could they do that with no money?"

"Unless they planned on making a little ATM stop along the way."

"Where the plane went down?"

"Be hard to flee the country without funds. The Chief clocked out at a quarter to eight, so we know they haven't gone too far." Renny took a right at the next intersection and sped for the police airfield. "To find them quick, we'll need a bird's eye view."

CHAPTER 36

Denise was happy she didn't sneak in a glass of wine during the afternoon. Right now, as she swam along the ocean floor, she felt as though she had taken three drinks on an empty stomach. She was grateful for the diver propulsion vehicle, as relying solely on her own physical strength to get around would be nearly impossible. She was already winded from the day's events, especially Cameron's death.

Whenever she panned her light, she feared that she'd come across his corpse. She heard the splash while she was getting changed. Something about that cemented the reality that he was dead, and that she and Nico were next. There was no use for them once the task was complete. The thugs would just see them as loose ends—witnesses to a violent crime. Worse, they considered Nico and her to be partly responsible for the merchandise being lost. In their eyes, she *deserved* the hell she was being put through.

Roughly thirty-six hours ago, she thought the worst thing that would come from visiting Cielo Nublado would be interacting with her ex. Had somebody told her that would be the best aspect of this trip by far, she would have told that person to screw off.

Flash forward to nine-twenty on a Friday night, and here she was looking for cocaine of all things.

She thought of Nico as she traveled the depths. Were the bastards leaving him alone? Or were they beating him senseless? In the middle of these thoughts, she realized that her concern was focused entirely on his well-being rather than her own. Just like his was for hers.

If any good came from this madness, if there was any light to be found in this darkness—it was that they found each other again.

Now, if they could get out of this predicament alive, that would be great.

A rush of water stirred her focus.

Movement. To her right. She panned her light but saw nothing but rock. Denise froze. Every shape she saw made her heart flutter. Each one was just a rock. Each one had a different size and shape. Bent, round, they all added to the tension.

A rush of water like that was *only* caused by movement. Not the current. Not a vent, as there were none down here. Only a mass passing by could do that.

She considered that whatever it was, it could've been a whale. An orca passing by could have caused such a rush. The mental gymnastics did little to settle her nerves.

The megalodon is dead. It was said over the radio. Nico confirmed it.

Such a fact meant nothing. Denise became hyper-aware of the yellow light piercing the darkness. The *only* light down here. In the world of deep sea predators, she was practically ringing the dinner bell.

The fact that the shark was confirmed dead meant little to her fragile psyche. SOMETHING had moved near her. Whatever it was, it was big. To generate a gust of water that strong, it had to be.

She switched her light off and turned off her vehicle. Darkness consumed her. Silence surrounded her. It did little to make her feel safer. If anything, it led her mind to darker places. Was this what death looked like? Was it just a dark void with perpetual silence?

It wasn't completely silent. There was the natural sound of the current. It wasn't overwhelming, though she could feel herself starting to drift forward. Give it enough time and it would carry her away.

Nico would like that. He'd think she followed his instructions and swam for the island.

Not an option. Not leaving him to be murdered by those savages up there.

There had to be a way to overcome the gang. Outsmarting them wasn't the biggest issue. It was a matter of brute force. They had the guns and the will to use them.

She would have to catch them off guard, but how? Stalling down here wasn't going to do her any good. The longer she took, the more impatient Thatcher would get.

Waiting in the dark, Denise didn't feel any more strange water distortions. She was now at the point that the darkness was more terrifying than what she feared was out there.

She counted to five, summoned her courage, and switched the light back on. Directly ahead of her was a massive shape, facing her like the head of a submarine. Below the nose was a massive opening lined with jagged teeth.

Air bubbles burst from her mouth as she screamed. She threw herself back, dropping the diver propulsion vehicle. This was it—this was the end. The megalodon was not dead. It was coming right at her. Her instinct was right all along. Outswimming a creature like this was futile. She threw her arms over her eyes and braced for the inevitable.

Which never came.

It took about two minutes for her to finally uncover her eyes. She winced once again at the gaping jaw. The light beam pointed at an upward angle, lighting the entire head of the unmoving 'predator'.

There were no eyes. Nor were there fins. In fact, there wasn't even a dorsal fin. In fact, there was nothing beyond the broken 'head' of the beast.

Denise looked back to the 'snout' and 'jaw'. Reality dawned on her. She was looking at the cockpit from the front half of Roberto Rosing's seaplane. It was upside down, the 'jaw' simply being the busted windshield lined with jagged shards of glass.

Fuck!

She fixed her mouthpiece and collected the propulsion vehicle. Panning her light to the plane, she couldn't help but laugh internally. Not that this situation was funny, but the relief helped to calm her nerves.

She moved around the cockpit and panned the light behind it. About two hundred feet back, a little to the right was the tail and fuselage. The wings had broken off during the descent and were scattered a couple dozen yards in each direction.

Now came a new anxiety. Either the briefcases were going to be inside the wreckage, or they were scattered somewhere along the ocean bottom. Should the latter be the case, they'd be near impossible to find in the dark.

Most of the fuselage was intact in the back half. Denise let the vehicle pull her closer, slowing it to a stop as she arrived at the severed end of the fuselage. Denise was a researcher and explorer. Most of the wrecks she had visited were a century old at minimum. She never dreamed that she'd be visiting the wreckage of a craft whose sinking she personally had the displeasure of witnessing.

Seeing the husk of the plane was foreboding in its own. She feared going inside, unsure if she could handle the sight of a crewmember's bloated corpse. Then she remembered the megalodon ate them all.

In she went. Rocks and pieces of ceiling layered the bottom. Like the cockpit, the tail was outside down. The seats above her were like stalactites hanging from the ceiling of a cave.

The light found something lying on the 'floor'. It was one of the submachine guns from the drug dealer's henchmen. She moved on past it. Nothing. No briefcases, no supplies—nothing.

She slammed a fist against the wall. Suddenly, she wished that the cockpit of the plane was, in fact, a megalodon barreling toward her. She was dead either way. Thatcher and Kris were not going to accept that the briefcases couldn't be found. She would be spending her entire night down here. Then there was the fact that it would take a while to ascend properly.

Denise turned around and panned her light in the direction of the plane's front half. There was a bit of the fuselage intact with that portion, though the fact was that she was standing in the main passenger section. It was unlikely that the package was there.

She looked down at the gun. It and the magazines were far back, as though they had been swept by the inflow of water. Looking back at the cockpit, she wondered if such a thing could have happened with the briefcases.

Might as well check. Not like I won't be here all night anyway.

As Denise crossed the ocean floor, she did her best *not* to look too far into the distance. The last thing she wanted to see were the sunken police boats that were scattered around the area. Those were actually piloted by good people with families and ethics. Unlike the scum that were on this plane.

Between the two halves were shards of hull and metal. No signs of the briefcases, unfortunately.

A fish darted in front of her light, startling her. She batted it away as she would a mosquito. At least it wasn't anything bigger.

The temptation to hesitate struck as she neared the forward half of the plane. If those briefcases weren't in there, she would probably suffer a mental breakdown. On the other hand, if they were in there, that only meant death was coming much swifter.

One could only take so much anxiety before completely losing her mind or simply growing tired of it. In Denise's case, she was sick of it. She arrived at the cockpit and beamed her light inside. There were rocks, crabs, metal shards, glass, and a couple of handguns which had been swept to the cockpit door.

Something metal and square-shaped caught her attention. Her blood rushed, stirring the unlikely hope.

She had to brush away pieces of seat cushions, floor and ceiling tile, and other wreckage to uncover the item.

Denise couldn't believe it. Both briefcases were right there in front of her, sealed and intact. An odd mix of joy and dread washed upon her. She was happy that she was no longer doomed to lurk in these dark waters, but now this meant she had to face whatever future awaited her up above. Thatcher was determined to have a little 'fun' before disposing of her, and Denise wasn't convinced Kris would stop him once they had what they needed.

She knelt by the handguns. Living in Texas, she had more than enough experience handling firearms. However, these had been under the water for many hours. The powder was probably wet by now.

Doom and gloom took hold. If only she could go up into the pilothouse of her boat and get that flare gun. If she had to pick any of those assholes to burn, it'd be Thatcher. But there was no way she'd get to it. Yet, her mind wouldn't abandon the idea.

Nico's voice filled her memory. *"Most seafaring crafts keep a flare gun in the cockpit in case of emergencies."*

Seafaring crafts… boats AND planes.

Son of a bitch. He wasn't talking to Kris when he said that. He was talking to ME! Protecting me in any way he could.

As she thought earlier, outwitting the thugs was their only chance.

Denise went into the cockpit and dug around. With a little effort, she located a little metal box containing the flare gun. Finally, she had a weapon. Better yet, she had the nerve to use it.

There were two cartridges. She removed the gun from the case and loaded one cartridge into the pipe, then tucked it under her air tank harness. Holding onto the other as best she could, she exited the aircraft.

The next step was to relocate the ropes, which was nearly as strenuous as finding the aircraft itself. To her relief, the light sticks secured at the ends continued to shine, making them easy to spot.

She secured the ends of the briefcases to the ropes and prepared to give them a sharp tug, only to stop at the last moment.

No. Let's make them wait. Give them something to focus on while I secretly line up a shot.

She smiled mischievously and began the long ascent to the surface.

CHAPTER 37

The atmosphere up on deck was getting tense. Nico, seated against the starboard gunwale, watched the drug addicted Thatcher pacing back and forth. The shakes were getting to him. Despite the cool breeze and lower nighttime temperatures, he was starting to sweat profusely.

His two companions were getting nervous. A man with a drug problem and a pistol in his hand didn't make for good company. There was no doubt that Thatcher's insides were churning right now. His brain craved cocaine, and his blood was scouring his body looking for any trace of the substance.

Repeatedly, Nico envisioned a plan of attack against the three killers. Originally, he thought of going after Allen Lo, as he was the smallest and most timid of the bunch. He'd probably be the easiest to overpower quickly. Now, he was considering going after Thatcher first. The guy was practically falling apart, which provided both advantages and disadvantages. Being shaky and relatively weak, he probably wouldn't be able to outmuscle Nico should he wrestle him for the pistol. The downside was his addiction was visibly worsening his temper, thus giving him an even more itchy trigger finger. Three times since Denise went into the water did Thatcher threaten to shoot Nico if he even looked at him funny.

Kris was carefully watching the water, particularly the two ropes that Denise was instructed to tie the briefcases to. He thought he noticed some light movement forty minutes ago, but nothing since. It wasn't the hard yank that Denise was instructed to perform once the packages were secure.

"What the hell's taking the bitch so long?" Thatcher said.

"It's dark down there. Give her time to look," Kris said. That almost made Nico want to chuckle. In a way, Kris was almost more psychotic than Thatcher. At least he was up front with his madness. Kris, on the other hand, seemed to dart back and forth between reasonable and completely insane.

Nico kept quiet. No need to stir the pot just yet. Equally as important was to keep still. More specifically, maintain the *illusion* that he was keeping still.

Slowly but truly, he slid his wrists back and forth, working the duct tape against the head of a screw. Never ever would he criticize Denise on the maintenance of her boat again. He couldn't scratch the tape heavily without making it obvious what he was doing. Slow, gradual movements, as though he was simply trying to stretch his arms.

"You know what happens after she's done," Thatcher said. His commanding tone was lost under a couple of sniffles.

Kris didn't even pay him a glance. "Yes. We take off for the Bahamas. Then figure out a plan from there."

"I meant with the scientist lady. It's been a while since I've gotten a little cooze."

That almost made Nico spring to action. The prick was such a lowlife he spoke of raping as though it was nothing more than a leisurely activity. Even Allen Lo looked uncomfortable. There were some lines that even murderers wouldn't cross.

The criminal mind was a complicated one. The standards they kept often contradicted each other. Each offender had his own particular line he or she wouldn't cross.

Unless you were Ed Thatcher, then there was no such thing as a line.

Now, Kris looked over at him, then back at Nico. At first, he seemed worried of their hostage overhearing this conversation. His posture shifted with a nonchalant shrug, as though to say *Who cares? There's nothing he can do about it anyway.*

"You sure you can even make it work? I see the way you're shaking."

Thatcher pushed his shoulder. "Damn right I can make it work. I'll whip it out right now and give it a go if you'd like!"

Kris winced. "No thanks." He turned his frowning face back to the water. "Do what you want with her. Just don't make it too noisy." The way he spoke, he didn't seem thrilled at the idea, but figured if it would mellow Thatcher out, it was worth it.

Thatcher smiled, then to showboat, he turned to Nico and batted his eyebrows. *Yeah, you heard that right. Whatcha gonna do about it?!*

Nico looked away, playing the part of the defeated man awaiting certain death. Meanwhile, he continued scraping that duct tape against that screw. He felt the edge of the bindings with his finger. He had created a tear. Perfect! Hardest part was over. Just gotta keep working at it.

"I see light," Kris said. Thatcher and Allen both hurried to the starboard side.

"Yep, she's coming up," Allen said.

"But she never gave us the signal," Thatcher said. "That bitch seriously thinks she can come up without our shit."

"Would you just chill for a damn minute?!" Kris balled his fist, desperately wanting to deck his partner in the jaw.

With them facing the opposite direction, Nico could work on the tape with a little more force. He scraped the screwhead back and forth, feeling the tear gradually widening. Almost there.

Now at the 'fuck-it stage' Nico pulled his arms apart with all his might, gritting his teeth. The tape stretched, the tear now forming a perfect triangle whose tip was working its way across its grey width. Finally, it gave. Nico's hands nearly flew to his sides. Had the thugs been facing him, they would have instantly realized what had occurred. For once, the greed of money and narcotics served a positive purpose, even if unknowingly so.

He adjusted himself to rest on his knees, making the inevitable spring to action easier. He kept his hands tucked behind his back to maintain the impression that they were still taped together.

"What's the holdup?" Thatcher said. "It's like she's just sitting there? Doesn't look like she's more than fifteen feet down."

"She said something about safety stops," Allen said.

"Fuu-UUUCK!" Thatcher spun on his feet then paced along the length of the deck.

"Here she comes," Kris said. Thatcher was quick to return to the side, his hand tapping restlessly on the gunwale as he awaited Denise's arrival.

The trip to the surface had been a strenuous one. Denise was still feeling the effects of nitrogen narcosis, and the few safety stops she rushed added to the lightheadedness. It wasn't anything she couldn't handle. She had her bearings and, more importantly, a focus on what she was about to do.

She yanked her goggles off as she surfaced and spat her rebreather out. Already, the three pieces of garbage in human form were staring down at her.

"What's the story, lady?" Kris said.

"Where's our shit?!" Thatcher shouted. It received another look from his partner.

"Where's Nico?" she said.

"You'll get pieces of him if you don't speak up," Thatcher said.

"I'm not telling you anything until I know he's safe."

"I'm alright!" Nico called from across the deck. "How 'bout you?"

"I'm good."

"Whether both of you will stay that way will depend..." Kris muttered. "Where are the briefcases?"

"Didn't you feel the rope tug?" she said.

"Bitch, you never tugged the rope," Thatcher said.

"Sure I did!" she lied. "Just pull the ropes up. You'll see for yourself!"

Thatcher had no plans to waste time calling her bluff. He went for the ropes and began pulling them in. He could feel some weight at each end.

"Got something. Maybe she wasn't flubbing after all!"

The others gathered by him. Just by how taut the ropes were, there was no doubt the briefcases were attached.

"Alright," Kris said to Denise. "Climb aboard."

She noticed the little grin that appeared on Thatcher's face simultaneous to that instruction. Her intuition screamed that the particular happiness he felt in this moment had nothing to do with the drugs and cash. Allen Lo's nervous glance at him only reinforced her suspicions.

Denise kept everything below the neck submerged. Her light was flashed off, preventing the orange color of the flare gun from coming into view. She proceeded toward the dive deck, only to stop as the briefcases were yanked from the water like a pair of trout.

"Yes!" Thatcher hauled the precious cargo aboard, dropped them onto the deck and opened them. The cocaine and cash were intact and unharmed by the water.

"For once, something actually worked out in our favor," Allen said.

"Damn straight!" Thatcher said. He dug a knife from his pocket and opened up one of the cocaine bags.

"Oh, Jesus. Already?" Kris said.

"Fuck off!" Thatcher said. He snorted a gram of the stuff and looked to the heavens. His face had a weird sexual look to it—which made sense considering something else that was on his mind.

Denise inched toward the dive deck, tossed her flippers aboard, then began to remove her harness. First, and more importantly, she tucked the flare gun between her knees, keeping it from view until she got the tank off her back. Clinging to the deck with one arm, she unclipped the harness and tossed it up.

Slowly, she pulled herself aboard. Peeking over the transom door, she saw that the thugs were preoccupied with their money and drugs. Kris and Allen stepped toward the structure, looking over the cash in the briefcase. Thatcher, meanwhile, remained in his orgasmic state of cocaine bliss.

He took another bump, moaned pleasurably, then looked over at her. He licked his lips. "Hey darlin'. You're looking gooooooood with your hair all wet like that."

Denise tucked the pistol behind her back. Her eyes went to Nico, who was on his knees, watching her. He gave a slight nod. He *knew*.

She returned a smile, surprising Thatcher. "Nicest thing anyone's ever said to me."

He closed the briefcase and stood up. "How 'bout you and me head down below for a little fiesta? I have something you'd be *very* interested in."

"Yeah? You sound pretty confident about that."

"Damn right I am. I got something hot waiting for you."

"Yeah?" She leaned forward, her smile revealing white teeth. "Maybe it's *I* who have something hot waiting for you."

Thatcher perked up. His eyebrows were practically on top of his head. "Oh, really?" He eyed her figure, mentally picturing her without the suit. His eyes lingered low to her pelvis. "Something hot, huh?"

"Red hot."

Denise pointed the flare gun and squeezed the trigger. A sizzling ball of fire struck Thatcher in the chest. Pain and panic struck at once. He staggered back, screaming, batting the fire with his hands, succeeding in singeing them as well.

Kris and Allen spun back and saw their partner dancing with a ball of fire attached to his shirt.

"What the—"

What they didn't see, until it was too late, was Nico springing to action. Kris was hit with a kick to the chest which drove him backward. The Chief focused his attention on Allen, hitting him with a haymaker to the jaw, then grabbing for his submachine gun.

The thug held on as best he could, but could not outmuscle his attacker. Fueled by rage and determination, Nico hit him in the jaw a second time, then put him in a haymaker. Allen gagged, feeling his airway closing. The curtains of sleep were threatening to come over his eyes.

Desperate and disoriented, he squeezed the trigger, spraying bullets across the deck. Kris, who was back on his feet and ready to resume the fight, ducked for cover as the deck splintered around his feet.

As the men struggled, the muzzle went high, sending bullets into the back of the pilothouse before it ran empty. Realizing Kris would be firing his pistol any second now, Nico released his choke hold, spun Allen to face him, then knocked him on his back with a punch to the nose.

Before the gunman even touched the deck, Nico was already sprinting for the other. He caught Kris mid-draw, grabbing his wrist and twisting it to the side beyond its flexibility. Kris let out a call as his fingers failed to maintain their grip on the weapon.

An elbow to the nose jerked his head backward. Blood splattered the aft window they fought alongside.

Kris yelled, pissed off from both the attack and his inability to overpower Nico.

As the Chief had predicted after the ambush earlier that evening, had he been prepared for them, they would've all been laying out on the deck. Just as Allen was now, and how Kris was about to be.

He released his grip on Kris' wrist, only to clutch him by the head. He raised a knee into the thug's midsection, weakening his stance. With all his might, he pulled his head downward, then raised his knee a second time. It struck Kris right in the nose, doubling the free-flow of blood that was already spilling.

An uppercut to the face knocked the criminal on his back. Kris floundered, furious at Nico for besting him, and at himself for letting it happen. He was halfway to his feet when a kick to his face returned him to the deck. Now, all he saw were stars—both the literal ones above and the metaphorical ones when one was on the brink of losing consciousness.

To his left, Nico saw Allen rolling onto his hands and knees. His right hand slithered near the Glock holstered on his hip. The guy was coughing, half-conscious, with barely enough of his wits intact to continue the fight.

Nico charged him, pinning his wrist with one hand and grabbing him by the collar with the other. He forced Allen back and slammed him against the gunwale. An elbow connected with his enemy's nose, stunning him once again. Nico wasn't done.

This was self-preservation and revenge all in one.

He grabbed a fistful of the criminal's hair and spun him to face the sea, clunking the spotlight with his shoulder. *Crack!* Again and again, Nico slammed Allen's head onto the gunwale like a gavel.

Teeth rattled around his boots, setting in the pool of blood which spilled from Allen's mouth.

Nico pulled back on his head for the umpteenth time, ready to smash it down again. By now, Allen was practically a ragdoll. His front teeth were missing, his nose flattened, his face bloodied. Despite this, Nico wasn't done. He was ready to continue the punishment.

He reared Allen's head back like a football and was midway through the next smash when he froze. His eyes steadied on the sea, where the spotlight was shining outward.

Something was out there.

At first glance, it looked like a distant sail. Then a metal cleaver. As it entered the light, he noticed it had the color of metal. But what really caught his attention was the eighty-foot mass it was attached to.

It was coming right for them.

No. No way. The Coast Guard killed it! They confirmed it!

It took several seconds of panicked flailing about for Thatcher to finally get the idea to tear off his shirt and throw it overboard. The ball of flame sizzled along the ocean's surface and sank, shrinking as it died out.

Thatcher looked down at his chest, charred by third-degree burns which blackened his tattoo of four nude women posing on a bed. From what Denise could see, they were holding pistols and what looked like a wad of cash.

She was so caught off guard by the violent reaction that she nearly forgot to reload the flare gun. Twice during the ascent, she nearly dropped the second cartridge. Now more than ever she was grateful she didn't, because physically besting a drug-fueled, raging Thatcher would be impossible at this point. She loaded the fresh cartridge into the flare gun and took aim.

Thatcher was already advancing, his eyes as demonic as the women in his tattoo.

"Bitch, you're gonna wish you didn't do that. I'm gonna tie you down and keep your ass there for days, use you as I please until I feel I've had enough, then—"

The next flare hit his groin.

Thatcher's anger reverted once again to full-blown panic. His chest burning to a crisp was one thing. His goods, however? No man could tolerate that. And just like with his shirt, the damn flare was clinging to his jeans. Attempting to brush it off only singed his fingers again. He couldn't even get his hands close enough to his belt to take his pants off.

There was only one thing his frantic mind could think of—water.

He threw himself into the ocean. Surprisingly, splashing down only triggered more pain. The saltwater stung his fresh burns and the flare was *still* burning.

Thatcher floundered along the surface, screaming and cursing, unaware what the red flare was attracting until it was too late. He felt the rush of water, then the reflection of the flare and spotlight on the greyish white skin, and the seven-inch teeth lining the open jaw.

The beast had been moving slowly since its recent feeding. Much energy had been spent, depriving humans of their short little lives and wrecking the inventions that carried them across the sea. *Its* sea. *Its* domain.

The small injuries near its left gills would take a while to heal, but the bleeding had stopped. The fish would still register pain in the area for at least a week, but pain to a megalodon was a minor inconvenience. There was no comfort in living in the wild. Pain was a reminder of the life that evolution had granted it.

As night set in, the beast was ready to feed again. Returning to the hunting grounds where it had found abundant prey at midday, it found itself investigating a phenomenon which reminded it of its original, deep environment. Lights.

In the world from which it came, lights meant that either prey was nearby—or a predator. It didn't matter how small the light. The megalodon had been tricked in the past, lured by little lights which seemingly belonged to a fish no longer than its pectoral fin, only to encounter a tentacled monstrosity. It had won those previous encounters, but suffered scars in the process.

So, it waited.

Only when the lights were up above, and the fish could identify its target, did the megalodon know it was ready for war.

And like an offering, the vessel had dropped one of its occupants overboard. A rapid heart rate, struggling movements, and a flickering red light served as a beacon, drawing the fish to its next meal.

Was it a figment of his imagination? Or a hallucination from the cocaine intake?

In the split-second he saw it coming, a trillion thoughts went through his head. Then the megalodon snatched him out of the water, enclosing him in a world of darkness. Not totally dark—his crotch was still on fire.

That's when Thatcher realized this fish was real. He was in its mouth, being swept to the back of its throat. It was swallowing him whole.

He passed through a small tunnel, only to stop midway. The flare was singeing the wet walls of the shark's throat. The walls began to contract. The whole body was thrashing about. Thatcher felt as though he was inside a giant bucking bronco.

In the blink of an eye, the current which took him to its stomach reversed. Moments later, he was back out into the ocean. The night sky was above him and thrashing water lapping around him. The momentum took him backward. As abruptly as he was regurgitated, his trajectory hit a sudden stop. Cold metal pressed against his back.

He was up against the bow of the *Manta Ray*.

Thatcher looked up at the ship, then ahead at the Megalodon. It was in front of him, snapping its jaws above the water. It had never tasted fire before.

At this point, there was nothing Thatcher could do but laugh. "Ha-HA! You fuck! What's the matter? Haven't tasted medium rare before?

Ha-ha—BLECH!" The fish swung its body to the left, smacking him with its caudal fin, leaving him pancaked against the hull of the vessel.

The red splotch that was previously Ed Thatcher proceeded to drip from the bow as the megalodon circled back for a go at the other human treats waiting on deck.

When he saw the fish smash the criminal, Nico wasn't sure whether to be shocked, relieved, or oddly amused. It was as though the megalodon had grown tired of Thatcher's conduct.

He settled on shocked when he realized the shark was coming back.

"Nico! Look out!"

Right after his ex-wife's warning came the scraping of metal behind him. He spun on his heel and saw Kris. He was on his hands and knees, spitting blood and a crown as he located his Glock. The muzzle grazed the deck as he lifted it.

Looking at him, Nico realized Kris had no idea that the shark was charging, or that Thatcher was dead. The sudden impact against the boat could've been a wave, or a dolphin, or anything. Hell, the guy was so disoriented, he probably didn't even notice in the first place.

He pointed the weapon at the Chief, pausing long enough for Allen to crawl out of the way.

"Gotta give you A for effort, Chief." The gun shook as he started to apply pressure to the trigger.

Nico shrugged. "You know the first step to getting a passing grade?" Kris hesitated, briefly debating as to whether he cared enough to hear the punchline before killing the fucker. Nico glanced over his shoulder, then back at him. "Not procrastinating."

The megalodon struck the boat, rocking it to starboard. Kris was suddenly on his back, his shots now aimed at the stars instead of the Chief. Now, he was aware that something was in the water. Then he was lost in another haze as the Chief threw himself onto the criminal, battering him with a hail of blows to the face.

Allen was back on his feet, though lost in a daze. Blood had smeared over his eyes, making his blurry vision a hellish red. As the boat rocked, the already off balance criminal stumbled back and forth.

As the boat rocked back, he ended up once again at the portside gunwale, peering down at the water. There was an odd 'hole' in the water. A hole lined with teeth, and quickly getting larger.

"Oh..."

The meg closed its jaw over the gunwale, breaking off a whole section as it pulled away. It splashed down, leaving a gaping hole in the side of the *Manta Ray*, and the still-standing lower half of Allen Lo. A piece of spinal column protruded from the severed waist like an antenna. The knees wobbled, then gave out. The remains toppled into the water, where they would soon be collected and reunited with the upper half.

Denise fell to her knees as the boat began to spin. She couldn't see the shark at the moment, but it was obvious it would keep hitting the vessel until it was resting alongside the plane.

They had a few weapons present, including a couple in the galley, but as she learned in the recent bloodbath, these weapons were not strong enough to penetrate its flesh. The only weak points were the eyes, gills, and mouth.

The bloodstream...

She recalled the original plan to drug the fish. It was the only chance they had. Except, instead of dosing the shark with sedative, she would inject it with cyanide.

Nico had Kris under control. Right now, she had to deal with the greater threat. She descended into the depths of the *Manta Ray*, nearly tumbling down the last few stairs after the shark struck again. This time, it hit under the stern. The crunch of metal that echoed through the vessel struck a nerve. Were the propellers knocked loose? Was there a breach?

She waited to listen for a potential rush of water. Nothing came. She continued into the lab and found the gun cabinet. If only she could've gotten down here while the gang had seized the boat. She could have hit one or both of them with sedatives, allowing Cameron or Nico to take down the last.

At least the criminals didn't learn that this tranquilizer gun was here. Knowing them, they would've discarded it just to prevent her from using it as a weapon.

She took the empty darts and the jar of cyanide. There was only enough left to fill two darts.

"Damn it."

Will this be enough? She thought back on what it took to put down a fifty-foot whale. She recalled it required two darts as well, and that was for a creature that was thirty feet smaller and already dying.

The shark was going to attack whether she had sufficient amount or not. If nothing else, maybe they could slow it down.

She loaded a dart into the gun and ran up the steps.

Nico landed another blow. By now, Kris' jaw was crooked, with multiple teeth missing. It was like a caricature of old cartoon villains, with crooked jaws containing only a few spaced teeth. Except Kris was a lot bloodier and bruised. Deservedly so.

Despite all the punishment, despite nearly blacking out twice in the last few minutes, he still clung to that pistol. Nico grabbed his wrist and bent it the same way he did before. This time, however, Kris was prepared for that technique. With no more fists landing on his face, he lunged upward, striking Nico in the throat.

Nico coughed and spat, his airway temporarily constricting. No amount of adrenaline could make one prepare for a crippling blow to the throat. All of a sudden, he was now the one on his back. Blood from Kris' mouth trickled onto his face as the thug smiled down on him.

The gun wavered between their two grasps, Kris slowly using his bodyweight to tilt it downward toward Nico. Slowly but truly, it neared his head. His finger squeezed the trigger. *Bang!* The bullet hit the deck, missing its target, but still inflicting damage. Gunpowder singed the left side of the Chief's face, making his ear ring.

"If anything good came of this, it's that I'm gonna get my full share of the cash," Kris muttered. "Don't worry, Chief. You'll get the bagpipes and the flag and the parades. Maybe not a coffin, considering where your corpse is about to go. But we can't all get what we want."

Nico sneered at him. *No way am I letting this bastard get the best of me.* He grabbed a fistful of Kris' hair, pulled him close, and headbutted him in the nose. The impact rang his own noggin, but it also weakened his enemy long enough for Nico to wrestle the gun free. The wrist-lock wasn't working this time. Instead, he would rely on good old-fashioned impact to shake things loose.

First, a little extra something to get Kris' bodyweight off of him.

Nico made a fist, extended his index fore-knuckle like the muzzle of a gun, then jabbed it into Kris' eye. The thug lurched back, yelling in a fit of rage and pain.

The Chief lunged upward, putting the prick on his back once again, then with both hands, slammed Kris' hand against the deck. The gun fell loose and slid out of reach.

A chop to the throat ended any fight Kris had left in him. Now, it was *his* airway closed. A taste of his own medicine.

Nico pulled the thug to his feet. Kris, head slung, only able to stand with the Chief's support, started to chuckle as he noticed he was being pulled to the side of the boat.

"You serious? You're gonna feed me to the shark? Isn't that a little beneath you, Chief?"

"Not really. Especially when I'm putting you to good use."

Good use. Kris knew what that meant, but having been beaten to a pulp, he didn't have the strength or even the will to resist anymore. He would just have to take satisfaction in knowing that the Chief wouldn't be walking out of this predicament either.

"The fish will still come after you after it eats me. You're just delaying the inevitable." Kris chuckled. "You seriously think the fish will have a full stomach after eating me?"

Nico looked past him at Denise, who stood behind Kris. She had the tranquilizer rifle in one hand and a spare dart in the other. They shared a nod—a gesture of mutual understanding of what they were going to do. Normally, they would think themselves as horrendous human beings for such an action, but then again, this guy was arguably more of a monster than the eight-foot creature trying to sink their boat.

Nico glanced at the shark. It was coming again toward the portside, eyes rolling back to plow into the hull. He turned his eyes to Kris for the final time.

"No, but eating tainted meat such as yours, maybe he'll get a little food poisoning."

Kris yelped as Denise plunged the dart into his back. Cyanide filled his bloodstream, immediately putting him into cardiac arrest. Breathing became impossible, both due to its effects on his lungs, and because of the seawater he was thrown into.

The megalodon slowed, detecting movement in the water. Unlike the last, this one did not contain a burning red light. It was a bite-sized piece of meat ready for the taking.

Hungry and burning up energy, its quick digestive system already through with its last victim, the megalodon snatched Kris and gulped him down whole. Its stomach acid began breaking him down, absorbing his flesh and blood, and any contents inside him.

Had there not been a man-eating predator circling them, Nico and Denise would've happily taken this moment to embrace. They had defeated the criminals that killed Cameron and took them hostage. Finally, they were alone.

That was also the unfortunate part. They were by themselves, with nobody to help. To make matters worse, the megalodon wasn't slowing down yet. It did seem uncharacteristically hesitant to attack again. It repeatedly circled their boat, its movements lacking any sign of aggression.

"Either it's full, or it might not be feeling well," Nico said. He looked at the tranq gun. "How many more of those darts are there?"

"Got plenty of darts. Cyanide, however... the dart in this gun has the last."

"And the odds of that finishing off the fish are...?"

"Slim."

"Well, we won't know unless we try," Nico said. He looked at the gap in the gunwale where the megalodon snatched Allen Lo. "And I know exactly how to get the bastard to open wide."

He took the tranq gun from her hands, then grabbed Kris' Glock off the deck. He moved to the breach and waited for the shark to make its pass.

Meanwhile, Denise went to the galley. There, she found Kris' shotgun, pumped and ready to go. Better yet, she found a couple of spare magazines for the H&K.

She returned to the deck, found the submachine gun and loaded it, then stood alongside her husband. Ex-husband—though she didn't think of him as such.

"What are you doing?" he said. "Back away. If this works, it's gonna come right at us."

"Look at yourself, Nico. You're not gonna be able to shoot the shark, then switch to the tranq rifle fast enough. Let *me* draw it in. You stand by with the dart."

"Denise—"

The shark was making its pass. Denise raised the H&K and popped off a few rounds. Nico took the hint. She wasn't backing down. Might as well go with the flow and hope for the best.

Denise waited long enough for him to shoulder the tranq gun, then fired a series of short controlled bursts at the dorsal fin. The fish twitched, its tail bashing the water, as though annoyed by the series of stings along its flesh. It turned and went for the boat.

The head came partially out of the water, the eyes locking onto the human treats waiting above.

No longer was there a question of its willingness to attack.

Nico pushed Denise to the side. "Go!"

The fish was breathing, jaws parting, serrated teeth dangling ribbons of clothing and flesh. Behind them was the back of its throat, coming right at the Chief. He squeezed the trigger and threw himself back as far as he could.

The megalodon hit the boat with a thunderous *crack!* Its jaws snapped repeatedly at the air, unable to reach the treat.

Nico was on his back, staring into the dark tunnel behind those layers of teeth. In the back of its throat was the dart, embedded in the soft flesh. He hit his target.

The moment of triumph was just that—a moment. Terror took hold as he realized he was sliding toward those jaws. The boat was teetering, the deck now a wet, slippery slope leading to death.

"Shit-shit-shit-shit-shit-shit-shit!" *Don't let those be my last words!*

More gunshots filled the air. Shotgun blasts this time, delivering tight groups of buckshot into the megalodon's gill lining.

The fish swung its head left to attack the new threat. In doing so, it was betrayed by its own weight. Splintering the gunwale and the deck, it fell back into the water.

Denise stumbled to-and-fro as the boat righted itself. Nico stood back up and looked at her, impressed and thankful. Those skills he taught her never wore off.

She pumped the shotgun, astonished at her own quick-thinking and marksmanship. "I might not have delivered on the chicken and rice, but—"

Nico pulled her close and pressed his lips to hers. Damn shark. He'd prefer to make that kiss last longer, but survival didn't leave much time for romance. Still, it provided a warmness to both of them.

Back to business.

Nico took the H&K and loaded the final magazine into its frame, while Denise loaded the remaining shells into the shotgun. Together, they watched the shark circle again.

It was sluggish, the back-and-forth motions of its tail having a lag.

"The drugs are taking effect," Denise said.

They felt a vibration under their feet and could hear a deep groan within the vessel. At the same time, they noticed that the deck they stood on wasn't even. It was sloping once again to port, and a little to stern.

Nico knelt down and looked at the side of the vessel. The hull was cracked wide open, allowing the ocean to infiltrate the ship. "Well, that plan backfired."

"Looks like we need a new plan," Denise said. "Any ideas?"

"You sure you don't have any more cyanide?"

"Positive." The ship groaned again, then tilted more violently. The water was rushing in fast. "Let's think fast, because ill or not, that shark will happily gobble us down."

Nico looked at the deck for anything to use, then settled on the tranquilizer rifle. "What about your sedatives? Would that finish the job?"

Denise didn't bother wasting time answering. She ran for the passageway, went below, only to stop midway down.

The water was climbing, killing the lights. She'd be traveling blind, searching for the right cabinet and supplies. It wasn't going to happen in the amount of time she could hold her breath.

She returned to the deck. "Good plan... should've come up with it five minutes ago."

Nico looked at his gun then at the shark. "Well, unless we grow wings and fly out of here, we're going into the water."

"Then we go down fighting," Denise said, raising her shotgun muzzle. "Give the bastard something to remember us by."

A hint of a smile came over Nico's face. Despite the dread of impending death, the fact that the love of his life was willing to go down like a badass made it a little better. Easier.

Still, he wished there was a way out. If only he had a chopper to fly them out.

His imagination made it worse. He swore he could hear the droning sound of helicopter rotors steadily approaching.

"Nico?"

He looked at Denise. She was looking to the sky and pointing. Right then, a spotlight embraced them.

Nico looked to the source. As though his imagination had materialized into reality, his department helicopter descended from the sky like an angel sent from Heaven.

God? Were you listening?

****

"There they are!" Renny said.

"Any sign of the bank robbers?" Carley asked. She was in the fuselage with her sniper rifle in hand.

"Not that I can see. In fact, the Chief and the missus look like they're packing heat. Doubt they'd be doing that if they were held hostage." As he moved the chopper closer, he noticed the tilt of the boat and the damage to the hull. "Oh, shit!"

Carley saw it too. "What the hell happened—" She got her answer as a dorsal fin passed through the spotlight. "You've got to be kidding me! I thought the Coast Guard killed that thing!"

"I guess they lied," Renny said.

"Oh my god. They're sinking. Ren, hurry. Let's get them out of there!"

"What do you *think* I'm doing?"

"I don't know! Probably thinking about girls on the beach!"

He shrugged. "That does relax me..."

She reached up and smacked him over the head. Even now, with the Chief's life at stake and a killer shark lurking below, he still felt the need to make quips.

Renny got on his microphone. "Hey, Chief. Is this a bad time to negotiate a pay raise?"

Nico moved around the deck in search of something. After a moment, he found the two-way radio, which had been dropped during a skirmish.

"Sure! I'll give half your salary to Carley!"

"I'm good with that deal! Take us down," Carley said with a thumbs-up. She unrolled the stepladder and tossed it out the door. It dangled twenty feet below them, swinging toward the people on the sinking ship.

The Chief urged the researcher to climb aboard first. She grabbed the first ladder bar and began her ascent, only to drop off and run across the deck.

"Go up!" Nico screamed.

Carley's reaction was louder. "HOLY SHIT!"

The explosion of water beneath them was enough for Renny to yank on the joystick. The chopper ascended, then stalled for a moment. The ladder went taut, then broke free.

The fish had seized it in its jaws. It headbutted the boat in the process, spinning it to starboard, then spat out the inedible ladder.

Carley put it in her crosshairs. The left side of its neck had two bullet holes from a large caliber weapon. She had heard the Coast Guard report from earlier that the helicopter sniper had hit it, thus driving it off.

No doubt, this was the same shark that wreaked havoc on the island earlier.

So, what did the Coast Guard report killing? Did they *think* they killed it, only to be mistaken?

Later would be the time for questions. First, they needed to get the fish away from the boat.

Carley squeezed off several rounds, successfully hitting the fish in the sensitive gill slits.

Renny moved the chopper to the north and lowered it, using themselves as bait as they did before.

The plan worked. The shark raced toward them with a vengeance. Cursing, Renny pulled the chopper up. The shark breached and snapped its jaws. The chopper jolted as its snout bumped against the landing skids.

"That was too close."

****

Nico and Denise watched as the flight team continued their dance with the predator. The sound of water seeping through the passageway, and the ocean climbing along the hull reminded them of their dilemma.

"We're taking a swim whether we like it or not," Nico said. "And they don't have enough bullets to kill that thing."

"Can they call somebody?" Denise asked.

"Won't matter. They won't get here in time." He held the tranquilizer rifle, squeezing the barrel with his fingers as though to strangle it. *Just one or two more doses would have finished the job.*

It was evident, despite its willingness to fight, that the shark was suffering from cyanide poisoning. Their plan was working, they just needed more of the poison.

Water swept the deck, pushing along equipment and wreckage.

"If only we had something to drug it with. Something that'll put its heart into overdrive," Nico thought out loud.

"Like—a cocaine overdose?" Denise said.

Nico looked at her. She was holding Thatcher's briefcase in hand. Inside were nine kilos of cocaine. An idea dawned on both of them.

"Wow—I'd never thought I'd be happy to see that shit," Nico said. "You think you can mix that with water and get it into some of the tranquilizer darts?"

"Yes, but it won't be enough. For a fish this size, it'll take all nine of these kilos to overdose it. Don't have enough syringes to pull that off."

Nico closed the briefcase and hurried to the ladder. As they climbed to the fly deck, the ocean consumed the main deck.

"You mind getting that flare pistol out for me?" he asked. As Denise went into the pilothouse to find the flare, he raised the radio to his lips to speak with Renny. "Hey, guys. I need a favor."

"A favor? Sure! We believe in good customer service! You want a quarter pounder with your rescue?"

After shaking his head and muttering "Jesus Christ", he responded, "Yes, that'd be great, actually. But first, I need you to lure the shark back towards us."

"What?! You insane, Chief?"

"Maybe. It's been a long day. But we're gonna drug the damn thing. It's our only chance of killing it."

"We came over here to save you from the shark. Not FEED YOU to it! As tempting as that salary remark makes it..."

"Have faith, Renny."

"Eh... alright. Just let me know when."

Denise returned from the pilothouse, flare gun in hand. It was loaded with a fresh cartridge and ready to fire.

The ocean consumed the main deck, and like quicksand, it began sucking the rest of the vessel down.

Nico looked at Denise. "You ready?"

"Yeah. But first..." She pulled him in for a kiss, a return for the one he gave her before. After a tender moment, she pulled away. "Just in case I don't get a chance to later."

"You will." With the briefcase in one hand and the radio in the other, Nico faced the north. "Alright, Renny. Bring the bastard over here."

"Aw, hell..." There was no sarcasm there. Despite his reservations, Renny steered the chopper toward the boat.

Carley hit the meg with a full magazine of rounds, successfully luring it closer.

Nico stood ready. The water was almost all the way up to the deck. It would take minimal effort for the megalodon to get them. To prevent that, Denise was ready with the flare gun, aiming it as though it were a .44 magnum.

The water rippled as a gust of wind passed over it. The chopper passed overhead, putting the boat between it and the shark.

****

The fish moved with heightened interest. There was easier prey directly ahead. Its vision, though compromised by whatever was in its bloodstream, was still able to comprehend the sight of two humans. They were almost at the water lever. Easy for a quick bite before resuming its chase.

The megalodon lifted its head over the water. Its jaws parted, its throat widening.

Before it reached the ship, something struck the back of its throat. Something small, not made of flesh, but material. Before it could spit it out, it felt extreme heat.

Another red ball of flame had appeared seemingly out of nowhere and had struck the roof of its open mouth. The fish reared its head back, swallowing the first item and its contents.

Its interest in the humans having faltered, the shark darted to the right and continued to circle the sinking boat.

Over the next few moments, it noticed something was happening within its body. Its heart rate, which had mysteriously slowed, had now increased rapidly. The shark's blood was racing. There was no amount of water that could quench its need for oxygenating its bloodstream.

All the megalodon knew was the discomfort that came with drug overdose. That discomfort grew more intense, like magma building under the Earth's crust. Its senses went into overdrive. It could feel every lap of water, smell every blood cell for miles, and see images that it could not comprehend.

Its heart, already strained by cyanide, was now overwhelmed by cocaine. It reached a rhythm surpassing the heartbeat rates during the most brutal fights the meg had ever experienced...and kept going. Finally, as though struck by a bolt of lightning, the valves ruptured.

The megalodon breached, mouth agape, spewing blood. It was dead by the time it hit the water.

CHAPTER 38

Nico gave Denise a boost, allowing her to climb atop the pilothouse. Renny was lowering the chopper. With the ladder gone, they had to do it the hard way—leveling the aircraft with them so they could climb in.

Carley reached down, grabbed Denise's hand, and pulled her aboard. The Chief pulled himself up onto the pilothouse and was ready to be hauled aboard.

"Oh, man! The chopper's low on fuel. Gotta go, Chief!" Renny called out. He tilted the chopper to port, pretending he was about to take off, then settled it back down.

Carley pulled Nico aboard, closed the door, then moved seats across from him. "Want me to slap him again, Chief?"

"Absolutely!" Nico said. The group shared a laugh. "But after you're done, text his wife again—suggest she treat him well tonight. Thanks for saving our asses."

"Agreed," Denise said. She pulled Nico close for her 'next chance'. That chance lasted several moments, sparking a smile from the sniper sitting across from them.

She looked over at Renny as he elevated the chopper. "I told you I have magic powers."

"Huh?"

"Like we discussed yesterday. I sensed they still had feelings for each other." She shook a finger at him. "Women's intuition is never wrong."

"Agreed again," Denise said.

The chopper turned and started its journey toward the island. As they departed, the four occupants watched the body of the megalodon as it began to sink. It was belly up, jaw slack, motionless.

Dead.

"Thank god," Carley said.

"Might have to brag to the Coast Guard that we *actually* killed the fish," Renny said.

"Yeah," Carley said. "Were you guys aware of that?"

"Yeah, the criminals were monitoring the transmissions through my radio—until they became shark food," Nico said. He watched the water passing beneath them. "Something doesn't make sense. They wouldn't DECLARE it was dead unless they knew *for sure*."

"But...it was right there, obviously," Carley said. "Unless..."

"Unless..." Nico's realization was concurrent with hers. He looked at Denise. "What are the odds that the meteor didn't just unleash one shark?"

"We haven't been able to explore yet, but considering the size and the ferocity—not to mention the other specimens Cameron and I discovered, it's not out of the realm of possibility that more sharks, or *species* have been driven out of the deep."

Now, they were all watching the infinite world of water below them.

"Species?" Renny said. "Like what?"

CHAPTER 39

Captain Samuel Grade gazed at the enormous carcass. The megalodon's tail was secured by a huge cable meant for pulling ships six times its size and weight. It took a bit of persuading to get the divers down there to attach the cable, but the task was ultimately done, and now they had the body.

The fish was dead. Really dead—the Bushmaster really tore the damn thing to shreds. It had lost so much blood, Grade suspected that it had lost thirty percent of its weight.

Roughly the same as I've lost in sweat.

Three other cutters were on the way, one of which was carrying the commander from Mayport. Grade wasn't looking forward to that meeting. His inevitable demotion drew closer along with the commander. It bruised his ego much as it did his career.

"Fifty-nine feet," one of the crew said. "That's the length."

"It's smaller than what they said it was," Grade said. "Eighty-feet my ass." Focusing on the failures of others was all he could do to make himself feel better. It had limited effect. Considering how his name was about to be dragged through the mud, he was starting to fantasize throwing himself into the shark's mouth. Already, he was thinking of his many defenses.

Unprecedented situation was the best he could come up with. It was true, but maybe not enough.

"Uh, sir? This is the Bridge. We've got multiple readings. Large bogeys at three-seven-five, portside. Moving towards us. Massive objects... We've got one surfacing."

Several bright spotlights beamed at the water. Grade lifted his binoculars to his eyes. His heart began another brutal drumbeat.

It was a dorsal fin. At least as large as the one they had.

"Another megalodon?"

"Sir!" a crewmember said. "Confirmed sighting!"

"Yes, yes! I see it."

"No, sir, over here. A hundred yards off the starboard quarter!"

That got Grade's attention. Sure enough, there was another dorsal fin cutting through the water.

"What in the name of—"

The Captain rushed into the bridge and stood over the sonar operator's shoulder. "Oh my God."

There were at least seven blips moving near the vessel, all of them representing sharks between sixty and eighty feet. They were circling the boat, likely interested in the blood that was spilled by their brethren.

"It's moving away!" a crewman announced through the comm. The Captain watched through the window. The spotlight followed the shark on the portside as it retreated west.

"The other one's moving too. Maybe they realized what we did to their pal."

"Uh, sir. I've got another reading. A *big* reading."

"They're all big," Grade said.

"No... this...this is *really* big, sir."

Grade returned to the screen. "Oh..." It was over twice as large as the shark they killed. Unlike the other blips, it was coming straight for the vessel.

The megalodons were all retreating, some to the west, others to the north. The way they moved made Grade think of the one they killed, how it abruptly retreated southwest seemingly out of nowhere.

"It's closing in..." the operator said. "Three hundred meters. Two hundred meters. One hundred... Fifty..."

Captain Grade returned to the deck just in time to see the ocean churn. He expected to feel the vibration of impact. None came, however. But the water was still writhing, as though angry that the Coast Guard had destroyed one of its deep sea demons.

And in revenge, it sent another.

The crew broke into panic as the visitor revealed its true identity. Instead of teeth and fins, it was armed with tentacles, each lined with suction cups as wide as a car hood. Protruding from those suction cups were three-foot hooks, like eagle talons.

Like cobras, they danced around the ship, taunting it before inflicting their awful wrath.

Captain Grade stood frozen. All of a sudden, he longed heavily for his previous predicament. Being court martialed was better than being eaten by a monstrous squid.

His drill instructor's voice echoed in his mind. *"Sucks to be you!"*

The End

SEVERED PRESS

facebook.com/severedpress
twitter.com/severedpress

CHECK OUT OTHER GREAT DEEP SEA THRILLERS

THE BREACH
by Edward J. McFadden III

A Category 4 hurricane punched a quarter mile hole in Fire Island, exposing the Great South Bay to the ferocity of the Atlantic Ocean, and the current pulled something terrible through the new breach. A monstrosity of the past mixed with the present has been disturbed and it's found its way into the sheltered waters of Long Island's southern sea.

Nate Tanner lives in Stones Throw, Long Island. A disgraced SCPD detective lieutenant put out to pasture in the marine division because of his Navy background and experience with aquatic crime scenes, Tanner is assigned to hunt the creeper in the bay. But he and his team soon discover they're the ones being hunted.

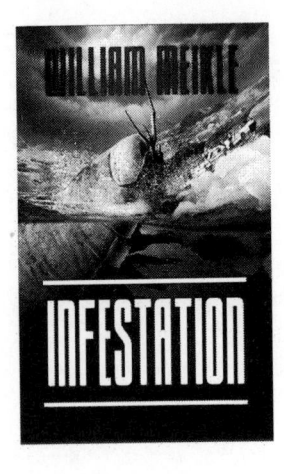

INFESTATION
by William Meikle

It was supposed to be a simple mission. A suspected Russian spy boat is in trouble in Canadian waters. Investigate and report are the orders.

But when Captain John Banks and his squad arrive, it is to find an empty vessel, and a scene of bloody mayhem.

Soon they are in a fight for their lives, for there are things in the icy seas off Baffin Island, scuttling, hungry things with a taste for human flesh.

They are swarming. And they are growing.

"Scotland's best Horror writer" - Ginger Nuts of Horror

"The premier storyteller of our time." - Famous Monsters of Filmland

SEVEREDPRESS

facebook.com/severedpress
twitter.com/severedpress

CHECK OUT OTHER GREAT DEEP SEA THRILLERS

SHARK: INFESTED WATERS
by P.K. Hawkins

For Simon, the trip was supposed to be a once in a lifetime gift: a journey to the Amazon River Basin, the land that he had dreamed about visiting since he was a child. His enthusiasm for the trip may be tempered by the poor conditions of the boat and their captain leading the tour, but most of the tourists think they can look the other way on it. Except things go wrong quickly. After a horrific accident, Simon and the other tourists find themselves trapped on a tiny island in the middle of the river. It's the rainy season, and the river is rising. The island is surrounded by hungry bull sharks that won't let them swim away. And worst of all, the sharks might not be the only blood-thirsty killers among them. It was supposed to be the trip of a lifetime. Instead, they'll be lucky if they make it out with their lives at all.

DARK WATERS
by Lucas Pederson

Jörmungandr is an ancient Norse sea monster. Thought to be purely a myth until a battleship is torn a part by one.

With his brother on that ship, former Navy Seal and deep-sea diver, Miles Raine, sets out on a personal vendetta against the creature and hopefully save his brother. Bringing with him his old Seal team, the Dagger Points, they embark on a mission that might very well be their last.

But what happens when the hunters become the hunted and the dark waters reveal more than a monster?

SEVERED PRESS

facebook.com/severedpress
twitter.com/severedpress

CHECK OUT OTHER GREAT DEEP SEA THRILLERS

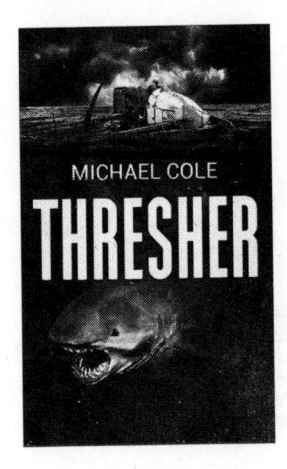

THRESHER
by Michael Cole

In the aftermath of a hurricane, a series of strange events plague the coastal waters off Florida. People go into the water and never return. Corpses of killer whales drift ashore, ravaged from enormous bite marks. A fishing trawler is found adrift, with a mysterious gash in its hull.

Transferred to the coastal town of Merit, police officer Leonard Riker uncovers the horrible reality of an enormous Thresher shark lurking off the coast. Forty feet in length, it has taken a territorial claim to the waters near the town harbor. Armed with three-inch teeth, a scythe-like caudal fin, and unmatched aggression, the beast seeks to kill anything sharing the waters.

THE GUILLOTINE
by Lucas Pederson

1,000 feet under the surface, Prehistoric Anthropologist, Ash Barrington, and his team are in the midst of a great archeological dig at the bottom of Lake Superior where they find a treasure trove of bones. Bones of dinosaurs that aren't supposed to be in this particular region. In their underwater facility, Infinity Moon, Ash and his team soon discover a series of underground tunnels. Upon exploring, they accidentally open an ice pocket, thawing the prehistoric creature trapped inside. Soon they are being attacked, the facility falling apart around them, by what Ash knows is a dunkleosteus and all those bones were from its prey. Now...Ash and his team are the prey and the creature will stop at nothing to get to them.

Printed in Great Britain
by Amazon